I0571252

Luck
of the
Draw

By

Rain Trueax

Luck of the Draw
is an original work of Rain Trueax.

All rights reserved.

Copyright © 2013   Rain Trueax

Prepared and presented by
Seven Oaks
Monmouth, ,OR.

ISBN-10: 0989807517
ISBN-13: 978-0-9898075-1-7

1

Chapter One

September 1974
Monday

The dusty green pick-up followed the ribbon of highway as it wound through canyons and over hills. Overhead hawks, and eagles rode currents of air. The dusty country was that of sage, juniper and rugged canyon rims. The man at the wheel kept a steady speed, easily skimming the corners and rough sections of road.

On the radio was a country western song. He listened for a moment trying to decide whether to change the station. *Please don't tell me how the story ends.* Geesus, he shook his head humorously. Another of those one-moment of love kind of songs. He twisted the dial until he came up with another station. More positive, yeah now that was more like it – *When they turn out the lights.* Oh baby he could go for that.

He wasn't much for thinking about love—win or lose. Sex, at least in a song, now that was more like it although he had little time for that either. He had a goal, a direction he was heading. Distractions only got in the way. Where it came to love, he knew what the songs said, but his parents, had they had that closed door kind of love? He almost laughed as he thought he wouldn't want to know. Who got that kind of fantasy relationship? He might know one couple and as best he could tell, they weren't heading for a happy ending.

Son of a bitch, he didn't like anything about the music. He lit a cigarette and quit listening to the words as he put his mind on autopilot. His hands and body took care of the driving without concentrating on it either. He wasn't a mystic, but he had studied enough Zen to know how it worked. There had been a time when he had felt the need to understand more about life. He had hoped maybe

1

somebody, with some kind of learning behind them, understood what it was all about and could explain it to even a dumb cowboy. Turned out there wasn't—not so far as he had found anyway.

He was still a young man, although older in experience than his years would have indicated; but his days for such spiritual searches were, at least for now, behind him. He understood operating in the moment. He lived a lot of those on a regular basis. He didn't need a name for it.

#

She walked into the store, taking off a sweater to leave on a hook at the back. "Hi, Dad," she said as she looked at the man folding merchandise at the back.

"How about tallying our invoices for this month?" he requested instead of looking up.

Beings he was her father and her boss, she smiled and said sure even while her own mind wasn't much in the mood for adding machines. She was more thinking of the painting she had been struggling with when she had left her little garage studio. Abstract, impressionist, neo-something? Her problem with painting was she hadn't found her own voice.

It's not as if professors hadn't tried to help her find it. Some, only after a great deal of frustration, had given up. It wasn't that she didn't have skill, but did she have vision? Was her talent in anyway unique? Did it speak to anybody else? Was what she had more craft than genius?

She sighed and wondered again whether painting was really for her. She felt this incredible urge to do it, to make it work, but the will to do something didn't equal talent. If it didn't work for her, what else might she do—besides work in her father's store for the rest of her life? She didn't have a clue.

She felt frustrated with her indecision, her inability decisively to walk any path. At twenty-one, she should be on one, shouldn't she? But she wasn't. She was drifting like a leaf in a stream with nothing she wanted that much or for that matter didn't want. Even a non-goal would have helped.

Interrupting her pensive mood, the first customer came into the store, and she walked forward glad to get a break from her tumbling thoughts and the adding machine. "Hi, Mrs. Thomas. How are you today?"

"Just had a bout of lumbago. I just don't know how I'll make it through another winter. You young things just don't know what it's like to get old."

"What did your doctor tell you?"

"Doctors, good God, missy, what do they know? They don't understand the suffering, the ache. I go in there and he simply ignores everything I say with that look they give a body. That sly smile says they don't care what's wrong, just want me out of there."

"Sorry about that. How may I help you today?"

The request was ignored. "Summer heat is hard on us old folks. You don't know about that yet being such a girl, but you'll see someday. And all that dust in the air. I blame that on the rodeo. I swear they start stirring it up when they get to town making it all worse even before the whole shebang starts. I'll be frightful glad when it's over."

"I'm sorry you aren't feeling well. Anything specific you need?" she asked trying to get the subject back to something with which she could actually help. She understood the old woman was lonely, wanted someone with whom to talk and it's why she visited the store so often; but she also had her own work to do—sometime.

"Oh that..." Mrs. Thomas worked up a frown. "I forget but give me a minute here. Let me look through your sale rack."

#

Gradually the terrain changed where development had occurred. Fields of wheat replaced sagebrush. Cattle grazed contentedly on small fields. Homes and farms came ever closer together. Now and then a business popped up.

Easing his position on the steering wheel, the driver permitted his mind to return to what was around him. Time to let reality get control of his rambling thoughts. He knew what he had to do and where it would take him. That's all he needed.

For a few moments, good times and bad, violent and peaceful, rushed into his mind, crushed together into a mental collage. Concentrating on driving was about all he could do to force the images from him.

Even though the approaching town was his destination, he hadn't wanted to go there. Sometimes a man did what he needed to do, not what he wanted. He knew how to handle that much. He had put off coming here way too long. This was a needed step, something he had to put behind him. It was time to bite the bullet.

3

Traveling as much as he did, one town got to seeming like another. On the map this one was just another little western hub. As he neared its center, he saw it had a kind of historic charm to it, old buildings still being used for real businesses. He liked that as so many of the towns he traveled through either had boarded up storefronts or already were twisting their former identities into tourist traps with gewgaws to attract the dollars of passers through. Maybe this one had no such opportunity, but it had left it with an authentic core. It hadn't forgotten its past nor ignored its present.

From seemingly nowhere, or maybe it related to the past and the present, the last argument with his brother came to his mind.

"Keep on like this, and you're never going to amount to anything," Martin had snapped.

"Might give me a little time on that one."

"By your age I had a real job and a kid."

"Martin, you are living your life, let me live mine."

"Mama was right about you."

Oh that always felt good. Bring in the parents, and accuse him of having no responsibility. He could have brought it back to Martin by telling him how much money he had in the bank and that at least he wasn't stuck in a marriage he detested. He didn't. They'd been through it all before. Instead of fighting to defend himself, he had sketched a wave and walked out the door.

A sign fluttered over the main street. "Welcome to Pendleton." A picture on one end was of a cowboy on a bucking horse. Down the street was another of an Indian. Brightly colored flags were strung between buildings. A celebration was about to begin. He passed under one that said "Let 'er buck." The town was decorated for a party, a big one.

His eyes swept from one side of the street to the other looking for a space big enough for the pick-up. Easing into one, he tossed his sunglasses onto the dash and rubbed tired eyes. It had been a long drive, but the bone deep weariness he felt went beyond it. Hot and dusty he still debated whether to check into his motel and take care of this later.

He hated shopping, hated buying clothes but had a few things he needed, most especially a change of shirts if he didn't want to have to find a laundromat in a few days. Between rips and holes, two of his shirts wouldn't stand up to another day's events. Once he hit the motel room, all he would want was a shower and maybe if he got lucky a few minutes to nap.

4

Luck of the Draw

Easing back on the sunglasses, he stepped out of the truck looking up and down the street. Penneys was two blocks down. Half a block up was an old-fashioned sign that read Connors Dry Goods. Now that was what stores should say as it gave the owner some credit while it told the buyer what was inside. He felt the heat of the pavement radiating upward as he walked the short distance. There was little breeze.

Entering the store, it took a full moment for his eyes to adjust to the dimness. It was a long narrow room with stacks of clothing running the full length. He hadn't seen one like it in more than a few years. On one side were shelves full of jeans, at the front racks of dresses and jackets. The aisles were narrow and confining.

Removing his Stetson, he wiped the sweat from his brow with his sleeve. Before he could figure out where he needed to go, a girl walked up to him. "May I help you?" She had a pleasant, melodic voice, but that wasn't the best part.

Her hair was a kind of burgundy red, her eyes big and blue. Geesus, she was too beautiful to be real. He let his gaze wander down the length of her, over the soft curves of breast and hip to the slimness of long legs then back to her face with its striking cheekbones. All of her looked like a woman should. It wasn't just physical beauty. No, it was also the way she carried herself-- proud, lady-like. She was something else. Everything about her looked expensive. None of it fit the old-fashioned store.

"If you need help later, let me know." She turned and started for the back. He supposed she hadn't liked being scanned like a new penny. Looking like she did, she should have been used to it.

"Actually, thank you, I could use some help," he said to stop her. She turned then. When he didn't immediately tell her what he wanted, she didn't smile and instead let her own gaze move down his body as his had hers. He knew what she was seeing. He wasn't a particularly handsome man, but what she would see had always appealed to the ladies. He was tall, pretty near 6'2", light brown hair, with a strong body, rangy in lines. Today he was in dusty clothes, scuffed boots that probably would not recommend him to someone like her.

Her eyes met his again as if to say—how'd you like it?

Well actually he did like it very much. He liked how she was tall too. She'd have the top of her head just above his chin with those heels. The package was prime, one he wouldn't mind unwrapping. He grinned and tried to remember why he had come into the store.

"A couple of shirts and a few other... personal items," he said as he zeroed back to the original purpose. After seeing her, he had another one; but he'd deal with that as he did everything else—go directly for what he wanted.

She led him to the back of the store and a table with shirts neatly folded in a myriad of colors. Cowboy shirts and work shirts not that far apart in style even if the men who wore each probably would be. "Any special kind?" she asked as she lifted one for him to inspect.

"Something that will hold up. Take a lot of hard use and another..." He tried to think what the other should be.

She moved down the counter to the work shirts. The light blue would cover it. This was going too fast. "Anything else?" she asked. By now he clearly saw she was eager to get rid of him. Well he wasn't eager to go. He gave her the half-cocked smile that usually got the girls interested. She looked away. Apparently not this one.

"Hot day outside," he said, knowing that was dumb thing to say.

"It usually is days but nights will cool off. What size do you need?" She had made a polite response. That was a start. Well actually not much of one. This wasn't going as it normally did, but he knew why. She wasn't the usual girl he met. He thought for a moment he was making a mistake here, possibly a big one. Stupid or not, he was moving forward.

"What size do you think I need?" he asked finally although he knew quite well.

She handed him a small.

"I look to you like I could squeeze into that?" He held back the laugh.

"Maybe you like your shirts tight."

"I might... on someone else." He gave her a telling look before he picked up an extra large for the length of sleeve as he tried to think of something else to extend the conversation long enough to suggest they get together later. "Got anything in silk?"

She looked at him as though he had lost his mind. "Does this look like the kind of store that would stock silk shirts or the kind of town that would need them?"

"No?"

She nodded. "That's right, no silk shirts."

"How about linen?" Now he was grinning and hoping she would too. She didn't.

"I really do have to get back to work if you have made your selection."

"I was hoping for purple but don't see one here. With flowers preferably. Big ones."

"Look, I..." She stifled whatever she'd been tempted to say. After all what could she say? He hadn't hit on her... yet. "We might have one with flowers." She began to move through the stack and came up with a yellow shirt with what looked like maybe daisies. It was ugly as sin, cowboy trim on it or not.

"You think that color suits me?" he asked, holding it up to his face.

"I can let you browse and when you are ready, I'll be in back at the cash register. I really do have work to finish."

He didn't like that idea. "Hey, I was just wanting to get to know you."

She definitely didn't like that one. "You really are a fast worker."

"With life, when chance hands you something you want-- move fast or lose it."

"An attitude like that could get you in trouble."

"It could. Anything worth getting though is worth a little risk, don't you think?"

"No, I do not."

She found a purple shirt finally, a plaid with nice blues in it, even in an extra large. Although he'd never worn a purple shirt, he figured he had to buy it. He added a blue checked shirt to the stack.

As she bent, he liked the way her hair had escaped its bun; the tendrils were wavy. "How about this one?" she asked, with another purple shirt in her hand. Uglier than the last if that was possible.

"Nah, one purple is my limit. I'll just take the blues for the days I'm not feeling purple inspired." Which would be pretty much all of them.

"And you said you had some other things you needed?"

"Boxers."

"In silk?" Now she smiled.

"I'll just check out what you have," he said smiling back. "Meet you at the register." He didn't plan that would take long.

With his selections, he walked to where she was sitting at a desk. She moved to the counter. "Cash or charge?"

"Cash."

She rang it up and when he handed her a fifty, their fingers brushed. She didn't like that. He did. He leaned back against the counter again, not in a hurry to leave as he considered how this was going to go, and he didn't mean the shirts. When she handed him his change and the bag, he made sure their fingers brushed again even though she quickly withdrew hers. She wasn't much used to playing he guessed. Young, not very experienced. Not the type of girl he usually wanted to see again, actually not even once.

"You live around here?" he asked, not making any move to leave as she clearly hoped.

7

"Yes."

"Lived here a long time?"

"Awhile."

"Got any longer answers?"

"No."

"You have had a lot of experience though." She gave him a look. "I mean in brushing off guys like me."

"It's happened."

"You are good at it. I'll give you that. Hey, you can brush me off too, but think of the opportunity you'd be missing."

"And what is that?"

She clearly hadn't been able to resist asking. He liked that. Now he had to come up with something. "Getting to know someone who isn't from around here. Somebody..." He needed a word that would draw her interest but one wasn't forthcoming. "New," he finally finished. Not smooth.

"New isn't always better. It can get a person into trouble."

"Staying out of trouble seems to worry you a lot."

"Of course, who wants trouble?"

"Sounds like a boring life. No adventure. Don't you ever take a risk?"

"Of course, I do." Her tone turned defensive.

"Well then here's your chance."

"You're a risk?" Now she was smiling with genuine amusement. That was getting him somewhere. He liked her smile.

"Actually I'm not, but you don't know that, do you? Not for sure. So that's where the risk taking comes in."

"Look, I don't need to be a risk taker—not about something like that anyway."

He crossed his arms across his chest. "Let's get down to brass tacks here. I won't be in town long. I can't keep coming in here asking you out. Asking you to have a cup of coffee with me or a dinner or whatever comes up. You brush me off and you miss your chance."

"Wow, now that scares me."

"It should."

"What if I went out with you and say you weren't really an ax murderer, but I came to liking you and then boom, you'd be gone. How would I like that?"

"Well if that happened, I'd probably like you too and be sure and come back one of these days and then we'd waltz our way through it again." Starting further along the line, of course.

"You do have a big serving of confidence."

He smiled at that. "Now where would I get if I didn't? Nothing ventured, nothing gained they say."

"Old sayings are usually just that—old and stale."

"Sometimes they make sense. How about it, Red?"

Her eyes darkened. He liked like how they could shift colors that way. "I really hate it when anybody calls me that."

"What's your name then; so I can call you something else?"

"What's yours?

"Billy Stempleton."

"You from a long way off, Billy Stempleton?"

"Not so far today. I drove up from Bend."

"I guess you are in town to see the rodeo."

"I'll be seeing some of it for sure."

"Have you been here before?"

"Too many years ago to remember."

"I haven't actually seen a rodeo," she said, her tone now taking on a more conversational note. "Where I came from, they didn't have them."

"You an eastern gal?"

"I was."

"Madison Square Garden has a big one every year."

"We lived outside Chicago and hardly ever went there."

He saw she was delaying having to decide if she did want to see him again. That was fine with him—if it didn't go on too long.

"I like this little town though, the rodeo, how everybody gets into the spirit of it." He knew she also wasn't thinking about rodeo.

"Big business."

"I guess although we haven't drawn in any new customers—with the exception of you. Maybe we need a banner out front or something."

The conversation was not going where he wanted. To further change its direction, a customer came in and she left him. He leaned against the counter, his ankles crossed in front of him, arms over his chest, as she helped the middle–aged appearing lady find what she wanted. He wanted to wait, if he could, until she finished as then he'd ask her out one more time. He had learned from the time he was little—want to ride a horse, you don't think about it too long. You just get on it.

He watched as she talked to the woman. She was a pleasure to watch. Not just pretty but that something more. She had class to her. He liked that, didn't come across it too often. She was also a challenge. He wasn't used to striking out with women and didn't intend to with this one as he felt increasing determination that she would go out with him. To do it, he would have to exercise something else--patience, which wasn't his long suit, as another customer entered. It seemed she'd never get back to the counter.

When she was, had rung up the second customer, when they were alone again, he asked it straight out. "I'd like to take you to dinner tonight. How about it?"

She'd had plenty of time to think about it. She studied his face though instead of answering. Then instead of a yes or no, she said, "Really, where are you from?"

"Lots of places but originally it *was* Bend-- really."

"It's not safe for a girl to go out with a man she barely knows...doesn't know."

"Lots of good things aren't safe. You would be safe with me though."

"Like you'd tell me if I'd not be."

"I don't know you either. I could be taking as big a risk as you--Red."

"Sara. Sara Connor, just so as you can quit calling me Red."

"So it's a risk for us both. You could be a serial killer for all I know." He grinned as he said it.

This time she smiled. "More unlikely than you being one. What was Jack the Ripper?"

"Not like anybody knows for sure. Maybe the queen."

She giggled. "All right."

"All right?"

"At my house. Dinner tonight at my home."

That wasn't what he'd been expecting., but it didn't take him long to decide he liked that idea a lot. Then she ruined it. "With me and my parents."

"Dinner with your folks? In your home?"

"Yes. Home cooked meal and all. Far nicer than going out to some restaurant if you travel a lot, right?"

"Let me get this straight. You still live with your parents?"

"For now."

"You are of age, aren't you?"

She nodded. He thought about that for a long moment. Clearly, if he intended to see her again, it would be at her home with her folks. He'd get some satisfaction out of the look on her face when he said yes as he saw she expected him to turn it down and argue for something else. A guy on the make maybe would have, but he was realizing he had been telling the truth when he had said he wanted to get to know her. He didn't have much time to do that, but it might be worth what he could put into it, and she was going to give him the chance.

"How are your people going to like you bringing home a stranger? And even worse wearing boots and a Stetson?"

"In case, you didn't notice, around here all the men wear boots and Stetsons. Anyway take it or leave it."

The more he thought about it, the more he actually liked the idea. He generally did pretty well with older folks. He hadn't met a lot of parents though, not of girls he wanted to date. The kind he generally went out with wouldn't want him to meet their parents as it was always a quick meeting and equally quick good-bye.

This was not how he had intended to spend his first night in town, but still it might have its pluses, not the least of which would be not having to eat greasy diner food. He thought about the down and up sides, then went for it. "What time?"

He could see he had called her bluff, and she was the one now a bit taken aback but she was game and said, "Six."

She bent over the counter and wrote her address on a piece of paper. Handing it to him, she said, "If you get lost, the phone number is there too."

"Not much town to get lost in."

"Then see you tonight—unless you are the one to back out." Her smile said she expected exactly that.

Outside on the street, he lit a cigarette wondering if he had lost his mind. He wouldn't be there. Except he knew he would. What he wasn't sure about was why.

Chapter Two

The motel was a long, modern set of buildings not far from the rodeo grounds. Billy, who was bunking with Tice McGraw to cut expenses, had left the choice of a motel up to him since he had ridden at Pendleton over the years. On the whole, he felt satisfied with the choice as he edged his truck into a spot in front of the office.

As Billy entered, a young man came from the back room. "Unless you have reservations, we're filled for the next week." His survey of Billy's dusty clothing and the pick-up outside had obviously labeled him one without a reservation. Just another broke cowboy was written all over the clerk's face.

"Under the name of McGraw or Stempleton." Depending on whether Tice expected Billy to be the one paying. He would be shocked if there had been anything more than a credit card number holding it.

As the youth checked the book, Billy looked around the office. It was small but clean. Not much of interest beyond a few travel folders. He wondered how a young guy could stand doing this day after day.

"Here it is. Room 15." The clerk's voice broke into his thoughts. He turned the book to Billy to sign. "Cash or credit?"

Billy pulled the roll of bills from his jean pocket, counting out enough to cover the whole stay before he replaced the roll. Although he had a credit card, he didn't use it. It was just easier to let his cash determine what he could do. No bills coming in when he was on the road; and if the cash ran out, he changed his idea of entertainment. He had the credit card only for ID when he wanted to cash the rare check. Checks were not exciting to those who would know he was a cowboy who might be on his way up or down. When he was on a winning streak, he stayed in motels. When he lost, which didn't happen much these days, he slept in the back of the truck with his sleeping bag.

"You entered in the rodeo?" the clerk asked.

Billy nodded.

"What events?" Now he had his interest or the big bills had.

"Bareback and bulls."

"You like doing that?"

"If I didn't, it'd be pretty dumb to do it, wouldn't it?"

The guy smiled sheepishly. "Sometimes a person does things they don't like so much."

"Got me there."

"Lots of times it doesn't seem like there's much choice. By the way, my name's Scott." They shook hands.

"There's always a choice," Billy said and smiled. "Just we don't always like the options we're given or the consequences possible."

Scott looked like he wanted to say more but instead chuckled. "Well, good luck, Mr. Stempleton."

"It's Billy and thanks."

"You do good at the rodeoing? On the circuit that is?

"Enough."

"We get cowboys in here but most are older."

"It's not an old man's game."

"Well, I didn't mean that old."

Billy took his key and walked back out into the heat. He pulled the truck around to in front of the correct door, grabbed his duffle bag and new clothing. He traveled light, just his gear in the box at the back of the pick-up, a few clothes, some papers explaining where his money was, cash, and that was it. If he kept winning, someday he might fly between events, but for now he was putting aside what he could toward his plans for the future. Save it now in case the day he'd have to quit came sooner than expected.

Inside, he turned on the A/C, the cool air instantly lowering the temperature in the small room. Two double beds, a bathroom, TV and a microwave. It was okay. Throwing his gear on one of the beds, he stripped and headed for the shower he'd been dreaming about for hours.

The cold blast of the shower was a shock but a welcome one as he let the water run over his head, down his body. Grabbing the small bar of soap, he tore off the wrapper. It was fifteen minutes before he left the shower to towel off. He lay on the bed afterward, only the towel wrapped around his loins when he fell asleep.

The door was thrown open with a vengeance and Tice's voice boomed loudly. "Goddamn, sleeping like a kid in the middle of the day. What the hell you think you're doing?"

"Whatever I was, I'm not now," he said, irked at his dream being interrupted. It seemed like it had been a good one, but he couldn't pull back the pieces of what it had been about. Something nice but he couldn't get hold if it again.

"Sleeping in the middle of the day ain't nothing for a grown man to do.... unless'n he has a gal with him." Tice laughed at his own joke.

"I thought you weren't coming 'til tomorrow," Billy growled, sitting up and lighting a cigarette, sucking the smoke deep into his lungs.

"Plans changed and here I am."

As Tice took his own shower, Billy pulled on jeans, then unwrapped one of the new shirts, the purple one, grimacing as he looked in the mirror. Well maybe it wasn't so bad. Yes, it was but he kept it on.

His eyes narrowed as he sat on the bed, elbows on his knees, thinking about the next few days. Two days from now, he'd be riding for the first time at the one rodeo he had put off entering. For the last five years, he had found reasons not to come to Pendleton. The whole reluctance had been stupid, didn't make sense, didn't fit his long-range needs, but he knew he'd done it deliberately in not entered a rodeo close to where he grew up, one of the biggest ones, one of the lucrative ones.

Billy wasn't usually a man to fear jinxes; to worry that fate would catch up with him somewhere. Something about Pendleton had him always finding an excuse not to enter. He could use any excuse like not putting his money down on rides that could cost him more than they could ever win. Well that was the truth in any rodeo. He hoped once he rode his first bronc, then he'd get past the feeling of someone walking on his grave. Surely he didn't think his father's curse would follow him here. Next September he'd come back and the whole thing would have seemed stupid.

He walked to the mirror and ran a comb through his hair. He tried to evaluate what Sara had seen. While not knock dead handsome, it wasn't a bad face. Strong jaw. That's good some say. Should mean strength. Behind that face though, behind that jaw, what was there? What kind of man was he really? What had that man accomplished?

If it hadn't been for the rawhiding his older brother Martin had given him, he didn't think any of this would be digging at him. Geesus, did any brothers get along. He wasn't a man to pick at himself or find fault with what he knew was the right thing to do. He saw himself as directed, having a purpose, and a man who followed his own drummer. Only Martin could make him doubt himself. The irritation could have made him regret stopping by to see his niece and nephew, but he didn't.

"Hey why don't you bring them on over to Pendleton?" he had suggested to Martin.

Luck of the Draw

"Are you crazy?" Martin had snarled. "The last thing I want is for Jessica and Joel to start romanticizing what you do. It's bad enough as it is."

"It's an honest living."

Martin had given him a sour look. "You call it a living?"

"So you'd rather I pumped gas," Billy had jibed.

"You could've done better than that— but yes."

Remembering the conversation had not improved Billy's mood. It had never been a secret how much Martin disliked rodeo as a lifestyle and disrespected anyone who tried to make a living at it. He saw it only worth getting broken bones; so if that was what a man wanted to do, there was something wrong with him. With Martin it all had to be his way or the highway.

He stubbed out his cigarette and ran his fingers through his hair, asking himself again why he cared what his brother thought of him. He wasn't going to follow Martin's idea of a good life. It wasn't what he wanted. Did he need Martin's approval? Hell no. Maybe though he always hoped he'd get it anyway, as deep down inside he had wanted his mother's approval but never had it.

Billy felt irked with himself over the whole, negative train of thought. He'd done more introspection heading to this rodeo and now than he usually did in a year—if ever. Generally he let it all ride on whatever happened—the luck of the draw and playing the hands as they were dealt.

When he had entered the path he was on, he was a kid. He couldn't say he had chosen it back then. It was just there from the earliest he could remember. When he had been drafted into the military, he did that too because what was the alternative? Being sent to Vietnam was another with no options at least for him. He had to go, run to Canada, or face prison. No thanks on the last two. Once he was over there it was another case of do it or face consequences. Nobody asked if he liked it.

His old man, having failed at it for himself, had tried to choose rodeo for both his sons. This one though Billy had chosen. He had not been pushed into it. He had found early on he had the skills it took, and he worked to get what he needed. He liked the exhilaration of a good ride but wasn't ignorant of the risks. Even with athletic skills, things went wrong. Each animal was different as was each ride. To last the eight seconds took a natural gift as well as muscular strength. Doing it for rodeo after rodeo took dedication. Avoiding injuries added in some luck.

Martin had given up the idea earlier than suited his father, but that had pleased his mother who didn't want either of her sons to follow in what she considered disastrous footsteps. She had begged her husband, well more fought with him endlessly, for him to give up the dream and get a real job. When he had, with the post office, it likely had broken him more completely than the original spinal injury.

At least it had until his father found another way to win. He'd lived long enough to see Billy begin to win buckles, but not long enough to see him take it all at Tulsa his second year full timing. His mother had heard about that success, but it really hadn't mattered to her. She saw it as about the long term and the long term was disaster even if it looked good for awhile. She belittled it every chance she got, none of which changed his mind. Now she was dead but he could still hear the words played over in his mind when he let himself remember. It was a lot of why he lived in the now and let the past go. The past didn't help what he was doing.

Whether his father had been realistic about the sport that was played at arenas of all sizes throughout the country, Billy knew he was. You could win it all, be on top one year but the next, it'll turn the other way. Logically, he understood some of Martin's disgust with it, his mother's fears. In a lot of ways it was gambling but with a man's life, his bones, his being. He thought he was taking it all into account. Maybe he was fooling himself as so many others had.

Though he couldn't put any real set of facts to the reasons behind it, Billy had gone out of his way to avoid Pendleton, the rodeo, that broke his father's back. He'd ridden at Sheridan, Casper, Calgary, Salinas, Forth Worth, Tucson, Reno, and the finals in Oklahoma City the years he had come in high on the rankings.

Maybe he had stayed away from Pendleton fearing this would be where it would all end for him too. Would it be payback time? Was it his turn to experience what his father once had? He shook his head laughing at his own fatalism. That was stupid thinking and going to guarantee an outcome he'd not like.

"Hey, kid," Tice said, coming in from the shower, not bothering with the towel. "What's the matter? You look like you're seeing a ghost there." Billy ignored the question, but Tice wouldn't let it go. "I saw that look on your face. Something is riding you. Don't bother lying to me."

Billy swore. "Can't you leave anything alone?" He felt more irritated at himself for thinking as he had been than Tice for picking up on it.

"What'd I say?" Tice threw up his hands defensively, which might have seemed innocent if it was not accompanied by a smirk.

Billy knew it wasn't Tice. It was himself, his own thinking. He justified himself anyway to Tice. "It was sure looking like the wind had shifted and a lecture was coming."

"You and Martin get in a fight again?"

Billy let out a groan. "What'd I just say?"

"Just want to help."

Billy laughed with disbelief. Why had he agreed to share a room with Tice? It was a lot knowing Tice hadn't done so well on the circuit but helping out a friend wasn't worth it if it left him open to his own insecurities being ripped open for discussion. He was doing enough damage to himself without letting someone else open a new wound.

"Shit, I can understand why you'd be edgy about Pendleton after what happened with your old man here," Tice said. "And not only that but you wanting to prove you can beat him. Don't get pissed at me over it though."

"How was your drive up?" Bill asked, not caring but wanting to redirect Tice.

"Fine. And this isn't over, not for you. You can say what you want but I know it's not."

Billy shook his head. "Drop it and if you can't, we won't be sharing this room which means good luck with you finding somewhere else since I paid for it."

"I can probably find a place fast enough," Tice smirked.

"Then do it."

"Don't want to."

"Then don't rag on me or you will."

"You done good this year, so far in the ratings, haven't you?" Tice said ignoring the irritated demand.

"I've done okay."

"Better than okay. I seen how it's been going. You are up there with the big boys. You been putting away part of it too, ain't you"

Billy was wondering again why he had ever agreed to sharing this room. He had felt an obligation to Tice for the years he had helped him get started. Geesus, some things weren't worth it.

When he didn't answer him, Tice went on, "Your trouble is your old man wanting you to be what he never was. He saw you as king of the cowboys and you aren't sure you are that man. Did you ever even want to rodeo?"

Billy snorted and walked to the window, opened the blind and stared out at the parking lot as Tice pulled on clothes. He was still talking but Billy shut him out. He owed Tice no answers.

He rodeoed for two reasons. One he was damned good at it, better at it than anything else, but the other was it would get him something he wanted more than victories in the arena, something that would be a hell of a lot more permanent. He had a plan and he was following it with no doubts about any part of it except riding at this Roundup.

What was waiting for him here that could change his life? A jinx? He could not keep thinking that way, or he'd be his own jinx and losing here just like his father had.

"You know, the problem with Martin is he's jealous of you," finally penetrated Billy's block.

Billy snorted. "Why would he have any reason to be? Martin has it all with a wife, kids, nice home, good job." He knew only part of that was true.

"He never pleased your old man."

"Dad lived with him until he died."

"Because it was all your old man could afford by then. He ragged Martin every day. I heard about it when Bob and I would talk. He saw Martin as a wimp—as much for letting him live there and taking it as anything."

"My old man had lousy judgment." No surprise there.

"Nobody can fulfill another man's dream," Tice said. "You can't do it either even as good as you are."

"I am not trying to," Billy said, lighting another cigarette before he laid back on the bed, his hand under his head.

"Why'd you not come here until now?"

"Tice, anybody ever tell you you talk too much?"

"Actually they have. It never changed much." He walked over to his duffle and grabbed out a bottle of whiskey. "Want a drink?"

"No thanks."

He took a swig and then lit his own cigarette. "You know, the key to life is knowing what you want and doing it. Never no mind what others want or think. It's all about what you want. Focus they call that."

"And that's how you live?"

"You better believe it."

Billy's smile was without humor. "Yeah right. Okay, get this-- I am doing what I want. I am a bronc rider because of me."

"You didn't add bull rider."

There was a reason for that, one Billy didn't find worth discussing. He put out a diversion. "No matter what Dad wanted, it is right for me—for now. I like how it feels when I ride and make it. I don't plan to stay with it forever. I won't stay until I'm broken."

"Everybody says that. It's hard to leave an addiction."

"For me, it's not an addiction. It's a simple fact of what I can do and how I can make money."

"Oh yeah, busting your body to pieces."

"Everything has some risks."

Tice laughed. "You have had how many broken bones?"

"Drop it. Nothing I've had has been life threatening."

"Well you need to let go of the old man's expectations for you."

Billy was tired of hearing the whole thing and knew he had to put an end to it as it was circling back around. "Look, have we finished?"

"All right. I just thought I'd say what I was thinking anyway even if you didn't like hearing it."

"Tice, I don't need a mother."

"And I wasn't aiming to be one. You can give me a bad time if you want over saying this but it's the truth and you know it."

"What I know is I am grown up, have faced a lot of things I'd rather not, and do know what I want now."

"Well just don't say I didn't try to tell you."

"There's not a chance in hell you'll hear me say that."

Billy lay back staring at the ceiling as the smoke drifted up. He owed Tice but not to the point of letting him rag him the rest of his life. Tice liked being the boss, calling the shots. When Billy was a kid that was okay. It stopped being okay two years earlier and had been obnoxious for longer than he could count. He felt sorry for his older friend, understood how hard it was on a cowboy at the end of his rides, but that wasn't his fault. It came from a combination of excess living and age. It had caught up with Tice earlier than it had to have. It did with most of them who lived it high wide and handsome to the end.

Tice, not being as tall as Billy, had in the past done a lot better at the bull riding. Maybe that was the problem. Bulls wore a man out sooner. Billy rode them only at some rodeos, not because he liked it but to get points toward all around. Unless a man was an adrenaline rush jockey, not many really liked riding a raging bull. It was a lot like what he imagined riding a rocket would be. A rocket that wanted to gore you when you jumped or were thrown off.

Billy saw rodeo differently than the old-timers. For him, it wasn't a wild and woolly lifestyle but a sport. He trained for it, kept his body in top shape and had studied what it took, perfecting his skills as any athlete would. His good years were just ahead for him—if nothing went wrong. Tice's were behind him, and he knew it even if he didn't voice it.

Sometimes Billy thought Tice was figured to ride his star as his father once had hoped. He wouldn't be letting that happen. He'd find a way to split from him. Nobody was going to dictate his life. The day for the break would come sooner than they'd either be ready for it.

He remembered when he was still a kid, the years when he'd looked up to Tice, when the older cowboy had helped him learn the ropes, introduced him to people who could help him when he made mistakes. He wondered if the man Tice had once been had changed, or was it that he never was who Billy had wanted to see.

Billy had taken two years off from rodeo when he got drafted straight out of high school. That led to Vietnam and a year he tried to forget, but he came back at just over twenty and hit the circuit with training and determination.

Men who lived like Tice, drinking, carousing, how could they expect to perform at their peak the next day? Well for a lot of years Tice had been good enough to get away with it. For that matter, he was still winning but not as he had even as he'd been lucky on the injuries, Tice was at the most five years away from the end. Even now he wasn't in the big money in the major rodeos and made most of his money at small ones that didn't pay as well. Pretty soon it'd be costing him more than he could win or bum off others. What would he do then? It's not like Billy would ask, but he saw it as the inevitable end for all riders who didn't learn to dismount before they got too badly broken up. That wasn't so much leaving it was having it leave him.

Tice never had never seemed to want a life doing anything but riding in these events. He'd never shown any interest in anyplace, anything else, certainly not in having a family or settling down. The women around Tice had always been just for sex on both ends. Some women who hung around the rodeo stars liked the money or glamour until the money ran out and they found out there was no glamour.

If Billy had learned much from Tice, how to treat a woman wasn't one of them. His own tendency had been to never get too close certainly not emotionally. He promised nothing and didn't get surprised when that's what he got.

In the late afternoon, because there wasn't much else to do, the two of them drove over to the rodeo grounds to see who had already checked in. It wasn't far, but they drove anyway, taking Billy's truck. Not walking was an old habit by now for Billy. Some was the cowboy boot with the heel and pointed toe, designed for riding, not hiking, but some was habit. If he could drive somewhere, he did. Workouts were regarded as separate from locomotion.

Luck of the Draw

They stopped to talk to some of the guys hanging around the office. Tice stayed shooting the breeze while Billy went on into the building. Inside there was heavy smoke from the cigarettes. Laughter came from one corner; low voices and loud mingled together-- some female. It all sounded very familiar. Tomorrow what now seemed relaxed would be chaotic as more arrived, and the whole thing began to come together.

When he made his way to the secretary, he handed her his RCA card and paid the fees for the two events for which he had entered. She recorded his number on the records under the event and handed him the number for his back when he rode. He also received one free pass to the rodeo. He looked through the mail to be sure nothing had been forwarded to him. He hadn't expected anything; so wasn't disappointed.

After the smoky room, the air outside felt fresh even with the dust and heat. The smell of the grounds was strong in his nostrils and he relished it. This was lifeblood. Where he belonged. Where he fit in. Having lived around ranches, cattle and horses all his life, this environment, although not exactly the same, nurtured him.

Bits and pieces of conversations drifted his way.

"You seen Benny yet?"

"You still owe me five bucks."

"In Casper, I drew Sun Bonnet and..."

"Where you bunking tonight?"

"Were you in Vegas? I didn't think I saw you there."

"Did ya hear Jerrod broke his leg? A bad one, not likely to ever be the same."

He walked over to the chutes, lit another cigarette as he thought he really should cut back. He stepped onto a rail and looked into the arena as he smoked. Pendleton was a little different from the set up for many rodeos. Around the edge was a ring of evenly plowed dirt, beyond that the grassy center. It was a bi-arena. The longest in the West—for now. A challenging one to ride because of that grassy center where most arenas were all dirt. In this one the horse bucked across it, hit the grass, which could change its stride or cause it to fall. Any of which could throw the rider onto a surface a lot harder than one that had been disked.

He remembered seeing it as a kid before he ever dreamed of being one of the riders here. It had to have been more than fifteen years, but he didn't keep track of dates to know how many exactly. Suffice to say-- many rodeos ago. He had had so much excitement at making that trip, his father wanting to talk to the cowboys, and most not remembering him. It had been less than his dad had probably hoped and dampened a lot of his own pleasure.

Beginning to feel a little depressed, he drifted over to the stock pens. If he didn't stop thinking of family, it'd throw off his whole game. He couldn't afford to do this to himself a time when his instincts needed to be at their peak.

Tice came up, slapping him congenially on the shoulder. "I was talking to some of the guys about us getting together later for some poker."

"Count me out tonight." Billy threw down the cigarette and ground it into the dust with his boot.

"Why? Early to bed for your beauty sleep?" Tice's laugh was not humorous.

"I have plans."

"What?"

"Why does it matter to you? I'm busy is all."

"A secret?"

He felt irritated. Why hide it? "A date... sort of." He guessed it qualified as a date. He hadn't thought of Sara since he had made it. Now he was thinking what a dumb idea it had been. Maybe he would stand her up after all. It was probably what she expected.

"What is sort of a date?" Tice wasn't letting up.

"Going to a girl's house for dinner. Dinner at six actually."

"That's hot."

"Her and her folks."

"Good gawd. You can't mean that."

"Why not. Home cooking. Sounds fine to me."

"Wait a minute. You knew her before?"

"Just met this afternoon."

Air whooshed out of Tice's lungs. "Good gawd." This time he added a few more coarse expletives. "I can't believe you done that

"Well believe it." Billy walked off but Tice followed him.

"Boy, are you nuts?"

"I swear you are acting more like my mother every time I see you."

"What kind of girl is she? Oh wait, never you mind. She's a *good* girl, isn't she? That's the only kind who'd make you come meet her parents. You are dating a good girl? Good gawd. I can't believe it." His laugh was raucous and sounded forced.

"You're wearing out my patience, Tice."

"Warning you is what I want to be doing. Her parents know what you do?"

"Why would that matter?" he asked with enough of a defensive tone to his voice that he wasn't surprised when Tice followed up asking if even she knew what he did. "It's not like it was a subject likely to come up when we just met. She doesn't at least not from me. It didn't matter."

Tice forced a laugh. "Given who she is to ask you to come to her house, one way or another, it will matter. It's the elephant in the room. You can bet on that. Jesus H. Christ, Billy."

"I'll let you worry about it."

"You get invited to her home, but it's not like she knows anything about you? I got news for you. It will matter to a *good* girl. Rodeo cowboys aren't exactly on any list of prospects."

Billy laughed despite himself. "I said dinner, not marrying."

"Good girls think beyond where it is to where it's going. That or they don't do nothing. You do know that, don't you?"

Actually Billy didn't know it, hadn't known a lot of women well other than his mother and that was sure no standard for determining all female behavior. Since he'd turned seventeen, he'd sexually been with some women, many older than him but nothing that mattered. On the circuit, he was like a sailor come into town and they all knew it. A fun time on both ends, maybe some sex but more often not. It was never with the thought he'd be seeing them again nor that it would matter to him or them. What the hell was Tice talking about?

"McGraw, you are making more out of this than it is."

"One step at a time."

"You ever been with what you consider a nice girl?" he asked with finally an amused smile.

Tice pretended to think. "Well maybe once... when I was five or maybe six. I learned quick though that they are definitely *not* the type to be with. They expect things, Billy boy."

"Like money?" he put a questioning tone to his voice. Now he was having fun with Tice but the older cowboy didn't recognize it. When he did, he'd be mad. That didn't bother Billy.

"No. Worse'n that. They want a ring."

"Damn, you are kidding!" He put shock into his voice. "What'll they do with the ring?"

Tice then looked at him and realized he'd been stringing him on. He swore a string of curses, a few combinations of which Billy hadn't heard used that way. Tice concluded it with a growl. "You wait. It's a ring through your nose is what it is."

"Look, it's just dinner and I like the idea of a home cooked meal. I haven't had one in a long time. Not like Martin would be inviting me over for any of Ginny's cooking."

"Ginny is a lousy cook."

"Beside the point."

"Well you are an adult, I guess, but you are going to be roped and lassoed afore you know what hit you."

Billy managed a chuckle but was not amused and more than a little relieved to see Nick Williams heading toward them. "You're just in time," he said taking Nick's hand as he extended it.

"You got a problem?"

"I'm being mother henned."

"Oh lordy," Nick said laughing and looking at Tice. "that's the worst kind most especially if it comes from a cowboy like this fella over here. I mean what can he know about mothering anybody?"

"Exactly."

Tice swore some more.

"How you boys been?" Nick drawled. "Been awhile since I saw you."

"I was in Bend visiting my brother's family for a bit. I haven't seen you around much. You haven't been in any rodeos I've entered not for awhile."

"Well, I had... a little accident. Laid me up. I am finally fit to ride again."

"The doctor okay that?" Billy asked seeing the new lines in Nick's face, noticing his slightly stooped stature. He remembered there'd been a lot of injuries before the last one. Nothing had been going right for him for a couple of years.

"Was I supposed to ask?" Nick feigned surprise.

"When'd it happen?" Tice asked.

Nick lit a cigarette. "Down in California, little rodeo. Hells' fire that I got laid low for not that much money. It had me down and out for most of a month. Then Jean. Well I know she wants me to quit but she won't say it. This time she pretty near said she'd leave me if I rode before I was totally healed. So I held off for... I guess this'll be four months."

Billy held back on saying anything. To him, it didn't look like Nick was ready to ride again. Was an injured cowboy ever? He knew from his own experiences with injuries that it took being leveled to stop him from getting back out sooner than doctors thought he should.

He remembered when he first had seen Nick when he was at the top of his game, the man everybody admired. The victories flowed and along with them the money. Sometimes Jean competed in barrel racing. She was a beauty and a pleasure to watch her on a horse. She was like one with her mare, Toni, until the year that Toni got too old to keep doing it. The horse was pastured back at her folks' and she didn't have the heart or maybe resources to train a new one. Nick and Jean had years of being the golden couple, the Liz Taylor and Richard Burton of the circuit for the glamour but even more respect they drew from their peers.

The thing with rodeo was when you're winning, everybody wants to be near you. When that stops, people avoid you, they don't know what to say. Kid though he had been back then, Billy had seen that with his father when he tried to befriend those he thought might have the magic that would rub off on him.

When it came time to let it go, Billy understood how a man could want to say to himself—quit damnitall before being killed. The thing is it didn't turn out to be so easy even if all along the man had known the day was coming. For friends of Nick and Jean, they saw themselves in the experience; and if earlier they had hoped for the magic to rub off, then they hoped the bad luck wouldn't settle on them.

People though still respected Nick to hell and gone. Who wouldn't with his strong body, the way he'd smile, and keep right on through pain or bad luck? Nick was walking straight into the face of adversity, whining wasn't in him, and when he held his head up, everybody hoped he really still did have more years ahead of him, years where he'd not be broken into pieces by the breaks of the game. And this was true whether they were among those who tried to stay close to the magic or those who ran away from the loss of it.

Nick had to be nearing fifty. That and a string of injuries meant he should have let it go some years back, before he ended up dead or worse— and worse did come along. Nick hadn't been willing to quit or else he had missed his window. If he didn't see the handwriting on the wall soon, it'd be a tragedy. Billy guessed that would leave Jean with nothing.

He tried to think of something to say but nothing came to him. It wasn't in him to criticize another man's choice or even to try and influence it. "How is your beautiful lady?"

"She's at the trailer. Come on over and say hi. She always has said you're the best looking cowboy she ever seen. Kind of hurt my feelings until she added except me. Of course, she had to add that or who knows what kind of a fray would have resulted." Billy chuckled. He'd heard that too when Nick and Jean went at each other full bore.

"You entered in saddle bronc?" Tice asked.

"Well I sure ain't entering the bulls," Nick laughed. "I've had my years of them. No more suicide rides for me."

"Well that shows you got some sense," Tice quipped.

25

They stood there, the three of them, smoking and talking of other rides and mostly the horses they hadn't ridden. With Nick, there were a lot of good times to remember, and he didn't dwell much on the bad. It wasn't the nature of the man. Billy admired that in him as much as the skill he'd had as a rider. The thing is, skill or not, there came a time when the human body just couldn't do it again, when the reflexes weren't as sharp. The spirit was willing or too stupid to know but the body gave out.

As they talked, Billy's mind was wandering to the speed with which a man could go from the top to the bottom. The luck of the draw was some of it but maybe that was true of a lot of life. The luck of the draw is why he'd had a year in Vietnam when his number sent him there. Likely it was also why he walked away without a scratch when the number was up for those standing beside him.

In rodeo, the wrong horse on the wrong day sent a man on a spiral where he lost his timing and confidence, where he had a body that had been broken so many places that it could not be brought back to what it once had been. If a rider started to doubt himself, it was the beginning of that end. It wasn't just luck though. It was being able to use what came along. He wondered if he'd have the sense to get out before his own slide started.

When Nick left them, Tice muttered, "How long you think he can keep going? I seen him dumped bad three times in the last two years. I don't know how he keeps paying his entry fees. And not just bucked off but really slammed. He keeps picking himself up and dusting himself off with that damned smile of his." He swore creatively.

Billy had done all he needed at the grounds and decided to head back to his truck. "You want a ride back to the motel?" he asked Tice as he found a nearby ash can and crushed what was left of his cigarette.

"Nah, I'll stick around and get a ride later. You enjoy your *date*." He smirked.

"You bet."

"And when you get bored, come on down to the bar. It's the one with the big sign down the street. The card game will be in the back room."

"Maybe."

"No maybes. You'll be there." Tice chuckled.

When Billy drove off, he wondered if Tice was right and he had been stupid to agree to going to a woman's home when he barely knew her. He knew Tice was definitely right on a different account. He likely should have told her he was a rider. There hadn't been a lot of time together, but he realized his reluctance to tell her hadn't been because he thought she'd be appalled. He had not wanted her to get excited at what he did and choose to go out with him because of it. Despite the attitude of Martin, his experience with women hearing he rode was usually more a groupie mentality where they ceased seeing him as a man and instead it was all about the romance of the rodeo. He hadn't seriously thought of it as a drawback up until now. He hadn't been with one like her either though.

So it hadn't come up and hadn't seemed important except maybe it had been and he'd missed his chance to reveal it casually. He still had a choice what he did about it. He could just not show up. He could call and make an excuse. He didn't have to go.

Chapter Three

Sara's room was decorated in neutral tones, one bookshelf along a wall filled with books from many genres. The bedspread was comforter with a brown pattern of stripes. There was a large window that looked out toward the street in front and which she had open to catch what breezes were possible. On the walls were posters of animals, three of her own paintings, and two mirrors, one full length and the other an old one with a circular frame.

She stood in front of that mirror, brushing out her long hair trying to decide if she would pin it up. The heat in her upstairs bedroom had her only wearing a slip; a sundress lay across the bed. As she stared at her reflection she wondered again what had possessed her to invite a perfect... scratch that, imperfect stranger to her home and worst of all to meet her parents. Had she been out of her mind? Her mother was difficult at best with something she had not planned. And this. Well it wasn't going to be a fun evening—if he showed up. Maybe she would get lucky and he wouldn't.

She glared at herself she applied some light make up and pulled her hair into a pony tail, sliding on the sundress. Why did she put herself through things like this? Always using lousy judgment on something other people would have handled so much more smoothly. She never seemed to make up her mind what she wanted and would end up moving in contradictory directions encouraged by impulses that challenged each other. This was a fine example.

She smoothed down the sundress, again looking at her image. Not enough breast or hip. It wasn't that she didn't want to have the curvy figure other girls found so easy to attain. Her adult form had come in as it was without many curves. Long legs were little consolation when she had so little on top to inspire men to daring deeds—whatever daring deeds were. The one plus was she didn't need a girdle or bra that made dressing considerably faster. She felt dissatisfied with what she saw, but there wasn't much she could do about it.

She should have told him no. Why hadn't she? Oh she knew part of the answer. She could remember the moment he had walked into her store with a strong, muscular body, moving like a big cat, slow, confident in himself. So sure of who he was. He had looked at her as though she was beautiful. He made her feel more confident than she knew herself to be. He had confidence. She wanted some of that for herself. At the same time, she wanted to knock his back a notch.

Well actually she had wanted several things at the same time as his gaze had spoken to all he could make her feel. She had never felt such conflicted desires, and that was saying a lot since her life was full of them. She should have never suggested he come to her home. It wasn't that she was afraid to see him alone. She had felt the devil in her to suggest he come here, and now she was going to put herself through a miserable evening.

Sure her parents always said bring home friends. She hadn't done that much. Well, in Pendleton, she wouldn't have as she hadn't been there long enough to meet many people. Lousy excuse, Sara, as it had been ten months and she'd had plenty of time to get involved with people if she had wanted to do so. It wasn't that she had made no friends. There was Cathy. She liked her well enough, but she knew the real reason she had held off on trying to be more involved was not being sure she wanted to stay. She didn't want roots, not yet.

She had dated Rory a couple of times although there hadn't even been good night kisses, not that he'd asked. She considered his taking her out at all more of a duty date for them both. He had shown little interest in her as a person. Basically it had only happened because their parents socialized and their fathers did business together.

Billy Stempleton was different, unique, like nobody she had ever met. He was... what the heck was he? She came back to the same thing. Something crazy had gotten into her even to consider bringing him home—let alone doing it. Part of her found him fascinating while the sane part said this guy is pure trouble. Her mother would only see the second part.

Billy looked like one of the local hands she had seen coming into the store now and again. He was clearly the kind who went from job to job with no roots, no plans, no future. All the more reason she should hope he'd not show up... except she knew she'd have never asked him if she hadn't hoped he would.

When she'd gotten home, before she took a shower, she had told her mother about the guest coming. Her mother had actually sounded pleased. She was a little more reserved when she found out it was someone from out of the area. "What do you know about him?" she had asked.

Well not a heck of a lot, but she rushed upstairs before her ignorance would become obvious. She planned to wait to come back down when he got there—if he came. She had no doubt that with her parents propensity for asking questions, she'd find out all the things she probably already should have known.

When she heard the doorbell, she ran downstairs to be the one to open the door. Standing in the doorway, hat in hand, he looked hot and uncomfortable already. She noted he was wearing the new purple shirt and that purple was clearly not his color. "Hi," she said as she ushered him inside.

'Hi," he said, handing her a bouquet of yellow and white lilies.

"They're lovely. Thank you. Did you have a problem finding the house?"

"Nope, biggest one up here, isn't it?"

"Maybe. I don't know."

"Nice neighborhood." He looked over as her mother entered the room. "Mom, this is Billy Stempleton. Billy, my mother, Ann Connors." She gave her mother the flowers.

"How do you do, ma'am," he said politely as her mother responded with equally polite words. She saw on her mother's face that she had a lot of those questions Sara had expected and they weren't likely to be long in coming.

Sara wondered how he would see her mother. Ann was still very attractive, her red hair now toned with gray but she'd stayed slim and active. She wasn't much like the image of a mother other than the questions with which she was already peppering him. She didn't waste time. "I think Sara said you come from elsewhere."

"Yes, ma'am."

"Please, not ma'am. It sounds ancient. Ann will do and is Billy really what you prefer to be called?" Her tone said William or Bill would be better.

"It's what I *am* called."

"Well then, Billy... what do you do?"

Wow, her mom was wasting no time with going into super interrogation mode. "Would you like something to drink, Billy?" Sara, forgetting her own interest in answers, took pity on Billy in an attempt to divert the conversation away from parental cross-examination. "We have fresh lemonade."

"That's be great. It's sure hot around here."

She filled his glass as her mother put the flowers in water and then continued with the questions. "Have you been to Pendleton before?"

"Years ago as a kid. From what I've seen so far, it hasn't changed that much."

"We are trying to get used to it. It's hard coming from Chicago as you can imagine."

"That's a big city for sure."

"Have you been to Chicago?"

"Not to spend time, just traveling through."

"Well this has been a difficult adjustment for me. No theater, symphony, boutiques, well you can possibly imagine."

They moved into the living room where Sara's father joined them, and she again did the introductions. "How long will you be here?" George Connor asked.

"A few days."

"Ah then it's for the rodeo."

"Yep."

"They tell me it's quite the show."

"Being only a kid back then, I can't say how'd you'd see it, but it was impressive to me."

Sarah wondered if Billy was regretting coming. She saw her parents as he must see them. Her dad was noticeably older than her mother, portly, balding, distinguished but in a casual sort of way. It wasn't hard to guess which parent had sought the move west.

"I think I saw you at the store today," George Connor said after an uncomfortable silence.

"Yes, sir. I had just gotten into town, and your store drew me right to it. I don't like chains. You have good selections."

Well that would please dad. She hoped they'd not think to ask how long they had known each other as it was a piece of information she'd slid over. Her mother would be imagining she had invited an ax murderer into the house.

"How long have you two known each other?" her mother asked and the cat was out of the bag.

"We met today," Billy said. The atmosphere got decidedly chillier after that. Fortunately the timer on the stove told her mother dinner was ready, and they adjourned to the dining room. The table was set quite prettily, but then it always was as her mother like good china, crystal, candles and flowers which she used to good effect. She had put the ones Billy had brought on the credenza. Sara imagined that through Billy's eyes the whole thing might seem shallowly ostentatious, but he said nothing except to compliment the food after they started to eat.

"Did you say where you live?" her father asked.

"I was born in Bend."

"That's Central Oregon, I believe."

Billy nodded, his eyes cool, giving away nothing of what he was thinking. "Since Oregon isn't home base for you folks, how'd you happen to find your way clear out here? It's not a town many would even know about if they didn't have family to draw them."

"The store was an opportunity I couldn't pass up. I had been looking at various small towns and then found this one, one family from the time Pendleton was established. Good reputation locally for me to build on. And frankly, I had had it with the big city," Mr. Connors said. "It was a hard decision for the family though as you might imagine."

"Where do your parents live," Ann went back into interrogation mode.

"Both are dead but they were in Bend when alive."

"Oh, I'm sorry." There the conversation died again as they finished the meal.

"Would you like a little glass of brandy?" Mr. Connors asked as they rose to go back to the living room.

"I'm not much of a drinker," Billy said.

"Coffee then?" Sara's mother asked.

"I would like that, thank you."

"Sugar or cream?" When he shook his head, she headed to the kitchen to bring back a pot.

"So you're here for the rodeo," George said as he settled into the big chair. "I have never been to one. Felt like they were kind of silly actually. Grown men riding animals that must be scared to death. Seems a shame to waste all that money on it." He took out a pipe and lit it.

"Some see it that way."

After pouring the coffee, Mrs. Connors said, "I suppose it's rather like the Roman gladiators." She handed Billy a cup. "A blood sport sort of thing with those who cannot egging on those who can hoping to see their blood spilled. Don't you think?

"Ma'am, I never thought of it that way."

"What other way is there to think of it?"

"There is the skill of the rider. I mean it isn't the easiest thing to stay on an animal like that. Especially the bulls who have an articulated spine that lets them go all which directions."

"You know quite a lot about it. Not your first rodeo, then I take it?" Sara's father asked.

"I've been to quite a few, yes."

"What about the poor animals," Sara's mother returned to her own concern.

"There are rules to keep them safe. They are well cared for. There are only those few moments in the arena where they try to get the rider off their backs... and sometimes stomp him while they do it."

"I just cannot see it as a real sport like say golf," her father argued.

"Well, everybody can see things as they want. I mean chasing around a football doesn't seem like much of one either if you break it down."

"It doesn't hurt an animal though."

"Other than the pig." Billy grinned. "In all the rodeos I've been to, I've yet to see an animal hurt beyond a sprain that wasn't crippling. Seen plenty of riders get it though. One fatally although that's rare."

"How did that happen?" Sara asked.

"Bull tossed him out and before anybody could get to him had turned back and gored him in the belly. They still couldn't get him out and the animal did it again. Bull wasn't hurt at all."

"Did they kill the bull for doing it?"

"No, but I do think it was his last rodeo. Maybe they put him to breeding. It's not like the rodeo wants a bull who wants to kill and now knows how to do it."

Sara shuddered. Her dad was obviously enjoying the subject and not ready to let it go. "You see and what was the sense to it, I ask you? Poor man died for nothing."

"Other than doing a thing he chose and loved. Would you limit people's choices?"

"Not specifically, of course."

"Just rodeos?"

Her father smiled thoughtfully. "Let the cowboys do it and the handlers or whoever else. Just convince the public not to go there. No profit in it and that would put an end to it. Free will and all."

"That's already the case."

"How do you mean?"

"Nobody has to go to a rodeo, do they? So it's already a matter of free will."

"Not for the livestock."

"That was a delicious roast Ann fixed tonight," Billy said smiling faintly. "Anybody ask the steer how he felt about that?"

Sara restrained a laugh and waited to see what her father's answer would be. It wasn't long in coming. "Well, there is no sense to it. It doesn't nourish our bodies. It doesn't require any brains to ride an animal like that. It would take more sense to stay off it in the first place." He laughed at his own little joke. ""Most of the cowboys likely don't have enough sense to figure that out though."

"Among other things," Billy muttered.

"They told us it'd be good for business in town," Sara said trying to get the conversation off blood and gore.

"Not mine. I don't see anybody new coming in. The regular customers are avoiding downtown. With the traffic, they couldn't park if they wanted. No, it's not good for any business but hotdogs and beer." He laughed again.

Ann Connors added, "They tell me that there will be a lot more drunkenness. I really worry with all the rowdies coming to town." Concern tinged her voice.

"Well fortunately for you folks, it doesn't last long," Billy said, his whole demeanor saying nothing was lasting as long as this dinner.

Before he could think of an excuse to leave, which Sara was sure he had to be considering, she decided to take some initiative. "I wanted to show Billy my studio." She hoped he didn't show his surprise at that, "and then thought we'd take a walk around town."

"Don't be out too late," her mother said with concern. She clearly didn't like this one bit. "Things could get out of control later."

"Oh, I won't. I'll just grab a sweater as nights sometimes get quite cool."

"Studio?" he asked as soon as they got outside.

"I paint."

"Seriously?"

"Well when I can. It's what I'd like to do but it's not that easy to make a living at it as you might imagine." She led him up a set of paving stones to the back where her father had converted an old garage into a studio for her. Flicking on the lights, she wondered what he'd think of her work. She hadn't considered that aspect when using it as an excuse to get out of the house.

He walked over to the canvas on the easel, studying it. "I am not an art critic, as you probably guessed, but this looks good to me," he said. "As much as I know about art anyway. At least I can tell what it is." He grinned.

Her work was mostly landscapes although she had painted a few of friends and people she'd seen somewhere to give herself some variety. She preferred plein air painting, getting out somewhere and painting what she saw. She knew she was a long way from being gifted at it but was pleased he was encouraging.

"I mean it," he said, seeing her skepticism. "I like them. The bright colors, the... uh not sure of the right word, but balance."

"Wow, you see balance?" It was what she always strove to achieve, the painting that would somehow depict the goal of life to find a balance between dark and light, growth and entropy, dream and nightmare. It sounded so grandiose to put it that way but inside her was this drive to make it happen on each canvas—except it never seemed it really did.

"It's ... uh something I tend to notice. I also like the feel of the land especially in that one of the river and cliff alongside it. Swallows flying out. Living matter and... well inanimate. Yeah, very nice."

She felt very pleased. "Thank you."

"You paint them all right here?"

"Actually I like best to at least start them out somewhere. I have a portable easel and when I can I get out there and try to ... well get the energy of a place if you can see what I mean." She picked up an older one of downtown Pendleton, "Although sometimes I'll see something right around here."

"I liked Pendleton when I hit here. It had the feeling of being a real town, not a strip mall sort of place."

"It is heading that way, I fear for everywhere. Malls are so much easier to shop although so far so good for Pendleton's downtown."

"You have your paintings in any galleries?"

"No. I am still learning... Well they really aren't good enough for that." She also knew she wasn't ready to have them rejected by a professional. It had to have surprised her parents that she had even wanted Billy to see them.

"Well they look good enough to me."

A few minutes later, they were outside and walking in the cooling night air. The one thing she really did love about Pendleton was the summer nights. The birds were singing in the trees, the breeze was just enough. Below she could hear the sounds of the city; but where they were, it was quiet with only an occasional car going by.

"I think I better tell you something," he said after a block.

She glanced over and saw a somber expression on his face. "Is it bad?"

"Well, it might seem bad."

"Then?"

"I happen to be one of those riders they were talking about."

"You *ride* in the rodeo?" She didn't know why she hadn't realized it from the start. Showing up as he had, not just the jeans, boots and hat, but the whole way he moved. She should have known. "What kind of riding?"

"For this one I entered bareback and the bulls. Sometimes it's saddle bronc."

"So... a rider rider. I was pretty stupid to not think of that, wasn't I?"

"It wasn't in your experience to expect." He looked over at her as though trying to decide what she was thinking.

"I wasn't expecting it for sure."

"I am sorry I didn't tell you when we first met. I had my reasons."

"And they were."

"About now, this is gonna sound silly given what your folks said tonight, but I didn't want you thinking more of me because of it." He laughed with what sounded like real amusement. "I didn't figure the other angle, that it'd be less of me."

"Cowboys in the rodeo have a groupie problem?" she laughed too.

"Sometimes it can seem like for a week or whatever you are the star, big hero type— unless you are thrown off. And yes, some have seemed to want to be with me just because of that. I kind of liked it being you didn't know and didn't care. Uh would you have cared if you'd known?"

She considered that. "I don't know. I might have even more figured you were a guy coming through and thought it wasn't worth getting to know you when you'd be gone right away."

"Can't deny that one."

"Sorry about my folks. They were kind of rough on you but didn't know it, of course."

"They're entitled to their opinions. It's not like I didn't know the viewpoint was out there. They aren't familiar with the rodeo world, have no reason to be. It's not much like a ballet." He gave a little laugh. "Really though, the livestock are not hurt."

"I believe you, and I am sorry for the..." She tried to think of a word but failed. Harassment came to mind but really it hadn't gone that far.

"Hey, it's okay. I have heard worse from my own family."

"You said your folks are dead now but they didn't like you being a rodeo cowboy?"

"Dad liked it. Mom not at all. And my brother thinks I'm a bum."

"Does that bother you?"

He thought about saying it didn't, but what was the point of trying to fool himself. "Some times more than others."

"How dangerous is it?"

"I don't think of it that way but there are certainly dangerous aspects, but heck, just crossing a street like this, a drunk can come wheeling down the road and bang. It's all over. In life aren't a lot of things dangerous but just once in awhile?"

"Well but those things we didn't choose. It sounds like you do choose it."

He shrugged it off but began to wish for a cigarette. If he smoked in front of her, would she see that as another black mark? "Where it comes to rodeo, I see it as a sport like any other. It's true you are dealing with a mostly unpredictable animal but that just adds an edge to it. Uh oh shouldn't have said that, should I?"

36

"I am guessing there has to be some adrenaline rush to it when you pit yourself against nature that way."

"You're pretty sharp. The whole thing is a variable for what you get out of it. I've had days I asked myself why I do it."

"But you keep at it."

"The times I debate it haven't lasted long."

"But you have thought it through and considered the risks as well as benefits?"

"I pretty well think through most things I do with a few exceptions." He gave her a crooked grin. "The truth is with most rides, it's just stay on until the bell rings and try to give as good a ride as you know how. If you gave a good ride, you get your money back and then some."

"You pay them to ride?"

"You bet your boots... well mine. And not everybody makes back those fees."

"But you do?"

"I can't say at every rodeo, but the vast majority. If that stops being true, I'll quit." He hoped.

"I guess if you weren't winning, you'd not be at Pendleton and likely finding something else to do."

"I've done well at it the last three years. It takes time to learn, and I have had my rodeos that didn't go so well. It's a lot the luck of the draw sometimes."

"Draw?"

"To decide which animal each man rides, the results are drawn— no favoritism. Pure luck which can give a bad or good ride."

He could almost hear her wheels grinding as she thought that one over. "Is Martin then your only relative living?" She surprised him by changing direction.

"I have a sister in Portland. Nora. She's a big city girl, but basically I come from Melmac plates and chrome tables not the china and silver folks."

"People should not be judged by what they own... and it sounds like you just judged us."

"Well, you are rich."

"Hardly. Dad is just someone who owns a small store. You saw it. It's nothing fancy. Actually he made more money in Chicago, but he hated it. He is a lot happier now even if my mom isn't. He hopes she'll find new things to like here."

"You're an only child?" he asked.

"Now. There was a brother, would have been a big brother."

"Sorry."

"I didn't know him. He died before I was born. I heard his name, saw some photos. It was one of those accidents that nobody can predict, like you were talking about. The result might have made my parents more protective. They never really have let up on that."

"Well they let you go walking with a stranger to them."

She smiled. "That is an improvement, I guess."

After a few moments, she said, "I like walking at night. The air is so still and hearing the birds in the trees. It feels. Well friendly, kind of idyllic."

"I guess."

"Don't you walk much?"

"It's not a hobby if that's what you mean.

They were now by the business district. He saw a small cafe was open. "Want another cup of coffee?"

"I'd like that."

They found a booth inside and sat down. Beyond the cafe was a bar and he could hear the music and laughter coming from it. "That's more what I'd have thought a rodeo type cowboy would be doing tonight," she said as their coffee was brought.

"I didn't lie to your dad. I'm not much of a drinker, and why would I want to be in a bar when I can be with a pretty girl?" He took a sip of the coffee. "You do look real pretty tonight."

"Well thank you."

"You told me about your dad and mom. What about you? Did you want to come to Oregon?"

"I wasn't crazy about the idea. I had friends in Chicago."

"A boyfriend?"

"Nobody special. I had been busy with classes and all. I could have stayed. My parents gave me the option. I wanted a break to think about what I was doing, whether it was what I wanted."

"What were you studying?"

"Art and history."

"So you should be in class right now," he teased.

"I could be, but if I went back, it'd be for winter semester. To be honest, I really didn't know what I would do if I got a degree."

"Teach?"

"I thought of that but what I wanted most was to paint myself. So many teach because they can't *do*. I wanted to be the one who could."

"Then why not do it?"

"Good question. I wish I had an answer. I guess I worry I'm not good enough. A lot of people can paint to a hobby level. Making it a career, that's another story."

"Believe in yourself."

She smiled. "Easy to say. Hard to do. I guess a lot of artists work on believing in themselves. It's not a black and white type of thing whether you are good or not good."

"Unlike rodeo where the horse or bull decides it," he teased.

"Exactly."

"We both have unorthodox careers then."

"You consider what you do a career?"

He gave her a calculated look. "What would you call it?"

"Well... I am not sure."

"It's not playing around. It is self-employment. I'll give you that, but I have a goal that goes beyond it."

Before she could ask what that was, she got a strong whiff of whiskey, garlic and onions at the same time she saw the man's face, and his hat was almost in her face.

"Hey, Billy boy, how you doin'?" the man slurred.

"Hank, you're drunk as a skunk."

"No kiddin'. Hey, who's the pretty gal?" He tipped his head back to get a better look at her. "Wow, Billy, she's a looker. She find you or you find her?"

"Beat it," Billy said.

"I think she's out of your league. Hey pretty lady, wanta dance with me?"

"Bye, Hank."

"Why dontcha introduce us?"

"Not like you'd remember in the morning if I did."

"Was that nice? Bring her on back and let me dance with her, huh?"

"I don't make her choices. Now beat it."

"You two come on back to the bar and have a drink with us."

"No." Billy's tone had grown less friendly.

"Hey, you're no fun."

"Nope, I'm not." He rose and took Hank's arm. "Time to get out of here," he said as he pushed the big man back toward the bar.

"You're no pal either."

"Tell me that when you're sober," Billy said before he turned back to her.

"A friend of yours?" she asked when he had sat across from her again.

"To some degree."

"Degree?"

"He's a man that I sometimes rely on—a lot."

"For?"

"He's a rodeo clown."

"I don't follow this world of yours. Why would you rely on a clown?"

"Another word for him would be bullfighter."

"You are definitely confusing me."

"When a cowboy goes off the bull, and he always go off whether at the end or the beginning of the ride, the clown is the distraction. That drunk, he is one of the bravest men I know and has saved many a cowboy. So try to overlook tonight. His job is a dangerous one."

"So he gets drunk before it all starts. I guess he's what my parents don't like about rodeo cowboys."

He chuckled. "He's kind of the old way. You know it's like any job. We aren't all the same. We don't face nerves the same way. That'd be true if this was football players too, wouldn't it?"

"I still can't believe it. You make a living at this?"

"For the last three years, a pretty good one."

"You don't do anything but rodeo?"

"Not anymore. When the money is good. When someone is winning, well it's the time to go for it. Those days don't last."

"When they end, have you thought what you'll do?"

"I have a plan for that, but you know it's years away. I could change my mind."

She studied him a moment, her thoughts not showing on her face. "Are you like dad says, the kind with a girl in every town, like a sailor or something?"

"Not me." He grinned.

"You did move pretty fast when it came to me."

"There were reasons for that. One I didn't have a lot of time to fool around if you weren't going to be interested. It's not like I could keep coming back. Two, I really wanted to get to know you. And three, if you ever want to do something, you do it fast and with confidence."

"Well, you did that."

"So what do you think, now that you know what I do? Scared off?"

"Not really."

"Going to tell your folks?"

"It doesn't seem it's something that matters to tell them right now. It doesn't involve them, does it?"

"Not to my way of thinking. So will you see me again?"

"It's kind of not going anywhere as it's obvious you don't have time for anything serious."

"You need serious?"

"You just want friends?"

40

"For now."

"Well friends are all I'd be open for with someone like you."

"Friends is a good start." His smile was soft and she realized surprisingly tempting. "With maybe open for options."

"I didn't like the way you said that."

His smile widened. "You worried about a little adventure in your life?"

"The kind where a person gets a broken leg?"

"That's always possible with an adventure."

"You'd be wasting your time if you hoped for it to be something... more."

"I wouldn't pressure any woman into something she didn't want."

"If I was going to see you again, with it being firm that it's not going to be anything serious on either side, what would we do? The rodeo doesn't start tomorrow, does it? Do you have to do prep or anything?"

"I signed in today. After my visit with my brother fell apart, I changed the reservation here to come early. I am free tomorrow. I work out in the morning but after that, nothing is on the agenda."

"Well what could we do?"

"You pack us a lunch and let's find a swimming hole. It's hot here. Maybe up toward the mountains?"

"Me pack a lunch? That sounded chauvinist. Why don't you pack one since it was your idea?"

"I thought all women could cook... or at least make a sandwich. You have the kitchen and all."

"Well I guess I could put together something. You'd be driving?"

"I would."

"Okay, I can provide a lunch."

"Good. I'll show up about eleven. How far off is the best hole?"

"I am not sure but I can ask."

They got up and walked out into the cooling night. "The air feels so good," she said, "just a little breeze, the city kind of quiet and drowsy sounding."

"Anything would feel good after a Pendleton summer day," he said with a grin.

"It's hot all right, but that feels good too most of the time. Not humid and sticky like Chicago can get."

"You sure have beautiful hair," he said, "all coppery-colored, the streetlight is shining on it real pretty."

"Thank you. I really hated being a redhead. I suppose I could dye it now but I haven't."

"That'd be a crime to cover that up with dye. I guess kids teased you in school for being different? Called you red?"

"As a matter of fact they did... in grade school. Nobody since then until you."

"I just did it find out your name." He reached down and took her hand. His was calloused and rough. "Can friends hold hands?" he asked.

She liked it and knew she probably shouldn't. "It feels okay," she managed, but it felt a lot more than that to be holding his strong hand. "Uh, how did you come to ride in rodeos? It doesn't seem it'd be the kind of thing a person would just wake up one morning and do."

"It depends on what part of the country you come from. A lot of riders are like me. They grew up with it. It's like football for small western towns."

"Dad hates football too."

"Well at least he's consistent. In the case of rodeo, I was just always around it. My Dad had rodeoed earlier. He taught my brother and me how to do it, and then others came along and showed me more, took me under their wings."

"It's hard for me to get past a parent wanting their son to do something that dangerous. It doesn't sound much like the parents I know."

"First off, it's not all that dangerous." When she gave a disagreeing snort of disbelief, he went on. "Second, excepting your dad, a lot of parents want their kids playing football. More get seriously hurt with it every year and those are kids not adults. This is just strange to you because you come from somewhere else. Rodeo and roping events, barrel racing, they are part of western culture. Most little towns have a rodeo of some sort. Some bigger than others. You grow up with it and it doesn't seem different."

"I guess not. But you said it was dangerous."

"It's unpredictable is a better way of putting it. It's not like you can set rules for it like soccer. But there aren't all that many injuries. If there were, there'd be less rodeos. Most rodeos get by with nothing more than bruises and sprains. Now and again though it turns ugly. So does driving to town or us to a swimming hole tomorrow."

"I never even thought of watching a rodeo."

"It so happens I have a pass. They gave it to me when I signed up. You want to come see one on Wednesday?"

"Your family won't want it?"

His no was crisp.

"Well if I can work it out with my Dad. The store sometimes is hard to leave although I have to think with the rodeo on, it'll not have much traffic. You don't have friends who'd want to use it?"

"My friends are in the rodeo." He dug it out of his pocket. "You should at least see a rodeo, you know to decide whether your dad is right about it."

"I guess that's so." She smiled and took it.

They walked on silently until they were back at her home and stopped on the sidewalk in front. "I won't come up," he said not that he'd been invited.

"But I will see you tomorrow?"

"Unless you change your mind."

"I won't do that."

"Your parents might not like it." He thought about kissing her but knew he wouldn't, not yet.

"They expect me to choose my own friends and use good judgment in that."

"And do you?"

"I used to." She smiled and then ran into the house. She knew he had watched her, that her parents were still up because the television was on. Once she was inside though she didn't go in to do more than say a quick goodnight then head up the stairs.

Closing the door to her room, she knew her mother would have liked more of a report on the evening which she was in no mood to give. She tried to think what she had felt being with him. His hand was strong, rough, and it felt right holding hers. It was a man's hand, one used to hard work. She felt the energy of him through the grasp of his fingers. It was not the energy of a friend.

If there was so much there with just having him hold her hand, what would it be like if they kissed? She didn't suppose his kiss would be the gentle tentative ones of the boys she'd met before him. That was the difference; they were boys. He might not be so many years older, but he was very much a man. That fact both tantalized and scared her.

She sat on her bed, the moon lighting the room almost as though it was morning. She thought about getting out a book to read, but she was in no mood for adding thoughts to her already turbulent brain. She took off the sundress and then laid back staring at the hazy ceiling. Was she using good judgment in going out with him, going swimming, going to a rodeo? Where was this heading?

It wasn't as though she'd never had a boyfriend, but frankly there'd been none she had taken seriously. It was more two buddies doing things. This could possibly take her to a different level with a man. She knew that despite what she had said to him. Was she ready to go? Should she go to that level with a man who would not be there in a week?

She knew the correct answer, the one her mother would want her to choose. Would she follow it? Or would she let her head not her heart make her choice? She could still walk a different road here. It wasn't too late. Not yet, it wasn't.

Chapter Four

Tuesday

Billy was up by six pulling on a t-shirt and jeans. Tice grumbled at the disturbance. No surprise since he hadn't gotten in until the bars closed and had been well soused when he dropped into bed.

"Shit. Where you goin', kid?"

"Breakfast then down to the office."

"Breakfast. Ugh! You going over there this early?"

"I've got plans today."

"Huh... How'd it go with her?"

"It was fine. I like her."

Tice rolled up on one elbow. "You score?"

Billy shook his head. "Geesus, do you ever take your mind out of the gutter, McGraw?"

"You must have gotten in early. Why didn't you come down to the bar?"

"Nothing there I wanted."

"And there was with her, huh? Well watch out. You know the way it works. Mom's home cooking, the good girl that you can't just leave. You'll be lassoed, dragged to the fire and branded afore you know the rope is tightening around your neck."

Billy shook his head. "You coming to breakfast, maybe some bacon or ham and eggs?"

"Shit." Tice shoved the pillow over his head as Billy chuckled closing the door. Outside the air smelled clean and fresh. He spent an hour working out with his weights, stretching, working on flexibility before he smoked a cigarette on his way to the café where he ordered coffee, eggs, bacon, potatoes, and toast.

As Billy waited for the food, he thought about what he was getting into with Sara. Tice had a point not that he'd admit it to him. Someday he might want a girl like her, but this wasn't the time for it. Traveling had always made avoiding that kind of complication easy. He moved on and even if he had felt interest, it was easy to let it go. He wasn't sure how easy it would be with her.

Part of him said it was silly to start worrying about something like that. She likely wouldn't be that taken with him. He didn't exactly lead a life of which she was apt to see herself wanting to be part. She probably had lots of men despite what she said. He couldn't afford a woman right now, not one to keep.

The men who had women traveling with them, well it didn't always work well for either of them. Some women worried too much; and if they didn't have a role in the rodeo, like Jean had had with barrel racing, the life could be pretty boring with no goals for themselves. The ones who stayed home, they often got tired of waiting and found someone else.

It wasn't ideal for the men either. They'd worry about how their women were doing. Try to keep them happy. Worry another guy was hanging around back at home. Lose their own edge. A man couldn't afford to lose his edge. Rodeo had enough uncertainties without adding rioting emotions. He admitted, at least to himself, that someday he had hoped to meet a woman like her. It would come later when he was near to giving up the circuit. At the beginning was no time to have that happen.

He was foolish worrying over it anyway. He'd have blamed it on Tice's warnings except he knew he'd been having some of the same doubts. He just hadn't voiced them. Right girl. Wrong time. It wasn't likely it'd get serious anyway; but if it seemed to be going that way, he'd cut it off quick. She deserved more than he'd be ready to give her. By the time he was ready, she'd have two kids with some local banker.

As he ate his food, he thought about having more time with her, going swimming, acting like he had a normal life. Maybe that's all he wanted—a moment of feeling as though he did have a normal life. Was that possible? Had he ever had a 'normal' life? He frowned as he sucked in a breath. He was kidding himself about this whole thing.

At the rodeo grounds, activity had picked up even though it was only eight and there was a full day before the events began. There were people all around the office and a lineup at the desk. The rides weren't posted yet; so he wandered down to the stock pens.

The Indian encampment was just beyond with tepees and as much activity going on as at the rodeo office. The morning sun shown on their canvas sides as they stretched between the arena and the banks of the Umatilla River. Some were brightly colored and decorated symbolizing tribal connections or identifying an owner. They came from the Nez Perce, Umatilla, Warm Springs, Cayuse, Walla Walla and more as they prepared for their own part, the parade and the entertainment as they used pageant to retell the history of the West—Happy Canyons.

He remembered his excitement as a child seeing it for the first time. The regalia, costumes, the first time he'd seen a real chief except in movies. The speed of those riders on their ponies, their skill had impressed him enough that he still remembered it all vividly.

He wandered beyond the tepees to the river. It was slow moving and relatively shallow where he walked. He sat on the ground and idly picked up a flat rock, skimming it across the water. Five bumps, not bad. He sat letting the sun soak into him as it rose slowly in the sky. It was so different down there, so much of what was above seemed a lifetime away from this slow moving river. The river didn't give a damn about any of it. The river never did.

When he walked back to the office, the lists were posted. He worked his way to the front of the cowboys clustered around it to find his own number and the draws.

Not bad, he thought with satisfaction. Opening day Apache would be his horse in bareback. He'd seen him ridden and not ridden. He was a good bucker and would give a show. About the bull #36, he knew nothing but that didn't bother him. He'd ask around to see if anybody else had and get some tips. That was one thing about cowboys, they were competing with each other, but they were in it together and most were willing to help the ones who might well beat them in the end.

He'd been silly to feel this town, this rodeo had a jinx on him. It was going to be okay. It would be like every other competition, no different. No ghosts.

Turning away from the boards, he saw Nick come striding up. He had a gangly youth with him of maybe nineteen. The youth was trying to mimic Nick's walk, his mannerisms, and not succeeding. Billy grinned seeing himself five years earlier walking besides Tice.

Nick glanced to the lists but then turned toward Billy. "Hey, want you to meet somebody. Billy, this is Denny Bauer. Denny, here's the cowboy I told you about. The best bronc rider out there right now."

The youngster's eyes turned speculatively toward Billy as they shook hands. The boy's hand was small, wiry with long thin fingers, strong for its size. He wasn't tall which would make him a good bull rider if that was what he was aiming to be. His face was lean, like the rest of him. "I seen you ride," he said with a cocky manner that instantly turned Billy off to him.

"Sounds like I fell off when you did," Billy said with a crooked smile.

"Nah, you won that day. Salinas. Remember it?"

Billy shook his head. "Can't say I do. That's been awhile as I didn't make Salinas this year."

Nick turned to the board now to study the lists and find his own draw.

"I wasn't riding yet when I seen you," the youth said.

"You entered here?"

"Bareback and saddle bronc," he said proudly. After a moment, he added, "Looks like we'll be competing."

"Looks like it."

Nick turned away from the lists and cursed which wasn't Nick's way.

"What's wrong?" the kid asked.

"Nothing."

"Well it's sure as hell is something," Denny said.

Billy looked at the boards to find Nick's draw. He said nothing but looked back at Nick with understanding. Nick had drawn a horse called Wildcat for a good reason. It wasn't just that the gelding was hard to ride, changed direction constantly, but Nick had a history with the animal. He'd been hurt on him two years earlier. It wasn't a superstition really. Every ride, every rodeo was different, but it wasn't what a man wanted to see for his first ride back after a serious injury.

He wanted to say something but couldn't think what would make it better. That was his trouble. He didn't have the words too much of the time.

Nick got a handle on his anxiety though and managed to say, "Well if the good Lord wanted me on that horse, it'll be okay."

"Something wrong with it?" Denny asked looking at the board himself.

Nick laughed shortly. "Nothing. Wish there was. He's in great shape at least he was the last time he slammed me into the chutes.

"You scared of him?" Denny asked looking incredulously at Nick as though fear never occurred to him.

Billy pulled out a cigarette and lit it. "Seriously you don't know yet that we're all scared sometimes, kid

"Not Nick."

Nick snorted. "Everybody, son. Everybody. Only a fool wouldn't ever know that sometime their number could be up."

"Not me," Denny said with the assurance of youth. "I never been scared."

"Well when the day comes you are," Billy said blowing out the smoke, "and that day will come, then you'll know what you're made of."

"What's that supposed to mean?"

He thought about not explaining it but decided to give it a try. "When you aren't scared, it's nothing what you do. When you are, and you do it anyway, that's when you know whether you have grit."

"I don't get it."

Billy hadn't figured he would.

"We're having some folks over to the trailer tonight," Nick said to change the subject. "Come on over, Billy."

"I might have a date."

"Might? A girl on the circuit?"

He shook his head. "Lives here. I just met her."

"And you want to bring her?" Nick lit his own cigarette as he gave him a surprised look. "It'd be fine. You bring her along. I always like to meet pretty gals."

"How do you know she's pretty?"

"Haven't seen you with one who wasn't."

"I am not sure how it's going to go, but we'll see."

"Hey, come on. I want to meet her even more."

"You seem too eager. I might lose her if I brought her, all those cowboys around, and you the leader of the pack."

"Like Jean wouldn't slit my throat first," Nick said with a laugh.

"A sweet lady like her, she'd do a thing like that?"

"She's part Comanche, carries a knife. Hell, there's a limit what she takes off me. I'm not pushing my luck. Hey, Denny, you coming tonight."

Denny who had seemed to be ignoring the conversation said sure.

"You bringing Susan?"

"We'll be there."

"Susan's his better half," Nick told Billy.

Billy hoped his mouth didn't drop open at that. He'd have to reevaluate how old Denny must be or else he got married straight out of high school. Brother.

"Hey, I'll see at least you tonight," Nick said giving Billy's shoulder a pat as the two of them took off.

Billy spent the next hour readying his gear. There wasn't much he had to do, but it was mostly killing time; so he wouldn't think about whether he was really going to be at Sara's in half an hour. Denny was married. God what the hell would drive a kid that age to get married? Nick didn't mention a baby.

"Hey, glad I caught you," Hank said coming up with a chagrinned look on his face. "About last night."

"Don't remember nothing," Billy said with an amused smile. "Something happen?"

"I wasn't so drunk I don't remember making a fool out of myself."

"Forget it."

"Hope I didn't scare off your little gal. I didn't mean nothing."

"I know that. She was fine with it. No harm done."

"She's sure a pretty thing."

"I noticed. How you feeling today?"

Hank chuckled. "Headache, of course, which led to Ibuprofen with a chaser of that pink stuff which is all why I do all my drinking a day ahead of the action."

"Jacey with you?"

"Yeah and she ragged me plenty about the drinking. Screw it, Billy, I need to bust loose once in awhile. Why don't women never get that?"

"Don't ask me," Billy joked, "not like I understand women at all." He hadn't had reason to try either.

"Well, you tell that little gal I am sorry if you see her again."

"Sure… if I do."

The expression on Hank's face grew somber, his eyes darkened. "Billy, you ever get feelings?"

"About what?"

"Like vibes?"

"Not unless I can't avoid it," he tried to make a joke but knew this wasn't really funny.

"I got one about this rodeo. Not that I'm excusing myself or nothing. Getting drunk ain't particularly smart on a lot of levels, but I don't feel good about this one."

Billy felt a chill go down his spine. "You afraid you'll get hurt?" he asked overriding his natural inclination to avoid talking about any of this. He wished Hank hadn't brought up the subject, didn't want to think more deeply about it. He wouldn't cut him off though and had to give him a chance to voice his fears. Except, did talking about them ever really help?

What he believed did help was a single minded pursuit of a goal, of doing whatever was required right in that moment with no thought of the next moment or day. When he found that concentration and focus broken, that's when he always got in trouble. He wouldn't say that to the older man. What did he really know of what worked or didn't for others? Hank was one of the best he knew at bullfighting and whatever Hank needed, he'd give it to him.

"Not so much me. Although that's always possible. Nah, it's the whole shebang, like it's going to go bad some way I don't know right now. If I could put my finger on it, I'd feel better. Damn, I sound like an idjit or one of them twinkies."

Billy wasn't willing to add to Hank's concerns; so he gave himself a moment as he lit another cigarette. "Want one?" he asked holding out the pack.

"Nah, I quit... again. I hope I make it stick this time. It's causing me to not breathe so good, can't run like I need to when I'm smoking. Jacey's been ragging on me something fierce. Says the kids'll be picking it up if I don't quit. Maybe I am quit now."

"I guess I should too but..." He left the statement dangling. He hadn't tried to quit but maybe he would someday too. After this season maybe... "On the vibe thing. I don't know what I believe about it; but if you ever get to feeling you oughta hang it up, you should do it. I believe that much about those kind of feelings. And I'm saying this totally unselfishly because the truth is when I go off a bull, there's no man I'd rather have rushing in to save my butt than you."

Hank gave a faint smile. "I appreciate you tellin' me that."

"Given that, I still say, if you ever feel you should quit, do it. Don't fool around about it. Just plain do it. Walk off the same day. Sometimes we don't get a second warning." He knew he was talking to himself as much as to Hank. He was talking to them all. Nobody would make them quit. Failure would do it eventually but it's not like a team would sit down and say you're out. They had to each do it for themselves.

Hank smiled, stared into space for a moment before he sketched a wave and left.

When Billy drove through town, the traffic was building with a mix of the people coming for the big event and those making it happen. The more he saw Pendleton, the better he liked it as a town. It was pretty with the hills around it, river running through the center. He pulled into a service station to fill up the tank on the truck and had to wait five minutes for that. Damn, Oregon needed self-service pumps. He thought about having it washed, but he had used up his allotted time.

He had only knocked lightly on the door before Sara's mother had opened it. She was wearing a casual tan slack-suit that emanated elegance. "Good morning. I am on my way out also," she said with a smile that didn't extend to her eyes. "Board meeting."

Sara came from the kitchen, picnic basket, that actually looked like one, in one hand and smiling broadly. "Yes, mom, we'll be careful," she said before her mother had a chance to request it.

In the truck, he asked, "So what's for lunch?"

"You'll have to wait to find out."

"Hey, tell me now. I like anticipation not uncertainty."

He glanced over to see how she took that. She was smiling. "Is food all men think about?"

"It's a close second." He looked down her form, enjoying the jeans and t-shirt. She did laugh but blushed too.

"Hey, I didn't know girls still blushed."

"I did not."

"Did so."

Her color heightened. "It's being a redhead, "she complained finally.

"Your red hair is real pretty. Don't ever apologize for it, baby."

Clearly she didn't know what to say to that, maybe wasn't so sure how she liked him calling her baby, and so changed the subject. "Did you go out to the rodeo grounds this morning?"

"I was up early, worked out, got breakfast and yes, got over there to take care of what needed doing."

"You work out?"

"Weights, stretches, sit-ups, pull-ups, push-ups, the usual to keep muscles honed and loose for when I need them." He wanted a cigarette but wasn't sure how Sara would take smoking; so he held off on asking if she minded.

"That guy last night, he really was a cowboy too?" He didn't blame her for wondering about a world that was all new to her.

"Hank asked me to tell you he was sorry. He was working off some steam before he can't afford to not do it."

"It feels like I am Alice and just stepped down a rabbit hole into an alternate universe."

Billy smiled. "We're flesh and blood like anybody else. Hank used to ride, saddle bronc and one of the best. Guess it got boring for him." He laughed. "So now he takes a greater risk."

"He's a wild one though, isn't he?"

"Actually, he's not. He's married, a family man. It might've seemed like he was hitting on you but he really wasn't. It was his idea of a good time to dance with pretty girls. He and Jacey have two kids. They are with her folks when she travels with Hank. This will probably the last rodeo she can go to for this year as the kids activities begin to pick up. She isn't with him all the time. Maybe you'll meet her."

"I'd like to meet some of the women. Do any compete?"

"Barrel racing but not in the riding events generally anyway. Not that I see."

"Kind of a guy's world then?"

"A last stronghold." He laughed. "Anyway like I said, he asked me to apologize. If you met him around the rodeo, you'll see he's a different kind of guy. He said Jacey didn't think much of his judgment last night either. He needs to take up yoga for stress."

He glanced over to be sure she understood he was joking. She at least smiled. "You know," he added, "it's a high stress job playing with bulls who have an ornery temperament. For Hank, it's only once in awhile he cuts loose. If it was all the time, he'd be off the circuit. You can't do that and this."

"So cowboys aren't wild like my father said or like a person hears?"

"I didn't say that, but it's a changing world. There are those who think carousing is the way to live, never mind the morning after, but it's a dying breed. Their bodies don't hold out between the rides and the boozing."

"Did you go back and join them after you took me home?"

He grinned as he glanced over at her. "Would it matter?"

"No, just curious is all."

"I didn't. I was not just saying it to please your dad. I'm not a drinker. Oh I have a beer once in awhile, a little wine with dinner, but alcohol is not my thing. The boys had a card game going and I was in no mood to lose the money I might make here before I wont it."

"So no vices?" she said with a teasing voice.

"I didn't say that. I drink a beer now and then, sometimes a glass of wine. Speaking of, did you bring anything to drink?"

"Cokes. If you want stronger, you will need to stop and pick that up," she said with a little laugh. She liked everything she was learning about him. "I didn't even think of getting any. I sure couldn't take my dad's brandy."

"We don't need it. What did you bring?" he teased.

"What happened to the adventurer?"

"I save that for the arenas."

"Well you took a risk coming to dinner at a stranger's house last night."

"A limited one... Of course, I hadn't met your mama yet."

Then she really laughed with him. "She's actually not as tough as she sounds."

"I'll take your word for that. What kind of board meeting was she going to?"

"I think an arts group but don't hold me to it."

He drove out of town toward a swimming spot one of the guys had told him about as she actually ended up not knowing of any. He couldn't resist watching her when the road permitted. Her hair was down over her shoulders. With the windows down, the wind blew it changing its colors with the light. She didn't seem to mind it being mussed. He liked that too. In fact there wasn't much he didn't like about how she looked. Then a thought occurred to him. "Where's your suit?"

"I'm wearing it under the jeans. Where's yours? Does this place have somewhere to change?"

"I doubt it, but I forgot to get one."

"You sure you didn't forget on purpose."

"Why would I do that?"

"Maybe you can't swim."

He snorted. "What does that mean?"

"In all the cowboy movies, how often do you see any of them go swimming?"

"Let's see riding, roping, branding, cutting." He used his fingers to add them up. "Nope, no swimming."

"So maybe a cowboy is like a duck out of water around a river."

"Since I am trying to impress you with all my good qualities, it's not likely I'd ask you to go swimming if I couldn't, now is it?"

"Well without a swimsuit, you won't be able to prove it... er uh." She got a decidedly uneasy expression on her face. "You wouldn't swim in the buff, would you?"

He laughed at the tone of her voice. "Would you mind?"

"Of course, I would. Plus you might get arrested... You might get me arrested. That would go over well at home. What kind of swimming hole is this?"

"Close to town like this, I am sure it's going to be family rated; and no, I wouldn't swim in the raw."

"Then..."

"Since it's a river, I can swim in my jeans."

"Boots too?" now she was teasing.

"Not this pair. I forgot to pick up the pair I use for swimming." He gave a mock expression of regret.

"How about the hat?"

"Only when it rains." They both laughed.

Luck of the Draw

At the river, he parked the truck along the road, stashed his wallet in the glove compartment before he locked the truck. They walked to the river's edge where the water looked cleaner than he'd been expecting and was, as he had guessed, a place with all ages along the banks and in the water. In the shade of a big cottonwood, it was almost cool. A rope hanging from the limbs of a large oak was obviously intended for swinging way out and jumping.

On a grassy knoll, she spread the blanket she had pulled from the basket. "Want to eat or swim first?" she asked.

"Swim," he said, sitting down to yank off his boots. He watched as she slid out of her jeans and t-shirt to reveal a white, two-piece swimsuit. It wasn't a bikini but was very flattering to her figure although he figured pretty much anything would be. He yanked his t-shirt over his head, pulled the belt from his jeans. The jeans were snug enough to stay up without it—he hoped as he rolled up the legs. He threw keys and billfold into his boots, laying the t-shirt over the top.

Getting to his feet, he followed her to the edge of the river. It was wide, had a nice pool in the middle with a sandy, gravel beach. She was already up to her knees when he entered the water. He watched her for a moment, forgetting his own need to go deeper. She was beautiful, more beautiful than any woman he'd seen with that red hair, the slim but curvy body. In a moment she had pushed forward and was swimming with long graceful strokes. "Come on in," she said turning over onto her back to look back at him. "Prove you can swim."

He grinned and moved quickly out into the stream and gave a shallow dive as he also began to swim. "Race you to the other side," she teased.

"What are the stakes?"

"There have to be stakes?"

"Of course."

"Well what do you want them to be?"

"How about a kiss?" He gave her a teasing smile.

She gave him one of those looks. "Sounds like a win win for you, but what about me?"

"Picky picky. So what stakes do you want?"

"Your hat for the rest of the day on my head if you lose."

He forced a concerned look. "That's my lucky hat."

"Well don't lose then."

"I have motivation not to for sure," he teased not much worried about the outcome. "So when do we start?"

"Right now," she cried, turning over and beginning a strong, obviously well taught, Australian crawl.

He dove, following swiftly, not catching up too quickly but staying close enough to enjoy being with her, letting her think she had a chance to win. She was a darned good swimmer, but his strength was way more than hers. When he put the effort into it, he was onto the rock and reaching down to pull her up by the time she got there.

"Ready to pay up?" he asked his hands on her arms.

"Now?" she managed to gasp, the water running in rivulets from her hair and body.

"You going to welch?" He gave her a look that said he had expected that.

"No, I wouldn't do that."

"And I don't want my first kiss with you to be because you had to," he said.

She smiled at him then. "It won't be." She reached up, her arms going around his neck. As her lips came near his, he waited, letting her be the one to bring them together. He tasted the water on her lips, the pressure of their warmth against his and he let that innocent kiss be all her doing. He knew there'd be more and then he'd teach her other kinds of kisses but not this one.

When they had broken apart, they waited on the rock letting their skin dry before they dove back to swim smoothly to the other side. Toweling off, they sat and she brought out the food. "Perfect picnic," he complimented her on the traditional fare—fried chicken, potato salad, carrot sticks and brownies. She handed him a Coke that had been nestled in a bed of ice. "This was worth waiting for."

She knew she was in way over her head as she watched him leaning back on the blanket. One knee was bent, the other leg straight out. He hadn't rolled his jeans back down, so his sinewy calves were part of the picture. That muscular chest, the long line of his torso, the ridged belly, it was heady stuff to a woman who had only been with boys up until then. It took her a moment to realize he had asked her a question. Her mind was anywhere but on talking after that kiss, after being so close to him.

"I want to know more about you," he said. "What kind of books do you like?"

"Seriously? That interests you?"

"Wow, that's quite a slam," he said with a laugh. "So I should not be interested in books? Who's the snob here?"

She couldn't deny it. "I am buying into a stereotype when I really don't even know what that is. Okay, my books... Well, I like mysteries like Agatha Christie. Non fiction biographies and autobiographies. How about you?"

"I'm not reading anything right now but when I do, I like books about nature and farming, of course."

"So non-fiction. How about movies? What kind of films?"

"Definitely comedy. If it's funny, I am ready to lay down my dollar to go see it. How about you?"

"I see most movies on television, the oldies like with Humphrey Bogart."

"You follow the news?"

"I hate to admit it but not so much."

As they ate, they explored different questions about things that weren't so important, questions where there were no wrong or right answers, but were part of every day living. She didn't really care a lot about what his answers were. Just to listen to his deep voice, the way he tended to drawl sometimes when he was not thinking about it, she liked it all. She wished they could kiss again but there were children playing on the water now in front of them. His eyes glittered as he watched her, listened to her questions, answered her and she knew he was wanting what she was except maybe he knew more to want than she did. She wished she could capture that look in a sketch and pulled out a pad from the basket.

"Do you mind if I draw you?" she asked, opening up the book to a clean sheet. He shook his head and she wasn't sure if he did or didn't, but she made some sketches, liking the one best that was a profile as he looked out toward the water, his thoughts hidden. Then for awhile she sketched the children playing along the sandy bank. He watched her as she worked and finally she asked him, "What are you thinking?"

He tried to think of the words. "That this is very nice. A woman. Peace. Life. The kind of thing that makes it all worthwhile." He might have used it as a line; but in reality, it was exactly what he felt. It felt real. It wasn't as though his life didn't, but his life was always about being on the move and constant change. That wasn't bad but just different.

"That's what a place like this is to you?" she asked

"That and more than that, a woman like you."

She didn't know what to say to that. "It is nice here, isn't it?"

He thought then about what he was saying and sat up abruptly.

"Does something being good worry you?"

"Right now. When it's something I can't keep."

"We knew that from the beginning. We really don't know each other."

"A day and not even all of that." He knew it felt a lot longer than a few hours. "I will be gone in a week," he added to remind himself more than her.

"I know."

"I am not promising anything."

"Neither am I."

"But you might want more."

"And so might you. I won't get serious about somebody who doesn't really want to be with me."

"I figured as much."

"We are talking about a lot of maybes that don't really exist. When it comes time for you to leave, you'll probably be glad to go and I'll be glad you are leaving."

"You think so? Life has a way of fooling us all. Not that I'm an expert on relationships but it seems to me the most trouble starts when we think we can have something the other person never intended to give. Or we think we can change their minds."

"That's human nature. Always hoping for more."

He nodded. "I'm biting off trouble here."

"I suppose we could just let today be it. Not see each other again even while you were here. Is that what you'd prefer?"

"To be honest.... no. Although it'd probably be smarter." His smile was wry.

"I find it not as easy as you to decide what is smart. I'm weak on forming goals. In this case though, if we don't think ahead... I can't believe I just said that, well, we can take what comes along until you leave. Maybe it'll be good memories for us both that we'll carry with us into the future, making life better someday with someone else for having had those memories."

"Can you really do that?"

"I don't honestly know what I can do right now, but I want what time with you is possible. We can be friends, right?"

"Sounds fine with me—if friends kiss sometimes."

She couldn't help but smile at his expression of innocence that she knew was anything but. "And we will have fun, won't we? When you leave, at least we won't regret not having the bit we could."

"Hey, Sara," a male voice said causing her to turn and realize that it was Troy. "I am surprised to see you here," he said looking not at her but rather Billy.

"Billy Stempleton, Troy Jerome."

Billy rose to take Troy's hand. "You from around here?" Troy asked. "I don't think I have seen you before."

"Farther west, Bend."

"Oh hey, I like it there. I go skiing at Bachelor. I bet you are a good skier coming from there."

"Haven't ever tried it."

Troy looked at Sara with more interest than he had shown when they were actually on a date. "Do you ski, Sara, I forgot to ask when we were out to dinner last time."

She thought that was rather interesting as Troy appeared to try and establish some rights to her. Rights she was pretty sure he had never wanted until this moment. She realized then that he had two other guys with him who she didn't know and Troy didn't introduce.

"I have skied a few times in New Hampshire, took some classes," she offered, "but I was totally lousy at it and gave it up before I broke a leg." When she started to stand, Billy took her hand pulling her to her feet.

"We should go sometime. Oh these two guys are Jeff and Royce. Or do you already you know each other?"

She shook her head and wondered how long before they'd leave. "You here for the rodeo, Billy?" Troy asked.

Billy nodded.

"It's a good show. I go every year. You going, Sara?"

"I plan to."

"Maybe we can go together."

That was funny in a sarcastic sort of way. Troy hadn't wanted to date her for months and suddenly he'd like to take her to the rodeo. Men made no sense. She answered, "No thanks but I appreciate the offer."

Troy looked from Billy to Sara and evidently ran out of innocuous questions. "See ya around," he said as he and his buddies walked off to go for a swim.

When they were gone, Billy asked, "He one of the not serious ones?"

She smiled faintly. "He doesn't even count there."

He grinned. "Good judgment." He bent and lightly kissed her forehead.

"Let's walk upstream a ways," she suggested. "I am curious what's around that bend."

Although going for hikes wasn't really his thing, he agreed and they walked barefoot along the gravel and sand bank. If he did much of this, he'd be buying himself some tennis shoes.

"Any rattlesnakes around here?" he asked, not happy with how the little pebbles were feeling on his tender bare feet. He might have been tough a lot of places but not bottom of the feet.

"Snakes? They have poisonous snakes here?" she asked after looking over to assess whether he was joking.

"It's not like I have been *here*, but most of eastern Oregon does. I have worked on ranches where they always had us carrying a gun. Don't much like the calves being bit by them."

She scanned the way ahead. "I don't like snakes."

"Just keep an eye out. They hang around water generally, crawl under or beside rocks. Nothing to worry about but just watch them."

"Have you been hurt?" she asked from out of nowhere.

"By snakes?" he asked teasingly although he doubted that what she was asking.

"In the arena, when you're riding."

"Hurt my pride more than once," he teased.

"That's all?"

"Ah, you want grisly details."

"Are they grisly?"

"Most injuries are not pretty. Actually I haven't been hurt much. Bruises and such, some strained muscles. I got stove-up some in Reno when I first went full time. Figures, huh? Well actually it wasn't the beginning for awhile after that."

"What does stove-up mean?"

She really wanted the whole tamale. He wasn't in the mood to talk about it. "You know right before a new rodeo is not a good time to dwell on past mistakes."

"I'm sorry."

"Not a big deal, but yes, I broke my left arm which was mostly bad because it kept me from riding for over a month."

"A bad break?"

"Is there another kind?" he joked. "But no, not a bad one or I'd have been out for longer. I suppose it could have ended my career before it began if it'd been really bad."

They turned around. He was still debating whether to ask her to Nick and Jean's to-do. Maybe she would not want to go anyway. That wantabe boyfriend sounded like he fit Sara's life better than he ever would. But the guy also seemed like a jerk. Ah hell, he would ask her to go and let that determine what happened.

"Some friends of mine, a nice couple, he's a bronc rider, they are having a thing at their trailer tonight. They said I could bring someone. Would you like to come?"

"Thing?"

"Get together, a do."

"Do you want me to come?"

She did have a knack for reading his mind. "If I hadn't, I wouldn't have asked."

"Okay then I'd like that. What does bronc rider mean?"

"Bucking horses and in his case saddle bronc."

"I am going to sound stupid but let me be sure I understand. Some of the horses aren't wearing… if that's the proper word… saddles?"

"Bareback means ridden with a strap around the middle. It'll all make more sense to you once you see the events."

"Well, I'd like to go tonight, meet other people from your world."

He was afraid she was making more out of this than he intended; but he had told her how it'd be; so that was going to have to be her problem. The thing was he didn't want to hurt her. She knew at least what she was walking into. His experience with women like her was pretty close to zero; so he might be the one who didn't know.

When they got back to town, he said, "I will head to the motel, take a shower and change, be back in an hour if you'll go out to dinner with me tonight."

"I'd like that a lot. Bye for now."

In the house, she was glad her parents were both gone. She debated what she should wear to a thing at a trailer. What kind of people would his friends be? Hopefully nothing like that Hank at the cafe. She would trust Billy that this wouldn't be the same kind of *thing*.

She knew she ought to be thinking ahead. She always thought ahead, figured all the choices, often making her incapable of decisions regarding pretty nearly anything; but she wasn't going to do that this time, not with this. Whatever she would have with Billy; and she took his word for it that it would not last beyond the week, she'd take it for the memories that would be left behind when he was gone. Sometimes in life, memories were enough, well that's what she'd heard.

She had never done anything like this. Maybe she would never do it again. Maybe she would be sorry later, but she knew this kind of opportunity for a possibly once in a lifetime experience only came along rarely if ever. It was a moment, would only be a moment in her life; but she wanted it.

Billy was the kind of person she had never expected to meet. It wasn't even the rodeo riding part. It was the whole way he strode through life, those boots, that steady look in his eyes, and those strong hands and body. She felt lucky she had ever met him, had this opportunity.

She smiled as she recalled one of her favorite Henry David Thoreau lines. "You must live in the present, launch yourself on every wave, find your eternity in each moment." It was crazy but she knew this was what she was going to do. She'd launch herself and ride this wave as far as she could take it.

By the time he had come back for her, he was wearing jeans and a colored t-shirt. She had changed into white jeans, a loose fitting brightly printed top, silver dangling earrings with turquoise stones. "Does this look okay?" she asked as she got into his truck.

"More than okay. You look great. How old are you, baby?"

She ignored the nickname. She didn't actually even mind it coming from him. "Twenty-one," she said.

"I was just wondering where you'd like to eat and thought you might like wine with dinner."

"But you don't drink... except for the occasional beer, she reminded him.

"And except for the occasional glass of wine with dinner." He drove the truck to a restaurant that was not near the rodeo grounds, good food, or so he'd been told, with a section in front with tables and booths for meals and a bar behind.

When they were seated and had ordered, she heard loud laughter coming from the lounge behind the restaurant. She hoped they weren't in for a repeat of the last such time. Billy sucked in a breath and then said, "Might as well get this over. I have someone I want you to meet. Won't take a minute, okay?"

He took her hand and led her to the back, down a long corridor to a large room with a bar along its length. They walked to a table with three men and a woman. One of the men watched them from the moment they had come into the room and grinned as they came up.

"Sara, I want you to meet a friend of mine, Tice McGraw. Tice this is Sara Connors. Those guys alongside him are Bill James and Shepherd something or other—bronc riders. The lady I don't know."

She gave a polite greeting to which Tice smiled, seeming to be sizing her up. He didn't bother introducing the woman with him even though she hung on his arm.

"Tice is the real deal, Sara," Billy said. "A cowboy like your folks were talking about last night."

"Oh," she said with a laugh.

"Now that don't sound complimentary," Tice said as he reached out and then took Sara's hand. "You're a right pretty lady, honey."

"Why thank you."

"Whatever the boy told you about me, it's all lies," Tice said eyes on her rather speculatively.

"What if it was flattering?" she asked.

"Well then it's all the truth." He looked at Billy then. "So this is your reason."

"Reason for what?" Billy asked.

"Why you ain't been around that much."

"I've been around. Just not when you were."

"She's a pretty good reason," Tice said again looking at her and continuing to ignore the woman at his side who was acting as though she felt anything but pleased at the interruption.

Billy put his hand on Sara's back and said, "We're up front having dinner, but I heard your voice back here and figured I better have you two meet."

"You coming up to Nick's later?

"We'll be there."

"Shit. I never would have figured that, Billy boy."

"We were invited."

"Both of you?"

"I told Nick I might bring a friend. It a problem to you?"

"Nah," Tice shrugged. "Just surprised me is all. K then. See you *both* later."

When they were back at the table, Sara asked, "You said he's a friend?"

"He and I are sharing a motel room this rodeo. Tice took me under his wing when I first started riding, taught me a lot of what I know about rodeoing. He was a friend to my dad." He didn't answer her question.

She kept back her thoughts about Tice, about the way he'd not only looked at her but seemed to put down Billy without saying it but implying it. She decided she was being foolish. "He doesn't think much of me, does he?" she asked finally as they began to eat their salads.

"It's not you. Tice is protective."

"And that was protective?" She gave a laugh.

He smiled. "Maybe. Maybe not. He likes it his way and when anything goes against that, he has to fight over it, wrestle it around 'til he gets used to it. I figured you better meet him now as you likely will later. And I sure didn't want him leaning over our table."

"And he doesn't like me because?"

"Did I say he didn't and what difference does it make what he thinks?"

"Maybe he thinks I'll take you from rodeo or is it more he fears I'll take you from him?"

"Well, you can't do either, can you? So he's just being himself. I ignore it."

"Do you?"

"As much as I can."

After dinner she suggested a short walk. He agreed even though he complained that he had more than done his quota of walking since he met her. He decided he might as well confront one issue. "Do you mind if I smoke?"

"I didn't know you did."

"Now you do."

"Well… it's not very good for a person; but no, I don't mind if you don't mind a vicious cough and killing yourself prematurely."

He grinned and knocked out a cigarette, lighting it as he took a deep drag on it before blowing out the smoke. "I think if health was a big concern, I'd have other things I wouldn't be doing. You ever try it?"

"Why would I?"

"It can be relaxing."

"Not when my parents found out. Besides I heard it makes a person's face look like tanned leather. Not so bad for a guy but definitely not good for a woman." As they strolled through the town, she asked, "Did Tice like your mother?"

His answer came after a moment. "I don't think Tice likes women period."

"He's gay?"

"Gay guys like women," he retorted with a smile. "No, he's not gay that I know of anyway. He uses women but like? No, I don't think I've ever seen him like a woman."

"What's the story behind that?"

He hadn't thought of the reason behind it. He supposed there must be one. "Not a happy home life, maybe. I really didn't know his family and they're not around now. You know with men, a lot of times, you just share one part of your life, not all of it."

"So he knows more about you than you do him?

Billy considered that for a moment. "You think he knows me?"

"Does he?"

"Just parts. Parts he needs to use for power."

"Wow, that's a pretty deep thought."

He laughed. "You figured being a bronc rider, I couldn't have one?"

"No, just surprised me a little."

"Where it comes to Tice," he said. "Maybe he just saw women as a barrier, in the way where it came to rodeo. Rodeo is his life. I don't know what he'd have without it."

"That makes it tough then when you said it cannot be a forever type of thing."

"He likely isn't looking that far ahead—although he should since he's had a lot more losing seasons than a person can afford to keep doing for long." He thought about it a moment and then added, "You know, where it came to my mother, he really didn't like her because she didn't like him and she hated rodeo. She feared the danger and resented how it took all my father's interest even when he couldn't ride."

"Your father got you into rodeo. Is that why you do?"

He took a long drag on the cigarette before he answered. "In the beginning, maybe so. I mean whoever knows why they choose things. Why do you paint? In his case, he wanted to go to them most weekends. I think he was trying to plant a seed in me well and Martin too. Dad had tried to make the grade but lost out early on and realized it'd never pay even its own way where it came to him. He blamed it on breaking his back at Pendleton but was that really why? He had been entering enough rodeos, but I don't think anything was heading to a championship buckle."

"So he wanted you to get that buckle." She looked down at the large one on his belt.

"Parents often want their kids to do what they can't, fulfill their dreams, don't you think? Maybe he did think he'd win through us. Mom hated that and did everything she could to block it. Pretty much Tice only was around if she was not."

"My experience with parents has been a bit different. Did... well maybe I shouldn't ask, but did your parents get along?"

"You name it and they disagreed about it. And when it came to Tice, Mom was even more adamant than usual. To her, he was a bad influence."

"Was he?"

He smiled "Could be. Martin doesn't like him either."

"Maybe for the same reason?"

He laughed. "Martin also doesn't like me. So I'd say it's the lifestyle more than particularly being against Tice."

"What's your brother like?"

"Solid, upstanding, Two kids, Jessica and Joel, six and four. Mom liked him best and I suppose Dad did me. That never works real well for the brothers, does it?"

"No, it doesn't."

"She wanted me to be a William. And I wasn't."

"Ah William and Martin. Nice names for boys."

"Except I was a Billy and that didn't fit."

"And Martin wasn't a Marty and so that didn't fit."

"Our parents did a real number on us, I guess."

She thought about that for a bit wondering if one of her parents preferred her. Did they compete for her? She hadn't thought of that before. "At a certain point we have to be who we are whatever our parents think." She was pretty sure she hadn't been living that truth for herself. Her problem was figuring out what that would mean to her life.

"You talking about me now or yourself?" he intuited.

"Both, I guess. I suppose that I have tried to suit my parents, make up for the son they never had. I started seeing that doesn't work before you came along. My problem is what I do about it."

"Is that why you haven't done more with your art. You are good, you know."

She considered that. "Maybe I've been afraid if I did go for it, I'd fail."

"Does fear stop you a lot?"

"I hate to admit it, but I think it has. I had to fight my parents to take the art classes and then had to admit maybe they'd been right when my grades were mediocre. It wasn't going to really work out to be a career. I wasn't good enough."

"Based on someone else's opinion—in that case teachers." He shook his head, seeing a sidewalk ashtray and grinding out his cigarette. "One school could have a set of agendas that another wouldn't. What'd gallery owners say?"

"I wasn't giving them a chance, was I? I worked on a vita but didn't finish it. I think that's the story of my life, not finishing things."

They walked a ways in silence before he stopped, reached out and took her into his arms as he bent and lightly claimed her lips except this time he pushed them apart with his tongue, surprising her with the feelings it aroused in her body. God, is that why they said no tongue when kissing, keep your mouth shut? She had had no idea how a kiss could reach her whole body. She melted into him not eager to see it end. She had known his kisses weren't going to be like any other boys. Make that man's.

When he had kissed her a second time, he lifted his head. "This okay?" he asked.

"If you have to ask, I must have been doing something wrong," she teased. Her whole body felt on fire in a way she'd never experienced. It felt good but probably was bad. She tasted the tobacco, and beneath that the man. It was heady.

As they walked back to the parking lot, as much to distract herself as to find out the answer to her question, she asked another question. "How long before your brother decided he didn't like rodeo?"

"I don't know. Maybe from the start. We were both entered into events from the time we were old enough. I was fifteen when I rode my first bucking horse to the bell."

"I can't believe they let kids that young ride them."

"It was a local event and not too rigid for checking on ages. I was always tall."

"Martin did that too?"

"For awhile but he didn't like it. He had different dreams, and besides he got bucked off a lot more regularly than I did."

"Maybe the problem with you and your brother is jealousy. Him of you and you of him. Could that be?"

Billy remembered Tice suggesting the same thing. "I don't see how. We both wanted different things, and he sees me as a loser. He tells me so regularly."

"Does he or does he see you doing what he wishes he could but can't?"

He considered that as they walked in silence. "I don't honestly know, but it doesn't seem likely. I mean he has so much going for him. Why would he want to be me?"

She smiled. "I can think of reasons. You are a wild wind blowing wherever you want, strong, powerful, free, living life right at the edge." She smiled. "You blow people right along with you. Why wouldn't he want a taste of that in his own life?"

"Ah and that's how you see me?" He was grinning now.

"I suppose I do, and it's both magnetic and repelling, kind of scary. I think you could suck someone right into you." She wished she had not said that. She didn't want him to know the power he could have where it came to her. She was only beginning to understand it herself.

"Don't be scared. I'd never hurt you." His arm went around her waist and she put hers around his, so they walked linked together as they approached his truck.

"You wouldn't want to, but nobody can really promise that. I might hurt you too."

He opened the truck door. "You might."

"We wouldn't want to, but it's just how life is and relationships— any of them."

As they belted their seatbelts, she asked another question that popped into her head. "So Tice was then your dad's friend first?"

"He was actually riding the circuit when I was in grade school, kind of between Dad and me for where he hit. He was riding high and wide in those years, making a lot of money and spending it just as fast."

"I guess with the travel that's easy to do."

He nodded as he started the truck engine. "It takes working to not let it happen."

"So during those years, your dad was praising him to both you boys, I am guessing."

"Oh yeah, be like Tice McGraw. King of the cowboys. Dad wanted me to ride like him. I'm not Tice. Didn't see things the same way, but I wanted to win,. It didn't happen big until Dad was dead. He never saw his dream come true for even one of his sons. Maybe it won't anyway. Every year, every circuit, I never know for sure how it'll be."

"And so you might be doing this to please your father even though he's dead?" She saw the muscle in his jaw twitch and wondered if she'd hit a tender spot.

"Can we really know why we do anything? We fool ourselves a lot," he said finally. "I've thought about the possibility, but I don't believe it's the reason. I I do it because I can. I admit I like the adrenaline rush from a good ride. But I don't plan on doing it forever. I am putting aside what I can, and this last year that was quite a bit. Someday I want a different life. Rodeo for me is good, but it's a way to get something else."

"But years down the road?"

"It will take a lot of years winning to get the kind of spread I want and enough money to run it right. I figure at least ten years on the circuit if I continue to come out on top, and maybe more if all goes well and my body holds out. I will probably buy the ranch sooner than that but not be able to actually run it for more years as I build up the place. What I buy will have to have some fixer upper aspects to make it affordable."

"And things like Reno put it at risk?"

"They don't help."

"How did you get hurt that time? Sorry. I forgot you didn't want to talk about it."

"Better I satisfy your curiosity now," he said with amusement, "than you imagine worse. It didn't really happen exactly during a ride. The horse was a chute fighter. In other words he wanted to get the rider off his back before he got out of the gate. It's hard in there, close quarters, you are trying to get adjusted and a horse like that makes it harder and dangerous even for the guys helping. The gate opened and instead of him going out, he backed up and knocked me into the timbers. When he started to go over backward, I had to get off fast to avoid being crushed. He kicked me going down. I was frankly lucky to get out of that one as lightly as I did. I woke up surprised to be in the hospital and not dead."

She shuddered visualizing it all too vividly.

"It goes with the territory," he said, "but things like that don't happen often."

"If they did, you'd be dead."

"Or working in a feed store somewhere with a gimpy leg," He laughed.

"Was Tice with you then?"

"He and two others helped get me out of there. You can see I owe him on a lot of levels. He's obnoxious, but I kind of understand that too."

"Because?"

"He's not doing as well anymore. He's like a lot of the old-timers, what else does he know?"

She mulled that over a moment before she thought of something else. "And you really mean someone helps you get on the horses? There is so much I don't know about your world. I have never seen a rodeo, not even on television or in a movie."

"Well it's not like they lift us on," he said with a chuckle. "There's a rig and you do need help to get the horse straight in the chute, get yourself settled right. Riders are there for each other. Getting on a horse when it doesn't want you there, when it's been bred to be good at getting you off, that isn't always easy."

"Wait, they breed horses to do this?"

"Same with the bulls. They are bred from those who were good buckers, who gave a good show, and they are only used for that. It's a good business for the livestock managers, and you can bet they take good care of the stock. It's their livelihood."

"This is quite a complicated world."

"Especially since there are big and small rodeos almost all the time around the West. It isn't that easy even deciding where will be best to ride although if a rider wants to get into the Finals, he wants rodeos that are approved."

"So let me see if I get this straight. Somebody has to authorize riders to ride."

"It's like any business or even say entertainment. You do have to get a card to get into the big rodeos. It weeds out the wantabes and those who aren't that serious about it. The rodeo is about a show as well as a competition. It'd be no fun if everybody got bucked off, now would it?"

"So there is a lot behind the scenes."

He nodded. "Riders help each other but there are handlers. And after the rides, pickup men in the arena to help a rider get off safely—assuming the horse didn't take care of that for them."

"And you ride them bareback?"

"A misleading term. There is a strap, goes around their torso. Same with bull riding, a strap to irritate the animal and for the cowboy to use to stay on. It's complicated; but if you come, it'll all make more sense to you."

"Bulls? I just can't imagine that one, men riding bulls. Isn't that dangerous? More dangerous?"

"It is the most dangerous and exciting event. And with bull riding, like I told you, there are clowns, like Hank, darting in to distract the bull when the rider gets off. They put on some show for the people in the stands, get some laughs, but it's deadly serious what they do. That way the bull goes after them and not you." He realized she hadn't said she would be coming.

"Big bulls... with horns?"

"Some of them and a kind of spine that lets them twist and do a lot of moves that make it challenging for the rider. Some bulls more than others and they will name them for that—like Twister. The better they are at it, the more value they have to the rodeo. You don't need to worry about them being mistreated. This isn't like a bull fight. These bulls are pampered except for that eight seconds."

"That's how long you ride them for?"

"On a good day."

Chapter Five

When they pulled into the trailer court where Nick and Jean were staying, Billy turned off the ignition but made no immediate effort to get out of the truck. It was easy to tell where the action was, and he just hoped the other people staying in the park were at the party. Music and loud laughter drifted from a good-sized travel trailer with pick-up trucks parked around it. He had some reservations about how this would go. Certainly not anything Sara would be used to. These people were nothing like hers. Maybe they should forget it.

She reached up and took his jaw, turning him toward her. "I think I want another of those kisses first... for luck," she said as she leaned to him. He brought his mouth down across hers, again teasing her with his tongue and surprised to find her meeting him and tentatively returning the kiss.

When they broke apart, he said, "Maybe we should forget this."

"Not on your life. I want to know more about your friends." She didn't wait for him to open her door and jumped lightly to the ground. They walked toward the noise with their arms around each other.

"Don't desert me totally," she said sounding a little more uncertain than she had.

"Not a chance. Think I'd leave you for the wolves to descend?"

The picnic table and barbecue in front of the trailer had people all around them, most of them men. Inside what appeared to be around a 35' trailer were most of the women. People were laughing, holding drinks and talking loudly. Did anybody hear what the others were saying? Sara doubted it.

If there was a cowboy style, it was hats, which might be Stetsons or tractor caps, accompanied by boots and Wrangler jeans. Some men wore bright cowboy shirts and others t-shirts like the one Billy was wearing. Was this supposed to be a barbecue? There was one going with what looked like hamburgers on it. If it was a party, it was like none she'd seen. It was chaos and yet there was a basic order to it, she guessed. Was it revolving around any one thing? If so, she hadn't yet seen what. The people were having a good time. That was the one commonality. Sitting, the men were slouched, standing they were leaning. If cowboys had a type, she hadn't seen that yet either. Most were lean though. Maybe that was what they had in common, rangy bodies.

There were friendly greetings to Billy as they joined the others. A few insults that were clearly compliments. Although he kept his arm around her waist, he was part of this and she was not even as he introduced her around. The talk was of rodeos, stock, towns, places, all things that excluded her. She felt uneasy. What was she supposed to do? Should she go looking for clusters of women?

The first friendly comment directed her way came from a handsome, dark-haired man, a swath of gray at his temples who left the barbecue to come over. "Hi. I'm Nick." His voice was deep and mellow. "And you're?"

"Hi. Sara here."

"Where'd Billy find you?"

"Picked me up in a store," she said with a smile.

"Wow, tell me the store."

She smiled at the compliment. "You are the host, I guess?" she asked pretty sure that was the right name and not likely to be more than one of them.

"Host?" he chuckled. "I like that." He poked Billy to get him to turn around. "Ignore this one at your peril," he joked.

"You don't see me letting go,"

Nick brought over another cowboy for her to meet. "Sara, this is Denny." Denny's eyes raked her up and down with the licentious, rude way she'd experienced from certain kinds of men. His type was nothing like Nick or Billy. A man can appreciate a woman without making her feel he only sees one aspect to her. They were clearly different breeds of men. The youth might just be putting on a macho facade. She did what she always did with such behavior, gave it no attention.

Billy's arm had tightened around her a little. As soon as Denny opened his mouth, she knew he'd been drinking and not a little. The three men talked rodeo which again left her staring into space. She understood nothing of it. They were talking of events of which she'd never heard, using words she didn't know the meaning of and occasionally when she did, she didn't like them.

Again, she felt a light hand on her shoulder. A woman's voice was a welcome relief. "Hi, I'm Jean and you're with Billy."

"I am Sara."

"Not your usual world, I take it."

She thought about that a moment. "Not sure I have a usual world."

Jean smiled more broadly, a petite, pretty woman with dark, long hair piled on her head. "It can be tough at first. These guys all know each other, and they talk shop whenever they get together. Boring!"

Sara laughed. "It's a foreign language to me."

"Come on inside and meet a few of the gals. Leave these guys to their gab."

Sara smiled gratefully and after letting Billy know she was going, if he would have even missed her, she followed Jean to the trailer. There were several other women talking in small groups. They were mostly young, some in jeans and others wearing sundresses. She could hear bits of their conversations but actually understood no more of it than with the men except that their traveling world harbored many difficulties at least from the snippets of conversation that she recognized.

"I told him if he left again..."

"Art promised to put in the sink but then..."

"The baby is colicky. She's with my folks but what should...?"

"We have been on the road twenty-thousand miles this year and now the truck..."

"We flew in. Since Joe took up flying it's been... only a few hours..."

"I couldn't stand going myself, regularly that is... Don't like travel and especially with the kids in school now and..."

"Thank god his folks live nearby as..."

Snatches of conversation with no connection. She found her own thoughts going inward, wondering how they all managed. Had these women been born to rodeo or found it through a man? In some ways their lives clearly weren't so different from other women and yet they added insecurity, financially and physically, with trying to raise families. It sounded like it led to a lot of loneliness whether they came with their men or stayed home.

"Want a beer, Sara?" Jean asked.

She wasn't a big beer drinker but felt it would be companionable and nodded. Jean took off the cap and handed it to her.

"Have you known Billy long?" Jean asked.

"A day," Sara said with a little laugh wondering what kind of girl that would label her to Jean. She took a sip of the beer thinking it wasn't bad.

"Ah just at the beginning. It's kind of unusual you know for Billy to bring a friend around."

"No girlfriends?"

"Not to say no women." She gave a laugh, "But none that he brought to meet us. No one that he ever introduced as important to him. Actually, I haven't really seen him with one woman for long either, not long enough with any to call them girlfriends."

"Well, I am not a girlfriend either. Just someone who met a guy she thought was interesting… I invited him back to our home."

"Our home?"

"My parents and mine. He met them."

"How'd that go?" Jean laughed.

"About like you would expect. They said some snide things about the rodeo. We're new to this part of the country, hadn't been around any rodeos. They didn't… well still don't know that he participates in them."

"That should be interesting when they find out."

"If they ever do." Sara shrugged. "Anyway, we had dinner. Later he and I talked and decided we'd like to know more about the other with the understanding it's going nowhere. He made it clear early on that it'd not be for longer than the time he's here—one week."

"And that was okay with you?"

"It might be all I want too. I don't really know. I am riding a wave that came into my life and not thinking much about what comes after."

"You do have the right philosophy if you want to hook up with a rodeo man. Can you live totally in the moment? It's not easy."

"I'm trying to decide that," Sara said with a laugh. "On anything else, I haven't managed. I've thought of myself as someone who likes to figure out where anything is going. It's worked out that by the time I'd make up my mind, I'd have missed my opportunities even if I then wanted them."

Jean laughed. "Tell me something about you."

"There isn't anything very exciting to tell. I work at my father's store. I kind of am floating between things maybe." She thought about mentioning her painting, but was it really what she did? After her conversation with Billy, she wanted to think about that before she brought it up to anyone else.

"I don't mean to interfere or be a *buttinsky*, even though I am being one and do tend to speak my mind. Don't hurt him."

Sara gave a surprised laugh before she could suppress it. "Wow, isn't that more my risk than his?"

Jean studied her for a long moment. "I might be all wrong about you, but you have a kind of toughness, reminds me of me actually. I think you will come out of this better than him if you break up."

"We can't break up. We aren't together."

Jean then laughed. "Right. With some people, from the moment they meet, they are together. If you didn't know that before, you know it now."

Sara thought about that before she asked the question that had most surprised her about what Jean said. "You don't think Billy is tough?"

"Not just him. Any man where it comes to emotions. Physical stuff, oh yeah, they can handle that, but emotional and it's a different story. But I don't mean to get out of line and I just did. Toughness is good in a woman especially if she wants to be with a man who rides the bulls."

"I am plain ignorant about all of this. He told me that's a dangerous event."

"It's the cherry on top of the sundae for the customers in the stands. They put it on last, as a climax to the rodeo for a reason. Big mean bull versus little cowboy and clown-- a disaster waiting to happen. I don't mean to say something can't go wrong in any of the events. God knows I know that. Rodeo is unpredictable and part of the breaks, so to speak."

"I'm pretty ignorant but interested in learning more." Her mind wandered elsewhere with something far more personal and debated whether to ask it. Then she decided to follow Jean's lead and just ask what was on her mind. "How long have you and Nick been together?"

"Let's see... We'll have been married twenty-one years in November."

"How did you meet?"

"I was sixteen, entering rodeos in barrel racing events which means I raced a horse down the field, around some barrels and back. Fastest rider, who has knocked over no barrels, wins. It along with trick riding tends to be a woman's game. Nick was a rider on the way up and like Billy not really wanting to get serious but one thing led to another."

"And you travel all the time? Isn't that hard on you?"

"It's not easy for me or him. Sometimes worse than others. For me it's what I have to do if I want to spend time with him. I..." She hesitated. "He's my life and this is what he is. You get used to it"

"Billy talks about doing something different someday."

"They all say that but it doesn't happen. Yeah, at first we thought we'd save some money and get a little place, small ranch, settle down and maybe even have kids. A ranch is the dream of a lot of riders. I lost the babies we tried to make and we realized that wasn't going to happen. We lost the money one way or another and now it's just a question of trying to hang on until we come up with something else we can do to survive."

She tried to think of something comforting to say. She didn't find the words. "That's tough."

"It's life. I figure the Lord doesn't give us more than we can handle."

"You're Christians then?"

"Yes, we are. I'm being snoopy again, but are you?"

"My folks go to church, Episcopals. I have gone but no, I can't say I'm a believer, not that I fault those who are... although some might fault me." This conversation was going a lot deeper than Sara had expected, but it was not making her feel uncomfortable. "I'm more of a I don't know what to think kind of person."

"Believing in something bigger than us, something that cares, helps if you are living this life. Whether it goes wrong or right it's good to think there is a plan, a reason, somebody in charge, who knows more than I do. Maybe it helps with any way of life. I do believe there is a reason for everything."

"I guess if I could believe it, I probably would. I am not sure how we get separated into believer or not."

"I won't be one preaching to you about it," Jean said.

"And I won't try to convince you to not believe." They both smiled.

"It's just always been there for me," Jean said, "from the time I was a little girl, the feeling there was someone helping, guiding me. Maybe it came because of my parents' teachings or well I don't know."

"It's good if it gives you peace."

"It used to but lately, well I've had a lot of fear for Nick. It's grown since the last accident four months ago. He was nearly killed. All our life together, I've tried to let him do what he needs to do, but after that I laid into him to convince him to take a long enough break to really heal. You know, those darned cowboys," she was smiling as she said it, "they don't think an injury should stop them. They go back too soon or just keep right on and then get hurt really bad. Part of me wanted to beg him to quit right then, but I couldn't do it."

"Why not, I mean if you are that afraid, it can't be healthy for you either."

"You... well you take a man as he is or you don't. I took him and I want him. I can't try to change who he is. I just wish... Well I wish he'd want something different. I am afraid if he doesn't, that it'll kill him." Sara saw Jean's eyes darken.

"And you couldn't tell him even that?"

"That seems wrong to you?"

Sara laughed. "Like I'd know. To be honest, what I know of relationships between men and women, well you could put it in a thimble. I should have said nothing."

"Like I did?" Jean said with a little laugh. "The thing is with Nick and me, I think if I told him, it'd weaken him. Like Samson with his hair cut. He needs me to believe in him. I don't want to be the one to add to his burden, and I know he's worried about money as it is. You know, traveling like we do, about the only work I can get is sometimes around the rodeos, taking tickets whatever. This time there was nothing"

"I wish I could help."

"I wish I could too."

"What makes them stay with it? The excitement?"

Jean gave a little laugh. "You think I'd know. All I can see is they experience something most never will. They can do something a lot of people admire. But it's more than that. Maybe it's like the ones who climb mountains, the ones who do that thing others can't but like to watch or read about."

"You know I don't get it at all. I have never been a risk taker. I can't imagine getting off on doing something that could cripple or kill a person."

Jean shook her head. "Maybe nobody who doesn't want to ride something wild and untamed can understand it and that includes me. Barrel racing wasn't really the same as it was more about the connection between me and my horse. Nick has tried to tell me what he feels, but he's not much for words. Whatever it is, it's something special for him, something that makes it all worthwhile, the risk, the injuries, even the uncertainty."

"And you think your fears would put that at risk?"

She nodded. "I know he's also worried about the future. Nobody figures they can do this forever. They try to time it so they get out before they are crippled by it."

"And you're afraid he isn't doing that because he has nowhere to go?"

Jean smiled. "Maybe now I know why I did want to talk to you. I didn't know why I opened up to you and now I think I do."

"We did seem to have an instant connection."

"Like you and Billy," Jean said with a broader smile.

"Maybe." Sara understood maybe better than Jean why she might've chosen to talk to her a stranger about such intimate truths. Possibly too she was trying to warn the new girl what this could mean to her life. She appreciated that and wished she had comforting words for a woman she was quickly coming to regard as a friend.

"Maybe he knows how I feel, and we're both trying to save the other from worrying. You can't be married over twenty years and hide much from each other, not if you live close like we do." She pressed her lips together.

Their intense conversation was interrupted by a young woman in a white cotton dress. Pretty, with long honey, blond hair, she seemed to be in her late teens. "I wondered where you got to," she said to Jean, sitting across from them, her gaze intently moving from one to another.

Jean introduced her as Susan, married to Denny. Sara remembered him as the young man with too much to drink and didn't envy Susan. It had to be hard enough to be married to a rider without adding in that he drank too much and appeared to have an eye for other women.

Susan was too heavy, but the curves were in the right places. She bubbled over with joy at her husband riding the next day.

"You don't worry about the events?" Sara asked.

"Why would I? Denny is a great rider. He's on his way up, going to be a champion. I really know it. It's exciting to me. All of it."

"We have been seeing quite a lot of Susan and Denny," Jean said with a tinge of amusement to her voice. "He started riding professionally not that long ago and has been hanging around Nick for tips, I guess. Wherever Nick is, I'll see Denny shortly after."

"Denny really respects Nick for all the stuff he knows, for sticking with it despite... well, you know getting old."

Wow, that was blunt and thoughtless, Sara thought. Jean didn't seem to mind though so she wouldn't take on a grievance for her.

"It's good you are supportive," Jean said.

"Oh I like it all. The excitement, him being so good at it," Susan said proudly. "We took all our money to make the fees up here, but it'll be worth it. We'll be rich someday."

"Not many get rich off rodeo," Jean warned her. "A few get to the top but most are somewhere down the way when they get bumped off the pile."

"Nick has a championship buckle."

"Yes, he does and what has it bought him?" Jean's voice was terse.

"Well it works for some to make money. I mean there's advertising and all, special appearances, you know," Susan defended.

"And maybe Denny will be one of them," Jean's voice softened. "Just never know, do we?"

"I know. Denny is good, real good." She then turned to Sara. "You don't look like a regular. Who are you with? I don't think I remember you."

"Billy Stempleton invited me."

"Oh wow," Susan grew rhapsodic. "He is soooo hot. I saw him outside. I could go for that too... if I wasn't married, of course. You two serious about each other?"

"We just met."

"Oh," she sighed, "love at first sight. How romantic."

"Did I mention the word love?" Sara asked curtly.

Susan stayed only a little longer and then wandered off to find her husband. Smart move, Sara thought thinking she'd do well to keep an eye on that one.

"How old is she?" she asked Jean.

"Seventeen. She's young and not just in numbers. She'll learn though if they stay with it."

"The school of hard knocks?"

"Rodeo provides plenty of those for the women and the men. Too bad people can't learn other ways, like through books or something. But many of us sure don't."

"I guess it's the most powerful way—personal experience."

Jean sucked in a breath. "Thank you for letting me talk it out with you." She stopped, seemed to consider and then added, "I am just frightened that by the time Nick figures out what he's doing is no longer working, he'll be dying."

Sara frowned. "I guess that's a normal worry for this... uh business."

"I keep repeating myself here but the thing is it's not an old man's game and old age comes faster here than a lot of other places. They just won't quit, some of them, and they go out on a gurney. That might be what it'll take to get Nick to give it up."

"Did you worry like this when you first got married?" She couldn't imagine living with that for over twenty years.

"I wasn't as starry-eyed as Susan but it was different back then. When you're young, you believe in yourself more maybe. You probably heal faster too. It was after the accidents started. You just sort of see it all escalating, know what I mean? The thing I come back to is what would Nick do if he quit? What would I do? Maybe that's what keeps him going—he wants to go out dying."

"That is a terrible thought," Sara said, not stopping to think of whether she should say it. "I mean for you. I don't know your Nick, of course, but that would be a terribly selfish way for him to think."

"He's not a selfish man. I doubt he's thought it through. You know how men are."

Sara smiled. "To be honest, not so much... I wish I could help."

"You... you might talk to Billy, try to get him to talk to Nick. He really respects him and might listen if Billy told him it was time to hang up his spurs."

"I don't have any pull with Billy. I don't see why he'd listen to me knowing nothing about any of this. I would though... well I'd say something if I got the chance but don't have any faith in it mattering. From what I have seen of Billy so far, he has a code similar to the one you are saying Nick has. He's more likely to agree with Nick than try to get him to change, don't you think?"

"Blasted, stubborn cowboys," Jean said with a little laugh.

"You know maybe you do have to talk to him seriously about it but after this rodeo is over. You say you don't want to break his concentration now, but can't you try when you are leaving here? Maybe it would be a relief to him. Maybe he's afraid he'd let you down to quit."

"I suppose that's possible." She sighed. "Dang, blasted, stubborn men." Then she grinned.

Sara and Jean walked to the front of the trailer where Jean offered her another beer and she took it to be sociable but felt like drinking two would be giving her a buzz which she didn't want. Out the window she could see Billy with the other men. He was talking and gesturing. Tice was at his right. She liked watching him when he didn't know. She'd had no time to do that. He stood taller than the others beside him, His face was lean, full of life. He was *hot* as Susan had said. It wasn't just his features, not that they were bad. But the energy of the man just swirled around him. She'd never met anyone like him, wasn't likely to again.

Seeing him with the other men, the way they appeared to listen to what he was saying, she felt he was respected by his peers. They seemed to wait for his opinion. It wasn't hard to see he was one of those on the way up. She supposed part of it was there are always those who gravitate to people like that.

Then he turned as though he sensed her eyes on him. He smiled, said something to Tice and walked to the trailer. "Man okay in here?" he asked with a grin as Jean gave him a hug.

"Some of them are."

He looked then the beer in Sara's hand. "Want some?" she held it out to him and he took a sip. "You gals talking about anything important?" he asked.

Luck of the Draw

Jean laughed. "We settled the state of the country and then the world, universe was next, but don't worry, we can pick it back up later."

Sara giggled. Politics were one thing she'd never heard discussed from any of these people.

"You ready to head out?" he asked, handing her back the beer for her to take another sip.

"If you are. I have liked being here though. I really like you, Jean. I hope we can be meet again."

"Whenever I come to Pendleton," Jean said patting Sara's shoulder. "We'll do tea... or a beer." She laughed again.

"I'll hold you to it," Sara said as she and Billy walked out into the warm night air. She was aware of his hand, the strong fingers, used to by now the calluses. It felt very right to be beside him even if it was only for this week.

In the truck, he asked, "Want to go straight home?"

"What did you have in mind?"

"Get out of town a ways, beyond the lights, and watch the stars."

"I like that idea." She wondered what else he had in mind and wasn't sure how she'd feel about that. Watching stars though, that would be fine. She moved to the center of the truck and rested her head on his shoulder. That felt right also as he drove, shifting gears, handling the wheel smoothly and with ease. It'd be how he'd handle a woman. She knew that. She just wasn't sure if she was up to a sexual relationship with a man she would likely never see again. It wasn't how she had seen herself. Maybe it wouldn't come up. Was it something he would want either?

"Did you really enjoy yourself?" he asked.

"Yes, I did. It was different. I had no idea what it was like for the women who are tagging along with a rider. Well," she laughed, "I don't suppose I know a lot more about it now. Your people are different and yet not."

"Explain."

"Well we all want a lot of the same things, love, to be needed, to contribute something to ourselves, our families, even the world. That's alike, but most people want security, I think, and there is not much of that in what you do, is there? So that's different."

"It can lead to security. If a man puts the money aside as he's going. It can buy a regular life someday."

"Do people give it up soon enough though? Or do they want that rush of excitement, wait too long and then it's a long slide down?"

He glanced over at her realizing she was talking about Nick and Jean. He wondered what she had been told but wasn't sure he wanted to know.

They came to a high point where there was a gravel road that led further onto a ridge. Billy turned down it and in a big opening, he stopped the engine. "Come on out."

He led her around the truck to the back, put down the tailgate and lifted her into the truck bed. He walked to the front, took a blanket out of the box and laid it down for them to lie back on.

He lit a cigarette and after a moment said, "I think that rush can be found other ways." He smiled over at her.

"You really began doing it right out of high school?"

"Not right out. The draft interfered for two years."

"You hadn't mentioned that."

"It's not something I talk about. You think eight seconds is a long time on a bull, try a year in 'nam."

She couldn't think of anything to say that didn't seem dumb. "It was bad?" was the best with which she could come up

"I don't know of anybody who was there and thinks otherwise."

"It looks like we're going to lose it."

"We never had a chance to win it. When people are fighting for their homeland, they will do anything. It felt... like a losing game from the start, but a man does what he has to do. I sure wasn't going to run off to Canada or go to jail. And rodeo is no deferment."

There was a silence as they both looked upward. "Do you know the names of the stars?" she asked looking up at a huge sky, stars twinkling in combinations she had never learned but saw as designs. The moon blocked some of them where it was glowing brightly as it rose higher in the sky.

He pointed to one. "That's Orion."

"Really?"

He laughed. "Nah, never learned them but doesn't that kind of look like a sword there?"

"A little bit." She sounded skeptical. "What do you think made all this?"

"Whoa," he said with a bit of a laugh. "You aren't expecting me to go all deep, I hope?"

"Well, maybe. Looking up there makes me think about it. It's all so huge, so forever in how it feels. Do you believe in evolution?"

Now he did laugh. "You and Jean really were going to settle the universe. I should have left you to finish it. Last time I take you to the back of my truck."

"You don't think about such things? Is it against the rules to ask questions and think while back here?"

"It might be. But okay, I'll play along. I believe in what I know of evolution. That life evolves, changes, and it's that which got us where we are which won't stay as it is."

"A god behind or doing it?"

She could hear the smile in his voice. "This might be curtains for us, but I don't think about it. I am not a spiritual man if that's what you were wanting to know."

"It's not curtains. I just wondered."

He took a puff of the cigarette blowing the smoke away from her. "I am here right now. I feel a blanket and a hard truck under my body, a woman alongside me, stars above. That's my spiritual belief—it is what it is right now."

"To be honest, I don't really have a set of beliefs for myself. Jean talked about it tonight, but I don't a lot. My parents might believe, but I am not sure. They live a form of it, but how much of that is for their place in the community? It does serve a social purpose."

"Maybe." He sounded skeptical.

"You don't like religion?"

"I like people like Jean and Nick who are religious, but for me, no, I don't like it, wouldn't like it unless things change a lot which I don't look for."

"Because it would limit what you do?"

He took a draw on the cigarette, watching as the smoke wafted upward. "My experience with religious people is they live life a lot like everybody else. No better, no worse. Some are hypocrites about it, Pious on Sunday and hell breaking the rest of the week. Some want a security blanket."

"And you don't need a security blanket?"

He thought about that a moment. "I might want one if I thought it worked. I just don't see it makes sense what they claim to believe. I don't believe in the stories, the philosophy of a god who intervenes that way. If it works for them, like Nick and Jean, then I have no quarrel with it as long as they don't try to push it onto me."

"So life just began here?"

"I can't say how life began. But neither can a religious person. They just know what somebody told them and they believe it."

"Somebody told some of us about evolution."

"Based on fossils, biology today. Now I am no expert on it either. I believe in what I see around me. I trust what I see and can touch."

"And you never think about it, really?"

"What do you think about it? I mean evolution? You have that college education. Did it convince you one way or the other?"

Now it was her turn to think. "Evolution seems obvious to me. It doesn't answer the question of god or gods."

"Is this what I get for bringing you to the back of my pickup?" He sounded amused.

"Well I have to admit; I never have lain in the back of one and looked up at the stars before. It might be what you get though from me." She smiled in awe of the blanket of stars up in that sky.

"So maybe you like a pickup bed?"

"A bit hard but yes, not bad and it does make me think about life, the world, you know the whole thing to look up at all those stars, so far away, so brilliant, all those patterns."

"You are a bit of a thinker?"

"Maybe too much of one and not enough of a doer. A person can think too much. Do you do this often?"

"Not with a girl. Never like this. But sleeping back here, I've done that. When the rides weren't going well, I'd put down an air mattress and sleep here. When I do that though— I sleep, not think," he added teasingly as he nestled her against his chest. "What did you really think of Jean and Nick?"

"I didn't talk to him long enough, but he seemed very nice. Salt of the earth kind of guy where his handshake is as good as a written contract. He has a basic niceness to his face—beyond the handsome part that is." She smiled.

"For not knowing him long, you did a pretty good analysis there. What about Jean?"

"Her I really liked. She's like him that what you see is what you get. She seems gutsy and strong." She thought then of what Jean had asked. "She's worried about him though."

He took another draw on the cigarette, staring straight up. "I think anybody who cares for Nick is worried about him."

"Have you tried to talk to him?"

"It's not my business. Man has to make his own choices."

"She would like it if you tried."

"You're kidding. She told you that?"

"I think she's feeling desperate, afraid, like it's all going to go really bad if he doesn't stop."

"No matter what I said, even if he listened, he won't pull out of Pendleton."

"You know that?" she pushed up on one elbow to look down at him.

"He's a cowboy right to the core. You finish what you start."

"Even if it might kill him."

"Nobody can know that."

She lay back staring up at the stars. She didn't understand that way of thinking. "What about factoring in the risks?"

"Everyone has to do that for themselves. You're out here with me and some would call that a pretty big risk, a man you only met a day earlier."

"I guess so."

"You didn't worry about it."

"I would have yesterday but not today. You won't do anything I don't want."

"Do you know what you want?"

"I won't tease you with anything I am not willing to do, if that's what you are asking, but right now, I am not ready to take it all the way with you. I wouldn't be probably if you were going to be living in Pendleton."

"I can understand that. I want you though, you know that." He lifted up on an elbow and lightly kissed her, his tongue again teasing her mouth open.

"I do know that but... Billy I haven't been with a man that way before."

"You're kidding." His surprise showed in his voice.

"Would I about something like that? Maybe you knew by... well I'm not experienced terribly even with kissing."

"You sure you're twenty-one?"

She felt defensive and knew she had no reason to be. "I was busy with college, work, other things. I didn't meet the right guy. A hundred reasons but there you have it."

"You plan to stay a virgin until you get married?"

"I hadn't thought that far ahead."

"But you don't want your first time to be with a man who's on his way somewhere else?"

"I am not sure right now, and you aren't giving me much time to be sure."

His laugh sounded genuinely amused. "I'm okay with this. We can still look up at the stars, right?"

"Not for much longer. If I don't get home by a reasonable time, my folks will be calling the police."

"Geesus, you are kidding about that at least. You're twenty-one."

"And still living at home. I maybe need to change that, but for now it's their roof and their rules."

He snorted as he sat up and ground out his cigarette. "I am finding this all a lot to take in."

"Well it's how some people live," she said a little defensively as she also sat up.

"I guess but not how..."

"Don't you dare say how I should live! For a man who makes his own rules, how can you find fault with mine?"

"I suppose I can't, but it does seem to me, as an adult, you shouldn't be having a curfew."

"It's not exactly that but look, I need to go home because I want to."

He helped her out of the truck bed, and they drove back into town without talking. The one thing she clearly saw was they came from two very different worlds and ways of thinking. At the house, he didn't ask to see her again or even if she would be at the rodeo. So that was that.

#

After he had left her, Billy felt angry but more with himself than her. What had he expected? He had known deep inside what kind of woman she was. It wasn't like he had been pressuring her either. Sure he knew what he'd want, how it'd be but then... damn, she was a virgin. He'd never been with a virgin. It'd have been as new to him as her if they had. Well Geesus, he was glad they hadn't.

He thought about going to the bar Tice had said he'd be. Drinking wasn't going to make his rides the next day go better. He headed to the motel, took a shower and tried to blank out his mind. Didn't work.

She didn't want a one night stand. He didn't blame her. She'd waited for Mr. Right; then along came Mr. Wrong pushing her for something... well he hadn't really pushed, but he hadn't hidden what he wanted. He could have gone at it differently, began seducing her. He wasn't sure why he hadn't other than he didn't want her that way.

If he'd been in a different place in his life, she'd have been a woman he'd have seriously pursued, put off doing anything else to win. But he wasn't at that place. Right now he had to concentrate on what he was doing. He couldn't let anything distract him from it. If he didn't follow this road, he'd never amount to anything. He'd be managing a grocery store or running a gas station. This was his shot at a life he couldn't get any other way.

Was it all about the glory? Maybe some. There was a thrill to a good ride, to the moments ahead of it, the aftermath, a thrill he couldn't deny. But it was more than that. This is who he was; and he had to work with that, not be distracted by a dream that didn't fit in. Focus was the secret.

Luck of the Draw

He let his mind wander away from that focus to the idea of marriage. At twenty-six, it was the first time he'd seriously considered it with even an abstract woman, let alone a real one. Marriage was way off in the future. He couldn't imagine Sara following him from rodeo to rodeo with a trailer like Jean had Nick. Nothing wrong with Jean or the other women that came with their cowboys, but that wasn't the life Sara had known nor what she'd expect.

He thought of what he'd have to offer any woman. His whole life was a gamble that he'd really get to the top, that he'd get enough years there to be able to buy the ranch he wanted, one somewhere along the John Day River with good water and grass. Those big enough to support a family didn't come cheap. He'd never have a chance to own something like that without these years on the circuit and not just being there but regularly winning.

He could see how it would be with Sara. If he married her, ridiculous to even imagine it is what she'd want, well she'd have him clerking in her old man's store. He would end up like what he had feared. Or even if he didn't do that, he'd be working a sawmill or in the post office like his own father. He felt restless just imagining that. No, he had a plan and he'd stick to it. She was not part of that plan.

He knew he was kidding himself. He suddenly wanted it all. The rodeo and that woman. He just couldn't see a way to make it work. What kind of place would she find in a rodeo? None. What a fool he was even to wrestle with it just because he had lain in the back of a pick-up with a girl. There really was no choice to make.

#

Nick and Jean lay curled on their bed, having enjoyed the time with their friends but relieved now that everyone had gone. The smells of tobacco and beer were still heavy in the air. It was hot inside, and they lay naked without any sheets, Nick smoking his last cigarette of the day. It glowed red in the darkness, the smoke curling to the ceiling. She lay in the curve of his arm, ignoring it was too hot to be so close. She liked the feel of his bare chest against her cheek, hearing his heart beat. They had talked of the party and the people there especially that Billy had brought Sara.

"You think they'll get married?" Jean asked, kissing his chest. She liked feeling the muscles flex under her lips. She didn't like the scars. His belly was still ridged with muscles, the body of a much younger man but under that, the torn muscles, the bones that had been broken proved he wasn't as invulnerable as he had once seemed.

He gave a laugh. "Aren't you jumping the gun there, babe. He barely knows her." His fingers teased her nipples making her feel her body coming alive to his touch, to the feel of him.

"Sure, but there's something going on there. Don't you see it?" Her mind wasn't really on that. It was on him, on this much beloved body and her knowing later they would be making love. She nipped his skin lightly.

"Women. They can't stop matchmaking for a second." He sucked in a breath as she moved more purposely down his belly.

"I didn't do that. It's not like I found her for him; but admit it, they are cute together. Can't you see him with her? Frankly she's perfect for him, and I like her for me too—as a friend." She let her breath touch him more intimately as a promise of what was to come. Encouragingly his body was responding.

"I don't know. She's not rodeo, didn't get raised with it." He sucked in a breath as she moved more purposely but determinedly went on. "A lot of women give it a try and have to let it go. I can't count the marriages I've seen go up in flames over it. Not many women like you, babe." She heard the smile in his voice.

"She's tougher than them."

"You're kidding. She looked tough to you?"

"Oh yes. She is. And she'd get him away from Tice's influence."

"Billy holds his own against Tice. Don't worry about that. One of these days that'll be over as a friendship whatever happens with the gal. You can see their break coming the way Tice tries to ramrod him. Billy has felt he owes him, but that won't last much longer."

"Well, I think she'd be a good woman for Billy. She might reach him where... Are you listening to me?"

"Sure, sure I am." He watched the smoke drift away and sighed. She knew he wasn't thinking about Sara and Billy. His mind wasn't on making love either at that moment. It was on the next day. She wondered if he would tell her that. She moved back up to lean on an elbow as she waited to see.

After a time, he said, "I drew Wildcat."

She frowned, hearing more from the tone of his voice than the words. She remembered the horse, the ride. How could she forget it? She remembered her determination that she not weaken him with her fears but maybe this was this something he needed her to say. She sat up and looked away, not wanting to let the fear swallow her. "Maybe you're not ready to ride yet. I mean have you really healed enough?"

He studied the tip of his cigarette, taking another draw before he answered. "I'm as ready as I'll ever be."

"We have talked of quitting. Doing something else. Maybe this is the time, could it be?"

"Could be-- after this one."

She didn't like that, but it was better than nothing. Would he really quit if this went well? She doubted it. Maybe she needed to lay it out for him, make it be about her. Maybe he would do it for her. Could she live with asking him that? She knew how much he loved her. "You know I've sometimes wondered what it'd be like to stay in one place, you know find a little church, a community. You could come home at night and..."

He interrupted her. "Come home after doing what? What else do I know, babe?"

"There would be lots of things."

He snubbed out the cigarette and laid back down, drawing her in his arms. "Maybe. We can talk about it next week. Just let me get past this one, okay?"

She knew it had to be, but she wished it wasn't so. She didn't feel good about this one. She would not tell him that though.

"Don't worry," he said as his hands went down her back. He began kissing her, his tongue delving into her mouth, his hands working their old magic until they both forgot about tomorrow.

Chapter Six

Wednesday

When morning came, Jean was up before Nick and moving quietly as she poured coffee into the percolator, added the water and stood back to watch it begin its magic. He had been sleeping soundly, and she knew he needed his rest. She wasn't sure if he had slept after they made love. She knew she hadn't, but she had kept quiet, praying, thinking, trying to make herself strong for him.

By the time the coffee was done and hotcake batter mixed, he came out, fully dressed even down to his boots. He sipped the hot coffee, savoring it as he always did. Then lit his cigarette.

"You know, if we change our lifestyle," she said, "Maybe you can also quit smoking. You know it's not good for you."

He laughed at that, a twinkle in his eyes. "Like I have such a healthy lifestyle now."

"Well, you could get one. Someday."

"I could... someday." He seemed relaxed, actually at ease. She began to feel more confident also. If he felt he could do it, it'd be okay. When she came over with the first hotcakes, he grabbed her wrist and pulled her onto his lap.

"Nick," she protested, not really wanting to leave him, "I have more cooking."

"Let 'em go," he said lazily, nuzzling her hair. "Anybody ever tell you you're a beautiful woman?"

"Just you every day."

"I should say it a couple of times a day. I don't want you to ever think I don't see it and think what a lucky bastard I am. With your hair down like that, you look like a little girl."

"Oh yeah, a thirty-nine year old kid." She laughed but felt pleased.

He pulled her hair back and looked at her more closely. "You can't really be over twenty-five, can you?"

She laughed. "You do have a way with words."

"You were the best looking woman here last night—nobody close."

"Liar or you need glasses."

"How long we been married, Jean?"

Now she felt uneasy. This was sounding like a summing up of a life. She didn't want him thinking fatalistically. Still she knew how men were with not keeping track of such things. Maybe she was making too much out of every little thing. "It'll be twenty-two years in November."

"Years get away from me. Seems like one just goes right into the other."

"Well that's how long it's been."

"How'd you put up with me that long?"

Now she really didn't like the way he was talking. Still he didn't look upset, didn't seem worried. She had to think positive. She had to be confident also for him.

"You're my man, my soul," she said finally smiling and kissing his forehead.

"It's been good though, most of it, hasn't it, babe?"

"You know it has."

"I sure never gave you a bed of roses."

"I only asked for you."

"I want you happy is all I want. I want to be the man who makes you happy."

"Why are you so solemn all of a sudden?" she asked feeling a chill in her heart.

"Nothing. Just old age maybe, the fall is coming. Remember I'm older than you. Hey is that something burning?"

"My hotcakes!" She jumped up and ran for the stove.

#

Billy didn't wake early. Part of that was rotten night of sleep where he tossed and turned and tried to put thinking out of his head but failed. It was surprisingly after eight when he fully opened his eyes. Even more surprisingly, Tice was already up and dressed. If he hadn't slept well, he'd slept deeply enough by morning to not have heard him as Tice was not usually quiet getting ready for a day—not when he was suffering from a hangover which with Tice was most mornings.

When Billy was finally outside, there was a hot wind blowing already, coming hard from the east. "Hotter than last year," Tice grumbled. "Never seen it so hot here this time of the year. This won't make it better on the stock or us." He went on complaining, but Billy had quit listening.

Sitting down to breakfast at the little cafe, Tice began on him about Sara. Billy worked on not hearing him but some got through anyway. "She's sure a looker. I'll give you that much; but boy, she's not in your league and you know it. You got nothing for a gal like that."

Billy signaled the waitress over for a refill on his coffee.

"She's got money. That outfit last night. Well it cost more than most women can spend in a year. Her folks must be rich, right?"

"Who knows. It doesn't matter."

"Well it does if you ever wanted—"

Billy cut him off. "This isn't your business, Tice. But she and I are history. Nothing to talk about there. A date or two. That's all it was or ever would have been."

"Seriously?"

"Not that it matters. I told her from the beginning I'd be leaving after the last event."

"Well if you mean that, you're making a good choice. She's not nothing but trouble for a man like you or me. A woman like that, she'd never quit wanting things."

"You don't have a thing to worry about, mom."

Tice grumbled but didn't give it up as he continued coming up with reasons why Billy was well rid of Sara. Billy quit listening. He had enough in the day ahead without taking on Tice's nonsense.

#

After a breakfast she barely remembered tasting, Sara went out to her studio, determined to paint and not let upset over how it had ended with Billy ruin her day. She had arranged to have the day off from her father and was keeping that even though she would not be going to the rodeo. Definitely not. With so few customers he didn't need her help and said he might even close early himself. She would make the most of her day with oils. She had done a few sketches which might work into something.

Mumbling to herself about irritating cowboys, she put a canvas on the easel, chose a few colors to start and began working with the brush but with no plan for her subject. Usually she had an idea or even a firm sketch but this was freewheeling with colors.

"How are you, honey?" her mother asked, knocking on the open doorjamb.

"Good." She hoped she wasn't letting her irritation at Billy show up in her tone of voice.

"May I come in?"

92

"Of course. I'm always happy when you come out here." She put down her brush and turned to face her mother. This would be a good time to discuss something important.

"I wondered how last night had gone. You didn't seem to want to talk after you got home. Was something wrong?"

"No problem. I was just tired, but I did have something I wanted to tell you."

"About that young man?"

"No, about me. I need to move out."

Her mother moved to a chair and sat down, her expression looking concerned. "I thought you were happy living with us, the studio, all of it. You can save your salary this way for the future. I..." Obviously this wasn't what her mother wanted to hear. "Have we done something?"

"It's not about you. It's about me. I need to get out of the nest, get a little apartment."

"Not to live with him, I hope?"

"Mother! I barely know him. No, this isn't about him. It's about me."

"I don't understand."

"Are you familiar with the writer Henry Miller?"

"This seems a bit of a distraction; but yes, he's the one who wrote Tropic of something or other, that obscene book."

"Well he wrote other things. A few years ago I wrote down something of his but didn't quite understand it. Last night I went digging to find it. I brought it out with me to tape to my easel.

She handed it to her mother, who read it aloud. "The aim of life is to live, and to live means to be aware, joyously, drunkenly, serenely, divinely aware." She stared at the paper a moment. "I don't get it. Drunkenly? What does that mean? This is kind of a lot all at once, dear. You want more freedom, is that it? You can have that here."

"Mom, I didn't get it either about that part and I don't think it means you have to be drunk but just live without the fear of doing the wrong thing and then not living at all."

"And that requires moving out?"

"I think it does. It's time for me to be building my own life, be responsible for myself. It's not just about freedom as such. It's about the next step in life. Fledglings have to leave the nest, you know."

Her mother sighed. "Perhaps you can think about it?"

"I have thought about it."

"For a long time?"

"Not so long but from the time I did, I knew it was what I had to do."

"Was this his idea?"

"This isn't about him."

"Oh well, if it's what you must, we will, of course, support you in any decision you make." She sighed and looked at her wristwatch. "I wish I had more time to talk about this, but I promised to meet some friends for lunch—on the other side of town to avoid the noise of the rodeo and all. Want to join us?"

Her mother was a practical minded woman, and Sara appreciated that more than ever right now. It would be okay with her and her parents and maybe better once she was out than it had been. "I appreciate the offer but need to work on this painting."

Her mother looked around the studio but didn't say anything about the canvases against the walls. Sara had never asked her what she thought of her work because she had been afraid what she'd hear. Her mother helped other artists get started but hadn't seemed to have much interest in Sara's work.

Finally she could stand it no longer. "See anything you like?" she asked.

Her mother turned to look at Sara. "What do you mean?"

"Do you like any of the paintings? Any at all?"

"Well they're fine, dear." Her tone said she was not taking a risk to go further in her analysis.

"I won't get angry. Just what do you think? Am I really a bad painter, Mom, or is it you just don't want me to be one?"

Her mother started for the door. "I am sorry I don't have time for this conversation now. We can discuss it tonight."

"I might be out tonight. Don't worry if it's late." She didn't know why she said that. She was not going to the rodeo. She would not see him. Except...

"You have a date with *him*?" The emphasis on *him* said it all.

"Nothing definite, but I do have other friends in town, you know. Just don't wait up if I am out when you come home. I am twenty-one. I will use good judgment regarding what I do."

Her mother sucked in a breath and left without answering. This was pretty typical for how their conversations had always gone. No direct confrontations. Well that was good as far as Sara was concerned for now. She finally saw at least one direction for herself, and so long as her parents didn't try to block her, she could handle not having their approval right now. She felt she would get it eventually if she proved she was right.

She set about getting the colors she wanted. She would paint and that was what she knew. The rest, well that was the iffy part. She'd start looking for a small studio apartment as soon as the rodeo was over. She would not go to the rodeo. She would stay away from Billy Stempleton. She was totally certain about the last. If she saw him again, he'd change her life, upset her shaky handle on her plans. She didn't want that... or did she?

#

The rodeo grounds were bustling when Billy pulled up having given Tice a lift. The odors of animals, hotdogs, popcorn, sweat, were all pungent and welcome to his nostrils. His boots raised up swirls of dust as he walked and the wind carried them as little dust devils down the grounds.

Handlers were working the stock, cutting out the ones for the day's events. All along the line of fences, he saw men on the ground or leaning against a fence, readying their tack. The ropers were out in a separate field warming up their horses.

He liked the feel of it all. He was part of it and that felt good inside. Yes, whatever his father might have wanted for him, this was in him also. Even the tense feeling in his stomach, the hope that he'd make a good ride, it was all part of it.

When Tice grumbled at his own following day's draw, Billy laughed. "You'd not be satisfied with a rocking horse."

"If it gave me good points, I would," Tice retorted. For the riders, drawing a horse that couldn't buck would mean low points and be as bad as being bucked off, well at least less bruises.

There was little time to kill before the day's events would begin. First the pageantry. Billy wondered then if Sara would use her pass. Probably not. It was best she didn't because if she was up there, virgin or no virgin, they were moving onto the next stage, and she had to know it as well as he did.

He took his chaps from the truck and strapped them to his legs, not adjusting them tight just yet. By the fence, he buckled on the dulled spurs he'd be using for his ride. He leaned against the fence, not looking outwardly as edgy as he felt inside. It was always this way as he waited for it to begin. He resisted the temptation to look toward the stands.

The bleachers and stadium were filling fast. Music was playing. Ten thousand people would be coming to watch the rides, see the show. Not likely he could have seen one red-haired woman in that crowd even if he'd been looking...which he wasn't. He had to make himself not. It was as well he not know if she was there to watch him. It might make him lose his edge. When he'd come to Pendleton, that edge had been what he had worried about losing. Now he wasn't so sure.

"Welcome to the Pendleton Round-up," the voice blared over the loudspeaker. "Cowboys, Indians, horses, cows, clowns, pretty girls. You want it. We got it. For the next four days, you'll see the biggest show in the West. The voice then told the audience to stand for the National Anthem. That was followed by the grand parade around the arena. Some came mostly for that as it was quite the spectacle with cowboys, Indians and colorful costuming.

Immediately afterward, Billy walked to the bareback chutes. He heard the anonymous voice droning on but no longer listened to it. His attention was now on the ride. He debated whether to hold the rein long or short. What would this horse do and how could he beat the clock. He'd know the answer soon enough and a kind of calmness came over him as it always did right before he settled down onto the horse's back.

"Scores on bareback will be determined by two judges. Half the points come from each. The scores are tallied with a certain percentage based on the horse's performance and the rest from the cowboy's. Riders need their horses to buck well, but, of course... not too well." The joke more or less fell flat at least with the cowboys who had heard it all too many times.

It began as Chute One opened and out came the horse and rider. His legs were up and came down at the right time to qualify. The horse bucked and twisted but the rider stayed with him until the right or rather wrong combination sent him over the horse's head to land hard in the dust.

"Too bad for Terry Hogan from Bellingham, Washington," came the announcer. "That'll be no score for him today. These boys pay to ride here and when they get bucked off, they only get one thing. Let's give him a big hand because that's all he's going to win today other than some bruises." The rider was standing, loosening his chaps, and dusting himself off as he walked back to the corrals.

Billy tightened his own chaps, walking to the fence, the leather of the chaps moving roughly against his jeans. As he climbed the fence, another rider was coming out of the chute. Tice came up beside Billy and they both looked down on Apache, a nicely conformed brown gelding.

The horse was uneasy, not liking any part of this, as he shifted position again and again. He especially didn't like the man now above him. Billy straddled the fence, easing himself onto the animal's back. He adjusted the strap and then moved a little forward; so that he was almost sitting on his hand. This strap and his own balance were all that would keep him on. He didn't try to soothe the horse as he might have on a ranch. He wanted him bucking and bucking good.

He nodded to Tice. "Let'er go," Tice yelled. The chute gate swung open and Billy was out, spurring high on the horse's shoulder with the first buck. Rhythmically then, he spurred as Apache surged across the ground, onto the grassy center of the arena for where for a second he changed his gait and then was bucking hard again. It was going to be good ride if he could stay on, stay in control.

Bucking, twisting, turning, and coming down hard now on his front legs, Apache did anything and everything to dislodge the rider. He was good at it but not good enough this day.

Billy was not thinking, no plans, no future or past. He was like the horse and totally in that moment. They were one, both operating on instincts that had been honed through many such rides. It was a magnificent moment, born of the now, flying like the wind; testing his strength and ability against that of a powerful animal. It was why he rode.

When the whistle blew, the pick-up man, Harrison, came alongside Billy as he let his legs drop down around the horse's body. It had been a damned good ride, and he knew the score would be high as he swung off by grabbing Harrison's waist and dropping to the ground. This was the way it was supposed to be. The horse, freed now of the irritating strap around his middle and that rider, spiritedly galloped off, glad to be escaping the arena for another day. At the cost of a few minutes of wild exercise, Apache had a soft life most of the time with good food and care. The spurs that encouraged him to do his best left no marks as they were dulled and intended only to encourage more action.

"76 for Billy Stempleton," came the voice. "That'll be the score to beat today, folks." He heard the stands come alive with cheers and clapping. He hadn't ridden for that though. It was good to know people liked it, but the big thing was that moment with the horse, the moment when it all went right.

As he got back to the fence, he was smacked on the shoulders by the other cowboys-- another sign of a good ride. Tice said only, "There'll be money on that one."

Billy again avoided looking toward the stands, but he couldn't help but wonder, for the umpteenth time, if she was there. Had she watched; and if she had, what had she thought about it? He felt like a kid in school wondering whether the pretty neighbor girl had seen him walk a fence without falling off. He was a fool. She would not have come.

He helped Tice as he had been helped. One of the things he liked most about working around the rodeo was how the riders helped each other. Even if they were competing and some needed the money more than others, they all worked to make each get the best and safest ride they could. You tried to beat a man's score but you didn't do it by undermining him. It was in many ways a unique fellowship, not that any would have called it that. It was just how it was.

"Next up is Tice McGraw from Bend on Donnegal. Tice is an old-timer here at Pendleton. Show these kids how it's done, cowboy." Tice's ride was a good one but not enough to top Billy's score. Still it would help him stay in the running for overall standings, and the next day's ride could bring anything.

Billy watched as Nick helped Denny Bauer get on his mount. They seemed to be having difficulty and Billy moved over to help. The kid couldn't get a handhold to suit himself. Already they had waited past his turn and the chute boss was putting on the pressure.

Finally Nick nodded, and they opened the gate. As Denny came out, it was obvious he was in trouble. His first jump wasn't good and his legs weren't where they needed to be. If he managed to stay on, he still wasn't likely to get any score. By jump two, he was going off and landing soft. There was that at least as he jumped up immediately.

Nick seeing Billy for the first time said, "Green. He got buck fever. He should have ridden that horse easy, just got too excited, I think."

Billy smiled even though he didn't much like Denny, he did like Nick. "I remember those days."

Nick shook his head and laughed. He stepped down from the fence and took out a cigarette. "Got to quit this habit," he said. "Going to kill me someday." With that he laughed and lit the cigarette. He held out the pack to Billy who at first shook his head and then changed his mind and took one. Drawing in the smoke, he asked, "Jean here?"

"Oh sure. She's up in the stands somewhere. She met up with Sara and they went off like long lost friends. Those two really hit it off."

Billy didn't say anything but at least that answered the question of whether Sara had watched his ride. Now he could only wonder what she had thought. He and Nick smoked companionably despite all the chaos around them. He thought about what Sara had said Jean wanted him to talk to Nick about. This wasn't the time but maybe after Nick's ride.

"How are things going?" he asked about as far into the whole thing as he was going to get.

"It's okay. I feel fine about today."

"Need any help?"

"Nah, I got Jim Gordon and the kid. If that ain't enough, I better quit like Jean wants."

"She told you that?" Billy asked as Denny walked up hearing the end of the conversation.

"That's not her way," Nick said. "She wouldn't complain, but I know how she feels. I feel her in my gut, know what I mean? Well you probably don't yet; but someday maybe, if you are lucky, you will."

"You can't quit, Nick, no matter who wants it," Denny said evidently rapidly gaining his confidence back after being thrown, if he had ever lost it. "You're the best. You have got a lot of good years left."

Irked once again at Denny, Billy said, "One of the things that is hardest to do and takes the most guts is knowing when to let it go. Every man has to decide that for himself. I hope I am smart enough to see that day coming before they have to carry me out."

"It's easier to say it though... when a man is starting out or in the heat of it," Nick said, "then to do it when the time comes."

"A lot of things aren't easy. It doesn't mean they aren't smart."

"Billy here just wants to cut down on the competition," the kid said sarcastically.

"Don't put your two cents in on this," Billy said, "when you're broke." The kid's face reddened and Nick gave an amused chuckle.

"Billy doesn't need to eliminate competition by talk," Nick said with another grin. "He does it with the rides."

The putdowns didn't quiet Denny for long enough. He glared at Billy, jealousy written all over his face. "I guess you got high score... for *today*." Emphasis on the today.

"Thanks for the congratulations," Billy said and Nick snickered.

"You were lucky."

Billy couldn't resist. "Luckier than you." He took another draw on the cigarette. It wasn't doing anything for his mood though; and when Nick turned to leave, he threw the cigarette down and ground it into the dust with his boot. He was irritated that he hadn't found something to say to Nick; but there was no time for changing what was going to happen, at least not today. Maybe tonight he'd talk to him. There was no disgrace in quitting. Then he wondered about Sara. What would she be doing tonight? He knew what he wanted her to be doing and he'd set about making that happen.

Tice, who had been listening to the discussion, said, "That kid doesn't much like you."

"I've had bigger disappointments."

They walked over to the fence where they could watch the saddle bronc. Neither of them were entered again until bull riding. When they saw Nick come out of the chute, at first it looked real good; and Billy turned to Tice to say as much. He'd been worrying for nothing. The horse bucked onto the grassy center, and it was the change of stride, combined with a quick turn, that caused Nick to lose his balance. When he fell, instead of landing clean, his boot caught in the stirrup. As the people in the stands screamed, he was tossed around like a doll. It seemed an eternity as Billy went over the fence along with other nearby cowboys.

The bucking horse came toward him, and Billy leaped for his neck, dragging his head down. Between his grip and then two others, equally quick, they had the gelding stopped and one cowboy managed to free Nick's foot, leaving him crumpled and motionless in the dust.

Billy knelt at Nick's side, putting his fingers to his neck to feel for the pulse as he heard the ambulance coming. This was going to be bad. Nick's face was gray, his eyes closed, but he was breathing. He had doubled up onto his side. The medics came running, put a brace on Nick's neck and then carefully lifted him onto the stretcher. Time was of the essence because although he wasn't bleeding externally there were good odds he was inside. As they were putting him in the ambulance, Jean was there, Sara and Susan on either side of her. Jean looked at the still form of her husband as they worked over him. "Is he?"

"He's breathing, strong pulse," Billy said. "Steady up."

Jean began to cry, and Sara was then putting her arm around her. Her face was as white as Jean's. Some introduction to rodeo.

"Is he... will he?" Jean asked the medics.

"We'll get him to the hospital, ma'am where they can assess that. He's breathing though and we'll do all we can keep him that way," one said as they moved the gurney into the ambulance.

"She's his wife. She needs to go with him," Billy told them.

They looked at her and then nodded. The doors closed and it sped off, sirens wailing as it hit the main road.

When Billy stepped away, he was aware Sara was beside him. He looked into her clear eyes and then took her into his arms. He did it as much for himself as her. She clung to him,

"I think I should go to the hospital," Sara said. "I'd like to have watched you ride the bull, but I think Jean needs friends with her."

"How will you get there?" he asked.

"My car. Try not to worry. I know it looks bad and it's going to be hard but you still have a ride to do. You have to concentrate on that. I think he's going to be okay. I really do. It's just a feeling I have."

"I hope that feeling is right. You need to go." She reached down and took his dusty hand, gave it a light kiss and then was gone.

Billy set his mind to concentrating on what he must instead of what he was feeling. Nick would pull through. He had to believe that. Sara, who didn't even know rodeo, had been right. He had to let his fears for his friend go and concentrate on the Brahma, or he would have even more trouble. The vision of Nick crumpled on the ground keep returning to him. He had seen a cowboy like that once before, with the gray face. The man had died. He gritted his teeth in irritation with himself that he hadn't tried to talk to Nick earlier, months or even years earlier.

And then his thoughts settled on Sara. She had come. She had kissed his hand. Even more important, she has gone to be with Jean, a woman she has only known a day, and yet she went to help her.

Focus. He was losing his focus. He had to shake all of this or he would end up like Nick. He knew too many who had had accidents. It was part of rodeo. Get himself together or lose his ability to do this and have to quit sooner than later. Or have it quit for him with one crippling accident. Then he'd be lucky to get a job in a store. Can't think this way. It'd kill him faster than the ride.

Tice came up but said nothing. Denny Bauer was standing off by himself looking shocked. It might have been his first time to see how quickly it all can end. It was not anything Billy could help him with, even if he'd had the energy to try, not given what the kid thought of him.

The mood behind the chutes was subdued and depressed. Everyone liked Nick. They all knew it could happen to any of them but didn't want to think it was going to with a friend. Serious injuries didn't happen so often that anybody got used to it. Break a rib or even a leg that was more the thing. Not something that caused a man's life to be on the line as it looked like Nick's might well be.

Mechanically Billy changed his spurs to the ones for bull riding. They were dulled as with the others but these had a small bell on them, intended to irritate the bull as if that was necessary. Brahmas were born mad and those that got into the bucking circuit were especially chosen for their dispositions. In case the rider and bell weren't enough, the tight strap around the bull's middle was the last incentive. Nothing to hurt him. Just irk him a little more. The bull needed to be angry and know what to do about it..

A rider had to consider one more thing. Those Brahmas wanted the riders on the ground sooner than later; and a goring could happen by accident as much as purpose. The whole event was set up to limit that happening with the clowns ready to jump in before the bull could decide who to go after.

His bull, # 36, was giving the handlers a hard time, fighting the confines of the chute, hating the men above him. This would be a good ride at least, he thought as he got himself in position to drop onto the bull.

Not only did each rider have a different outlook toward the bulls, but each bull was different. Intelligence level, meanness, a lot of things played into how the bull would react. Not all bulls were killers although all of them disliked being ridden. That was their job. Sometimes a man knew a bull's reputation, but Billy knew nothing about this one except he was edgy and ready to get this done.

He had seen riders, before they rode, get physically sick from the nerves. Others swore profusely as a reaction to the tension. Billy just wanted to be quiet. There was little lightheartedness and only some dark joking around the bull chutes.

He couldn't say exactly why he rode bulls but he knew the tension he felt before a ride was greater than anything else in his life, anything he'd ever know anywhere else. This was, as Sara had suggested, life on the edge. Whenever he thought he'd quit riding them, stick to bareback and saddle bronc, he always came back to the challenge. Maybe this time he'd get it right, he'd find that rhythm that told him he could be one of the great bull riders. Maybe he was the kind of man who now and again needed the ultimate challenge and in rodeo, for him, that was the bulls.

He adjusted his chaps and pulled on his glove. Stepping up on the fence to stand over his bull, he signaled to Jack Peterson who was his flank man and fastened the strap around the bull's middle. They worked silently, sweat pouring off both of them. Tice pulled the rope that had been rubbed with resin and tightened it through the knot just behind the bull's shoulders.

Billy wiped the sweat from his brow with his sleeve, pulled his hat down firmly on his head, then settled himself onto the huge bull. He wrapped the braid twice across his palm and through his fingers, holding it palm up. Between his thighs and knees, he could feel the power of the animal under him.

As he signaled to let it go, time stopped. Everything seemed crystal clear as though in slow motion. The noises, the people, everything faded away. He barely heard the voice saying his name and Bend Oregon. And then nothing beyond him, the bull and the gate existed as the chute opened and he and the bull were in the arena. Billy spurred and fought to keep his balance as #36 bucked and twisted, stomped and tried all his tricks to dislodge the rider on his back.

Billy's position was none too secure and he held onto the handhold for dear life. This wouldn't be a pretty ride if he managed to hang on long enough. The hold he had was all that kept him from going off over the bull's head, right between those horns—if he was lucky.

Would that whistle ever blow? Then he heard it or thought he did. Either way, he was going off. He jerked the rope with his free hand and jumped, hitting the dust rolling, getting up the instant he hit and heading for the chutes.

The bull's rope had fallen off but that didn't improve his mood as he turned and headed for Billy. Bulls were a lot faster than men, and he knew that he'd not make it to the fence first until he saw from the corner of his eye Hank darting in before leaping back to his barrel, distracting and annoying the bull as it offered him the option of a second enemy, a more annoying challenge.

Billy ran for the fence aware the bull had decided he, who had been on his back, was the most irritating. He heard the thundering hooves behind him and made it over the rails seconds ahead of the bull who slammed into the wood and angrily turned to blame someone else for what happened.

Catching his breath, Billy watched as Hank tweaked the bull for awhile, then jumped again into the barrel as the bull charged it. People laughed not realizing how dangerous it was. Rodeo clowns were more bullfighter than clown even if the audience didn't recognize it.

Relieved to be on the other side of the fence, Billy saw Denny coming up to him. Just what he needed. "You sure got over that fence fast," the youth taunted.

"Just as fast as I could," Billy said looking as the bull was still trying to get Hank. The other clown, Morgan, began harrying him. When the bull switched to him, Hank got himself up on the fence, letting his baggy pants fall almost to his knees. He pretended fear and Billy didn't doubt some was real. How could it not be? The clowns came close to death with every ride. All it would take is stumbling at the wrong time, misjudging a turn.

Finally the bull grew tired of the game and when the gate opened, he made his escape.

Jack, Hank's brother, came over to see how Billy was. "Thank your brother for me. He saved my bacon again." He ran his fingers through his hair and put his hat back on.

Tice came up with his score, which Billy had not heard when it was called. It didn't seem that important to him now either. It was not good enough to take the day, but it was respectable. He still had a chance for the overall even in bulls which wasn't his likeliest shot at scoring money or points. Right now he didn't care one way or the other. He was tired, spent emotionally, and all he could think about was to get to the hospital. He wanted to know how Nick was, but something more was there, waiting for him.

Chapter Seven

At the hospital, Billy felt his usual reluctance to enter. He supposed nobody liked them even knowing they were necessary. He forced himself to cross the threshold. In the corridors he smelled the odor of antiseptics and disinfectants. They turned his stomach.

In the waiting room, Jean, Sara and a few others were doing just that. Jean was standing, a little apart, looking out a window. He talked to her a moment, heard her monosyllabic responses and knew she was probably praying and didn't need him. Sara was on a couch at the back of the room. He hesitated only a moment before he went to her. He didn't ask himself why that was where he wanted to be. "What do they know?" he asked.

"He'll be in surgery a few hours probably. They weren't sure, couldn't promise anything regarding the timeframe. They were guessing from his vitals that there would be a ruptured spleen, definitely internal bleeding, his ankle... It was evidently shattered, but they won't know what else until they operate. They said he has a good chance of surviving and that's what we have to hold onto." She took his hand when he sat down. Hers was cold. The way she was looking at him said as much as her grasp.

He felt hot and dirty. Slouching back on the couch, he was aware how exhausted he really was, emotionally and physically. Although he'd seen injuries in his years on the circuit, nothing like this and nothing happening to a man for whom he cared so much. Surviving didn't mean coming back to full strength. Would Nick be crippled, ever walk with that old, lazy grace or worse?

Sara's voice came to him as though through a fog. "Do you have a headache?" She shifted her position and began working the large muscles of his shoulder and then his neck. He had not realized how tense he was until his muscles began to relax. Her fingers were surprisingly strong, and he felt himself begin to let go of the day.

Jean came to sit beside them. "I don't know what I'll do if..."

"He's going to be okay. You heard the doctor," Sara said. "You can't think any other way."

Jean sighed. "I don't know. I dreaded him riding this time. I felt like... Oh I don't know what I felt. Just... I should have told him. I should have made him quit. I wish..."

Sara moved to put her arm around Jean then begin to rub her back as she had Billy's. "The doctor told you that he thought he had a very good chance," she repeated because she knew Jean needed to hear it. Besides she wasn't sure in her traumatized state how close Jean was to a collapse herself. She had obviously been living with fear a long while. Now it had happened, the worst she imagined short of his death. Surely the worst wouldn't also happen.

"Doctors say things like that."

"I thought he was telling the truth. It really seemed like it. You have to keep believing it. You believe in prayer, in God, so trust that now."

"I do," Jean said with a little cry, "but it's hard. I ... I really haven't got anything without Nick. He's my life. My everything. I can't imagine life without that man in it."

She looked so small suddenly to Billy. She sat there with her eyes bleakly fastened on the door the doctor would come through. All her hope was based on something she had no control over. He wished he also could put his faith in that prayer she claimed would help. He couldn't. He had seen too many things go wrong with people who totally believed and those who believed in nothing.

The rain fell on the just and unjust. He had seen that in Vietnam, seen sudden death where there was no way a man could figure a logic to who lived and died. He wanted to believe in a god who would save people who prayed, but he couldn't do it now and maybe never did.

Sara was talking to Jean, her voice low and caring. He didn't try to understand her words but was glad she had them. He didn't.

An hour later, a man in hospital garb came through the door. "Mrs. Williams?" he asked and didn't waste time telling her the news was positive. "WE stopped the bleeding. He got a transfusion and his color is much better. Broken ribs, of course, bruised but not destroyed internal organs. The big issue for the future will be his ankle. It was broken three places. We pinned it back together but... well, he'll need physical therapy to walk normally again, but we have every reason to believe your husband is going to recover. He is in Intensive Care."

"May I see him?"

"He's still under the anesthetic, but of course, you can be with him."

Jean turned back to Sara and Billy, then to the others sitting there watching her. She took Billy's hand but her eyes were on Sara. "Thank you. It was good of you to be here for us."

Sara smiled and gave her a quick hug. "I'll be back later."

Jean followed the doctor from the room.

Billy stood then and looked at Sara. They had things to talk about but unless he asked, he knew she'd not come with him. Asking her to was complicated by a lot of things. Nothing had really changed. "So what are you going to do now?" he asked.

"What do you want me to do?" she asked bluntly.

He didn't have to think long on what that was—sensible or not. "I want you to come with me." There were no fancy words in the end. Just the simple statement. Take it or leave it.

"I have my car. I'll need to drive it home."

At her house, she went in just long enough to leave her parents a note. She came back out still wearing the red jeans and a striped shirt. "You look beautiful," he said as he kissed her lightly before turning on the ignition and driving off.

"I didn't really know what to wear to your rodeo."

"You just need a pair of boots instead of sandals to look like a real cowgirl," he said with a smile and reached across to take her hand. "You have the right spirit though whatever you are wearing. I liked how you went there for Jean."

"I like her. She'd have done it for me if the need was there."

"Some who have known her longer weren't there."

"Well, we all do what we can, I guess. At our own speed. How did your bull ride go? I was disappointed to miss that, but glad to see you are in one pice still." She managed a smile.

He shrugged. "I scored, didn't get bucked off, but I won't win money on it."

"Maybe tomorrow."

"I'm really too tall for it."

"You're kidding."

"No. The guys who do the best on the bulls are well under six foot. More like 5'8 or 9'."

"If you know that, why do you enter it?"

He gave a short laugh. "I ask myself that regularly. The last time being today."

"Ah, then I am not the only one who does things they don't want to do?"

"I suppose we all do. I get something from it though or I'd not do it."

"Something? Like?"

"That adrenaline rush you were talking about."

"The opposite of security," she teased.

"Definitely that. So what did you think of your first rodeo? I am guessing not so much after you saw one of the most brutal accidents I've even seen." He shook his head. "You'll never believe me now when I say it's not that dangerous."

"I admit it was exciting. Especially watching you ride that first time. I knew it had to be dangerous before Nick, but you made what you do look easy actually."

"Good thing you didn't see me on the bull. You'd have been less impressed."

"Maybe. I have a feeling though I'd still be impressed."

Despite his upset over Nick, he smiled then, pleased with her, with himself and the world for at least a moment. He knew he was being foolish, but he was that little boy who had walked that fence and the pretty, little girl had watched and then applauded. The moment was sweet.

"I have to take a shower," he said finally.

She nodded.

"Where do you want to wait?" He knew he should have picked her up after he'd cleaned up. He just hadn't wanted to let go of that moment.

"I can't wait in your room?"

He looked over at her trying not to read too much into that. "If you want."

"I want."

At the motel, she followed him into his room. It felt strange with him opening it with a key, a place she'd never been and yet one that might mean so much to her life. Inside it was neat, no clothing strewn around. She realized she'd never been in a man's hotel room. Another life first.

He went to take his shower while she sat in the chair by the window. She stared out at the parking lot, the road, and sky beyond. She waited knowing that he was near and that felt good. She liked hearing the sound of the spray, even more knowing he was naked under it.

She had felt so far from him when she went to the rodeo. Oh she wasn't going to go. She definitely would not watch him ride. But in the end, she had not been able to stay away. He was a stranger and yet in a strange sense, he was not. She knew he'd want her to be there even if he hadn't said it. How had she known? She had met him only two days earlier. That was nothing in terms of time. It felt like forever, as though he'd always been part of her being. Was that feeling enough to change her own life? She knew he would not be part of her reality after this week and yet he would be part of her from now on even though not in a physical sense. Damn how strange life was.

When she had told him what she felt at the rodeo, she had done as Jean had said she did. She had left out her fear. Her stomach had turned in knots as she had watched him come out of that chute on a seemingly wild horse. The ride lasted forever even if it had only been seconds. Then it was over. He was safe and on the ground and striding back toward the chutes. It was exciting then but still seemed so unreal that even now she found it difficult to believe it had happened.

If she had gone to the rodeo, not known him, never lain in the back of his pickup and watched the stars, never gone to Nick and Jean's trailer and met those people, perhaps then it would have been different to watch those events, not have them impact her as they had. It wasn't simple entertainment to her. It was real people with real consequences. And yet... real? What did that mean anymore?

Like Alice in Wonderland, she was finding herself a part of a strange, almost alien world. She was not just an onlooker. She had known the man who had crumpled into the dust, the man whose wife had screamed his name as she had realized what was happening to her beloved, a man she might never make love to again. Two days ago, people like this had not been part of her life. Now what would having known them do to her tomorrow?

When Billy had shown up at the hospital, dusty, sweaty, and looking totally spent, she had felt a surge of protectiveness. She had wanted to comfort him, be comforted by him. He was not a stranger. He was hers in some way that would never end and she knew that whether he went off at the end of this week and they never saw each other again.

There was no way not to relate Nick's accident to Billy. How did Jean live with any of that? She had seen what it did to her even before the injury, how Jean had been holding herself together for Nick. Could she do something like that for any man? Pretend it was okay when it was not? Or could she somehow find herself part of his adventure and not have to shake with fear, instead to feel increased strength through what they were doing together? She might never know, might never be given the opportunity to find out. Maybe she would reject it if she was given that chance.

If she let herself see Nick's crumpled form change into Billy's, she'd be incapable of thinking straight, of doing anything. Showing her fear likely wouldn't be crippling to Billy as it might've been to a man married over twenty years, but she knew it would bother him. If he cared for her at all, and she faced the possibility that he might, then her fear would endanger him, not strengthen but weaken.

Sara had lived a life that respected and valued safety and security. She had made choices based on that. Had those feelings limited her life unnecessarily? She didn't know except one thing, and she had to hold onto that one thing or it would be destructive for her. He would go at the end of a week. However, forever might not be part of what she needed from a man right now. She needed the moment. Forever? What did that even mean?

Something was traveling through her brain, firming up a decision. She wanted what he had seemed to offer in the back of that pickup. She would only have memories when this was finished, but she didn't want him to go without those, and as many as she could cram into these few days. This wasn't about a wild desire she could not control. He hadn't done much to stir that up anyway as they had talked before anything could happen. She felt what was possible though, as though an energy surged through her that was as real to her as if they had gone forward and done the physical act of becoming one.

Did he love her? Probably not. Did she love him? She wasn't sure. Was love something anybody could define or write down what it had to mean for another? Did it have anything to do with the kind of connection she felt to him?

Sometimes there came turning points in a person's life—change points, call them what one would. Walk one way or another and it'd all be different for the future. She used to think such moments would take much thought and planning. She knew now they didn't.

She saw herself becoming the kind of woman who would walk forward without counting every bit of the cost. She hadn't been that woman, but it wasn't too late. Billy, or at least knowing him, had already changed her; and it was a change she welcomed.

Melodramatic to think it but she had started this week feeling like a girl. She would leave it a woman, and it wasn't just about whether she and Billy had sex. She was going to begin walking her own path and that also meant moving out of her parents' home. She was going to walk with the moment. She didn't want to let this opportunity with him go without experiencing it fully. If it was possible, she didn't want her first time sexually to be with anybody else.

She realized how ironic it was that Billy who seemed to walk with uncertainty, with danger, who was on the road, a man without a home, he had been the more goal directed. She had what seemed like security but it had been restricting. It had meant letting things happen by the plan of others. That was about to change.

The water stopped. In a few moments, he'd walk through that door and he would have every right to expect she had a reason for being here. Seeing Jean with Nick, knowing how many years they had had together and then how it was today, when Jean faced losing him, she knew nobody gets guarantees. *The moment. It's all any of us have.*

When he opened the door, the moisture of the shower entered the room behind him. He was only wearing jeans but he walked over to his duffle and pulled out one of the work shirts he had bought from her. Instead of putting it on, he lowered himself to sit on his heels in front of her. "I wondered if you'd be there today," he said smiling up at her.

"Did you want me to be?"

He nodded. "It's seemed likely you'd have given me up as a bad job."

She smiled then, reaching out with her finger to touch his lean jaw. "Are you?"

"It is one possibility."

"Well, I did want to see a rodeo." She knew her eyes had to be warm with what she was feeling. She wasn't sure how much he'd want to hear. She ran her fingers down his arm tempted to go further and follow a path to his chest but she held off. If this was going to go anywhere, it had to be him. She wanted it to be him.

"I liked how you helped Jean too."

"And you didn't expect that either?"

"To be honest, not really."

"So I'm not the kind of woman a man can lean on?"

"I had pegged you as more like your mama's china." He smiled.

"Something you take out for holidays?" she asked with a laugh, feeling amused and seeing that he thought he'd offended her. "You might be surprised that china is stronger than you'd expect. It might get chipped but it doesn't break that any easier than pottery." She bent forward lightly kissing his lips-- the first kiss she had initiated. He deepened the kiss without touching her with anything but his lips and tongue. The kiss went clear to her toes.

"You know what you want here, baby? You sure?" he asked. Seeing his answer in her eyes, he stood, reached down and picked her up into his arms, carrying her to his bed. He went to his duffle bag and rummaged around before he came back to her, a small package in his hand.

As they sat on the bed, she put her hand behind his neck and pulled him to her, the kiss deepening as her tongue tentatively moved into his mouth. She felt it all through her body as his arms tightened around her and the kiss grew in intensity. Somehow, she wasn't sure when it happened, her shirt was open and her bra unfastened. Her bare chest was now against his. It felt as though she was going into him, becoming one with him just when he touched her. How could that be? The sensations grew as he pulled her shirt off and stroked her bare back and then moved to her breasts.

He laid her back on the bed and lying beside her began to kiss her breasts, suckle them. Nothing in her life had ever felt so right. The kisses deepened and her own hands learned that touching him, playing with his body was adding to her joy.

She heard the sound of the door opening and Billy jerking away all at the same time. He tossed his blue shirt over her and rose. Opening her eyes, she saw Tice in the open door, the sunlight highlighting him as his crude expletive and laugh filled the room.

"You said you were going to the bar with the boys," Billy said.

"Son of a bitch. Well who would've figured. Sorry about interrupting your uh whatever this is here." Tice's laugh had no humor in it.

Sara got off the bed, reaching for her shirt and bra. She went into the bathroom to get dressed. She supposed she should have felt embarrassed; but other than not wanting Tice to continue to see her bare breasts, she didn't care about the rest of it. When she walked back out, the subject had changed; and Tice was doing most of the talking, berating Nick for not quitting when he should have, while Billy was looking out the window and ignoring him. They both turned when she entered.

"So how did you do on your last ride?" she asked Tice.

"You didn't stick around to see?"

"She went to the hospital to be with Jean," Billy said through his teeth, obviously barely holding onto his temper.

"How is he?" Tice asked as though he had just remembered that it wasn't just about whether Nick should have quit but also whether he would survive.

"They say he'll make it, but he'll have a long haul ahead."

"He should have quit."

"Like that's so easy to do."

"How'd you like the rodeo that you did see?" Tice turned and asked Sara.

"It was interesting and more so for knowing some who rode in it."

"I'll bet," Tice said with a smirk.

"We're going. See you later," Billy said as he finished buttoning his shirt, stuffing it into his jeans, and buckling his belt.

"Hey I could get lost. Sorry I spoiled the mood," Tice said with a chuckle as Billy gathered up keys and wallet.

Outside the air had cooled a little with a storm front moving in. Only a few steps from the door and before Sara could get into his truck, she glanced up and straight into the eyes of one of her mother's closest friends. There was no hope that Cheryl Jefferies hadn't seen and recognized Sara coming out of the motel with a stranger wearing a cowboy hat, but she hurried on past without so much as a hello.

"Well that finishes it," Sara said with a laugh that reflected no humor as she stepped up into his truck.

"Sorry Tice was rude. I shouldn't have gotten that started without realizing he might be coming back." He knocked a cigarette from the pack and lit it.

"Oh it gets better... Before it's through I might need one of those too. That woman that just passed, acting like she didn't know me, she is a good friend of Mom's."

He swore under his breath. "This is our day, isn't it?" He drew the smoke deep in his lungs, blowing it out the open window as he turned the truck out onto the road.

"Well, it could have been worse... even with Tice." She gave him a little smile as she thought about what she needed to do—if anything. Would this qualify as using good judgment to her parents? Would the woman go straight to her mother? Well, let's see walking out of a motel room with a man. What were the odds she wouldn't?

"You want to go to your home and beat her to the punch?"

She thought about that and didn't like the idea. "How about you buy me dinner... or I buy you dinner? I think there's also a dance at the rodeo grounds, isn't there?"

"And you want to go?"

"You won, right? I got to see my first rodeo... part of it anyway. Despite all the rest, shouldn't we celebrate?"

"Where do you want to eat? The sky's the limit. I think I am safe to say that in Pendleton." He grinned.

"What about the barbecue over at the grounds. I hear it's really good."

"Seriously? Better than a restaurant somewhere?"

She reached out to stroke his neck her body still heated from their lovemaking. She wanted so much but for now she felt it was maybe lucky they'd had it slowed down. "Seriously."

At the grounds, it was easy to find where the food was being served. They followed their noses and the lines. In hardly any time they had filled plates and went looking for free tables—of which there were none. "How about down by the river on the grass?" she suggested and it was where they went.

They were both hungry enough that they didn't talk while they ate. When she was finished, Sara licked her fingers. "Delicious. I don't know when I've had better barbecued chicken."

"It was good but not that good. I mix up a mean barbecue sauce," he disagreed.

"I will have to test that someday, but up until today, that was the best."

"How long since you ate?"

"Breakfast. How about you?"

"Same. Want to go back for more?"

"No, it was enough, but you go ahead.

He thought about it and shook his head.

"How about a walk down along the river?" she asked. The path was an easy one as it followed the almost like a canal river as it passed through town.

Next to the rodeo grounds was a small park, pleasant, cool with big trees and soft grass. They found a peaceful corner, back from play equipment and lay back on the grass. She plucked at a stem, teasing his lips with it. She looked up at the sky and saw that there was now a star visible or maybe it was a planet but it didn't matter.

"Star light Star bright first star I see tonight," she said repeating the child's nursery rhyme.

"And what did you wish for?"

"Can't tell you or it won't come true." The truth was she hadn't wished. She would never have asked for a healing for Nick as that seemed way too important for wishing on a star. For herself, she had what she wanted right at this moment, and it seemed wishing for anything more would lessen it. "How about you? Do you have something you want to wish into existence?" He didn't answer right away, and so she added, "Like to win the all around for this rodeo?"

He shook his head. "My wishes are further into the future, but they do take winning at rodeos like this one. It won't happen right away but someday. A little ranch, enough cattle to pay the bills. Good grass, water, barns, a house. Sometimes, when I was small we'd live for awhile on places like that, staying in the hired man's housing."

"Do you know much about ranching?"

"Some. I have a lot to learn. I know what it was like when my dad worked such places and later when as a teen I got jobs for the summer at one ranch or another, sometimes haying, helping cut the cattle, moving them, brandings, the usual stuff. The accounting end I know less."

"You liked it obviously."

"What I saw of it. It's a good life for a family. A place like I want though, I wouldn't be able to own any other way than this. I wouldn't really wish for it though. Might jinx it." She could hear the smile in his voice.

"What was your childhood like besides going to rodeos?"

"It was what it was. A lot of moving. Father who was never satisfied. Mother who wasn't happy. I guess I miss what it could have been more than what it was." In the growing darkness, she could barely make out his features. "You know," he said, "I like rodeoing but never figured it'd be a forever thing for me. I hope I have the sense to get out in time to still have a body I can use."

"Was what happened to Nick really because of his age?"

"Some of it for sure. You lose reflexes, a lot of injuries make the muscles not so responsive. He just didn't want to give it up. A younger man could get his boot jammed into a stirrup wrong though." He hesitated, then added, "It's not the kind of mistake Nick would have made years ago."

He didn't add that he wondered if some had been Nick losing focus as he knew Jean wanted him to quit. Was he feeling divided, and it cost him big time? Emotions and those kind of events didn't go well together in Billy's experience. It wasn't fair to blame Jean, but he couldn't see their relationship not being part of the dynamics that kept Nick there or maybe even cost him judgment when out on the horse. A man couldn't go being afraid for her and being wholly there for himself.

"Do you like the traveling part?" she asked interrupting his thoughts. "Seems like you'd be on the road so much that there'd be nothing but travel."

"It's not my favorite part for sure although." He took her hand and kissed her fingers. "I do meet some interesting people that way. I can take time off when I want but when it's going well, the money's flowing, it seems a good time to stay with it." He grinned. "I admit too that I like the adrenaline rush when it all comes together, me knowing I can do it and feeling it all flow; then comes the challenge to do it all again. But I know nobody can do it forever."

"Jean was right about Nick then?"

"Most likely but you know things happen and they aren't always the kind you can plan, and that's true whether it's your life or mine."

"Boy do I know that," she said with a teasing smile. "A guy walks into your store, and bingo, the whole game changes." She took the blade of grass again, moving it across his lips.

"Well, for what it's worth, I wasn't expecting all it was either."

"So where is this place you expect to find your Shangri-la?" She wanted him to kiss her again, teach her more about kisses, but she also liked playing with him, delaying the moment that would happen.

"There are some real pretty ranches southwest of here. Any of the forks of the John Day River would be good. It pretty near drains all of eastern Oregon. A place like that would give a man water, grass, some land to raise alfalfa, timbered slopes for the cattle to graze in the summer, maybe sell some logs, a nice spreading house with a view of the distant ridges. There's a lot of red rock in that country, nice canyons."

"I've never been to the John Day River or really seen much of Oregon. It's pretty there?"

"Very pretty with swimming and fishing holes." He looked at her then. "Good place to raise kids."

"You want kids?" She sounded skeptical.

"Sure. Someday, and I hope I can give them the kind of life my parents never managed. You don't want babies? I thought all women wanted babies."

"I've never really thought about it but probably... like you, someday. I haven't felt in any hurry for it. You'd have to give up rodeo if you had children, wouldn't you?"

"Would I?"

"The women I heard, those at the gathering, they sounded like it's pretty hard to be the one left behind when a man is gone all the time. Leads to a lot of divorces, I would guess. And a father wouldn't be much of a factor in the kids' lives if he was gone all the time."

"I do want to be the father when I have kids; so guess you are right about not traveling then or certainly not when they get old enough to go to school and they couldn't come along. When I get married; and I don't plan that for a long time off, I don't want a divorce. I want it to last."

"I guess most expect that when they get started but things don't always work. Do a lot of the riders do what Nick did—hold on too long?"

"Most aren't as good as he was to have to worry about that choice," he said with a smile, taking hold of the hand teasing him with the grass and kissing it again.

"Nick still didn't want to stop."

"It was more he didn't know what else to do. He never talked about a ranch. Can you see him keeping a little store? There comes a time a man either puts his money into something solid or it's frittered away."

"And he will quit now?"

"That choice is gone. Assuming he does live through this, It sounds like between that smashed ankle, his age, and the internal damage, I think he'll have to quit. Nick might be stubborn but he's not crazy. The question though is back to what will he do? I would hate to see him working at a fast food restaurant. He doesn't have any education, any experience doing anything but what he is. I hope he doesn't have a gimpy leg."

"Jean could work too if she wasn't always traveling with him."

"He won't like thinking she has to do that."

"She has not chosen how it was up until now. Maybe it's her turn to make some choices, don't you think?"

"Maybe." He pulled her down for a kiss. He parted her lips with his tongue, moving into her mouth, teasing and exciting her whole body. She knew it couldn't go far with kids playing a short distance away; but it was enough for her to know she wanted more, a lot more with this man. She liked playing with him, feeling him next to her. Even when they didn't touch, it was as if their energy was meeting and caressing. She had never known anything like it and wondered if she ever would again.

"What about the dance tonight?" she asked after they'd pulled apart and laid back.

"You can dance?" he teased.

"Can you?"

"Western two-step. You better believe it."

"Well, I haven't done that but can probably pick it up. Should we stop by the hospital first, check on how Jean and Nick are, see if there is anything Jean needs?"

After one more slow, lingering kiss, they got up and went back to the truck, driving to the hospital. They learned little other than that Nick was still in intensive care. Jean was with him, and they didn't ask to have her notified they were there. Before they got to the exit though, they heard her call to them. The three of them went for a cup of coffee.

"How is he doing?" Billy asked as he sipped the strong brew from the vending machine.

"Holding his own. He woke up once, talked to me, or I think he knew it was me. He's in a lot of pain and that doesn't seem to be helped enough by the morphine. I've seen him hurt so often that you'd think I'd be used to it, but I'm not."

"He's going to be okay though?"

"They say he should recover, but his ankle, well I don't know and his hip socket got pulled out. He maybe can do what a normal man would but not what he's been doing all these years. He's likely going to rehab before he can really leave. His spinal cord was bruised but thank god he won't be paralyzed."

Sara wished she knew something to say that would comfort Jean, but she didn't have a clue. Only Nick could say those words.

Jean turned to Sara who hadn't taken a sip of her coffee yet. "You make him quit." She gestured toward Billy. "Don't you go through this. Make him quit before he's crippled and an old man before his time. He won't have enough sense to quit either, but he's young enough now to find something else. Get him to do it."

Sara didn't say anything realizing Jean just had to get this out of her system.

"You don't know what it's like to see your man lying in the dust, broken, maybe dead or crippled. If he doesn't quit, you will know someday; and it'll kill you like it's killing me."

Sara looked at Billy and saw the remoteness in his eyes. He said nothing, but she felt his withdrawal. Until she had this shock, Jean had believed a woman couldn't ask that of a man. Limited experience though Sara had had, she knew Jean had been right.

Lovers, no matter how much they cared, could not tell each other what they must do when it came to a big choice, to something that impacted who they were as people. If they couldn't handle the choice of the other, they could walk off, but they couldn't and should not try to rewrite someone else's path to suit themselves. She might have even said as much to Jean if she hadn't recognized how close Jean was to a breakdown; and if Billy hadn't been standing right there. As it was, she kept her mouth shut. She sipped her coffee, looking down at her knees.

She remembered then a quote by Tagore, one she'd memorized. 'Let my love like sunlight surround you and yet give you illumined freedom.' The words fit this situation for what it'd be like if she loved Billy.

With some man, someday, she'd learn to love that way. Love but don't hold too tight. Even if she had thought she loved Billy, he'd not have wanted such words from her, not now. She would though share it with Jean someday that she knew she had been right. Jean might blame herself for the accident, but she would be wrong to do so. Nick had made his own choice.

Luck of the Draw

If she had loved Billy, she wouldn't let her love box him in, try to change him into something he wasn't. She would not let love do that to her either. This wasn't the right time for such words to Jean or Billy. It was how she wanted to live, but the knowledge was new to her. She had to live with it for awhile to be sure she could really follow that road.

She thought then of how complicated life became once one entered into a relationship with another person. It likely was what would impact parenting too. Love but release. Not easy but it had to be the right way. It would take learning to live it fully. Until now it hadn't been something she needed to know or had a place to apply.

The other side of it was working out one's own path. Follow it with wisdom and insights without trying to force the beloved also along it. She felt as though she had found her own a path and couldn't believe how rapidly it had come to her and in such an unexpected way. Applying it wisely could take a lifetime.

When they finished their coffee in silence, Jean went back to Nick; and Sara and Billy left the hospital. "A penny?" she asked before they got to the truck.

"Not worth that much."

"Want me to be the judge of that?" She had hoped they could talk about this, but it was clear Billy was not in the mood for that. "Can we still go to the dance?" she asked instead of saying what she was thinking.

As he drove to the dance pavilion, he said no more than was required to be polite. He was closing her out. She thought about trying but decided she would not try to push through the barrier.

When they entered the building, they stood for awhile watching the dancers. His hand was at her waist, but he said nothing. She could see his thoughts were far away and guessed it was related to what Jean had said or maybe what he had been thinking all along. It wasn't up to him to protect her from her own options, but she wasn't going to say that either.

The couples swung past. The songs were country western, and none she knew. Some were slow and some fast. Finally he turned to her, took her hand and led her out onto the floor. The song was a slow one and they found they danced well together. He was tall, looming over her, the set of his jaw determined, a dark look in his eyes. When that song ended, they stayed for the next and the next.

Dancing became a mindless thing as she let her body follow his lead. He was a good dancer, probably the athlete in him, and had a natural sense of rhythm. It was easy to follow him.

Half an hour or was it an hour or more later, he asked if she'd like something to drink. They had only taken a few steps that way when Tice showed up. "Wal where ya been, Billy boy, Billy boy?" he slurred. "Don't tell me. I know."

"You're drunk," Billy growled.

"Jest a mite. I see you're still with…" He looked lasciviously at Sara. Already a few people were standing watching them. Tice voice was anything but quiet. There was a woman with him but she appeared as drunk as he. Tice looked again at Sara. "How about letting me take a turn with her?" He reached out, but his hand was knocked away by Billy.

"Hey pards share, didn't you remember that?" Tice said now turning his gaze to Billy. "Hot little piece. Just a dance, how about it?"

Billy grabbed his shirt front. His voice was low but icy. "Shut up," he said with a hard smile, his voice not much above a whisper meant only for Tice's ears.

Tice laughed then and swung his fist toward Billy's face. Billy easily ducked. A sharp push would have been enough to send the drunk to the floor but clearly Billy now wanted a release of his own as he raised his fist and slammed it into Tice's belly doubling him up. Tice tried once more to hit out. He was fighting a battle he couldn't win between his own drunkenness and Billy's quick moves as he landed a sharp uppercut to Tice's jaw that sent him sprawling to the floor where he lay gasping for breath and swearing as much as he could muster.

It all was over in a moment or less but it had been enough to draw crowd interest. Billy took her arm firmly and led her through the gaping people. The ones who looked as if they were part of the rodeo didn't appear surprised. Town people looked aghast.

"We better be out of here in case somebody called the cops," he told her and she saw the wisdom of his words. It wasn't as if she wanted to call her parents from the jail to come get her. Oh that would go over well.

Outside she thought of what she had seen. Her first real, in person fight, if you could call it that. It had happened so fast. The sounds of fists landing on bodies, boots moving, and finally Tice falling were ones she'd never heard before; the energy was quick and angry. It made her stomach upset as she thought about it; so she stopped thinking of it.

When they were in the truck, driving away, he said, "I'm sorry about that."

"Don't blame yourself. He was the drunk one."

"He will be all apologetic in the morning probably—not that that helps. I blame myself for the motel room earlier. If he hadn't seen that, well he'd have not said what he did tonight."

"I was as much part of that choice as you. And the fight wasn't all your fault."

"Not *all* my fault?" he asked looking over at her in amazement. "Where do you get that? I didn't start it."

She knew she wasn't being smart to start an argument at this point. Billy was strung tight as a wire, and she wasn't much better. She couldn't resist saying what she thought. "You didn't start it, but you know you could have avoided it."

He sucked in a breath. "Sara," he started to say and then stopped.

"You know it was true. You wanted to hit him, and finally he gave you enough provocation. He might have deserved it, but you could have walked away."

"Little Miss Protected again. You know so much about fights, don't you?"

"Well, no, I don't, but…"

"Sometimes hitting someone like Tice, someone who is asking for it, is the only thing that will get through to them. I didn't hurt him."

She wanted to argue, but she knew it'd do no good; so she sealed her lips with a set and she knew mulish expression that he clearly saw when he glanced over. For the first time she noticed that his knuckles on the steering wheel were bleeding.

"Well you did hurt your hand," she said with anything but a tender tone to her voice.

He flexed it, a bit tenderly, she thought, but shook his head. "It's fine. Just scraped it a little maybe on one of his fancy buttons."

It was his right hand and he definitely did appear to be favoring it. That made her angry again, but she managed to ask with less than an angry tone, "Maybe you should have it looked at by a doctor.

"Sara, let it go."

"Is that all you can say to me? Over and over again it's me who has to let things go, telling me things we can't talk about."

"I'm the one defending myself here."

She reached for the door handle as soon as he stopped the truck in front of her home. "Good night," she snapped, but he was also getting out. "There is no need for you to walk me to the door.

"There's one need. Lights are on inside. In case that lady earlier or something at the dance gets back to your folks, I will go in with you."

"What for? To make it worse?"

"I am going in." His lips were tight, the expression in his eyes resolute.

She tried again anyway. "It's not necessary."

"It is to me."

Upon entering the house, Sara knew her parents were in the living room looking toward the door expectantly. It wasn't that late, only a bit after eleven. They usually would have been in bed, and the look on their faces told her at least some events of the day had come home. For a moment she felt like a child, but the feeling didn't last. She was an adult, and they would treat her like one, or she'd be looking for an apartment in the morning.

Billy's boots sounded unnaturally loud on the wood floor as they walked into the living room. Her father stood by the fireplace with his hands behind his back and her mother was seated stiffly on the sofa.

"Cheryl called us this evening with some information about your activities." Her father sent a stern look her direction ignoring Billy totally. "Would you explain what you were doing coming out of a motel room with I am assuming this man?"

"I am an adult. Do you have a right to ask what I was doing?"

Her father was taken aback as he hadn't expected an assault but rather a submission. Her mother gave it a try. "Our family has a reputation in this town that we must uphold. We own a business that depends on people respecting us."

"I am sorry you feel that way about it. I am not you and what they are owed is your pricing merchandise fairly and treating them with respect. I don't think what your daughter does should have any bearing on you. They might even feel sorry for you."

Sara was in no mood to feel guilty. Actually she didn't feel guilty. She was angry at Billy and was taking it out on her parents with her response not being much different than his had been at the dance.

"Well what about the rest of it?" her father asked.

"And that is?"

"A brawl at the dance." Now he looked at Billy for the first time. "Troy's father called to tell me that a man my daughter was with there got into a fight, disturbed the peace."

"Sorry about that, sir," Billy said. "I didn't mean it to get out of hand but a cowboy made a crude comment about Sara and tried to put his hands on her."

"Was that true?" her father asked turning back to her.

"That's what happened. I am just amazed at the speed with which the gossips have been operating. That happened just moments ago."

"Our friends have been concerned."

"Or had something they thought was juicy. There really wasn't that much to any of it. It was hardly a brawl. Billy hit the guy when he tried to grab me and wouldn't take no for an answer. There was no brawl as Mr. James put it. It was over about as fast as it started."

Billy inserted, "And as for the motel. I had to stop by to change my clothes. Sara could have waited in the car, but it didn't seem like a good idea as hot as it was."

"It's the appearance that we care about," Ann Connors said.

"Then next time tell your friends I am of legal age," Sara said. "It's really not their concern."

"I think they were worried about you."

"I doubt that very much."

"And…" The wind was clearly out of their sails as they both seemed stymied for what more to say. Finally George Connors said looking now at Billy, "I guess it all did sound worse than it was. It's not like we think Sara would go wild just because the rodeo came to town."

"She didn't," Billy said firmly.

"I'm sorry, Sara," Ann Connors said. "I… we jumped down your throat. We were worried but you are right. You're an adult and have been taught to wisely choose your friends. We should have trusted your judgment. I guess we were just edgy with all the excitement of the big show here."

"Have you been to the rodeo yet?" Billy asked wondering if they would see him there if they went and how that would go over.

"We haven't planned to go," Ann answered. "George is too busy, and I have had plans every day that made the timing wrong."

"There's always next year," Billy said feeling relief. He wasn't ashamed of what he did but having heard his brother's take on it and the earlier comments from Sara's parents, it was going to be better for her if they didn't find out at this point. Maybe at no point. The likelihood if it ever would have to matter to them was pretty slim and growing slimmer.

Ann Connors said, "I'll fix us all some coffee. You will have some, won't you, Billy?" She sounded much friendlier than she had only moments earlier.

"Unless he'd prefer brandy with me," George said getting the decanter from a sideboard.

Billy was uncomfortable about either, but he accepted the brandy taking a sip. What he really wanted was a cigarette. He wasn't about to press his luck with that even having seen George smoke a pipe the night he had dinner with them.

When Ann and Sara returned from the kitchen with coffee, he began thinking of excuses he could use to leave. He didn't belong here. He moved over to the fireplace, one boot up on the hearth before he wondered if that was taboo. Since nobody said anything, he left it there, staring into the dark fireplace nursing the brandy he had no desire to finish.

For a moment there was silence and then a bit of small talk about the weather. When a break came in the polite conversation, he said he had to leave and set down the barely touched glass. Sara said she would go to the door with him. They walked out onto the porch with no objections arising from her parents.

He stepped down a step and then looked back up at her. "I don't know if I'll see you tomorrow or not."

"I understand." She showed upset in her eyes but didn't try to convince him otherwise.

"We'll get together though... later. I'll call you."

"Sure." She had her lips tightly together. He saw she knew this was the end but maybe she would be glad it was. "Call me... sometime," she said and walked back into the house. He wasn't sure if he had seen a tear, but it didn't matter. This was not going to work for either of them.

Chapter Eight

Thursday

Jean had spent most of the night at the hospital beside Nick's bed. They transferred him from intensive care to a room but the drips and tubes were still in place. He looked up at her once but didn't say anything. She believed he had recognized her.

Okay, so he'd live. She had that much. He would recover, but what would they do? He couldn't think of riding again. The doctor had made that much clear. When Nick was up to it, they'd have to talk about it. She dreaded that moment. Another fall from a horse would kill him, and it wouldn't take that much. That broken ankle was unlikely to stand up to riding as he had been doing.

The doctor had added, "I know these men. They aren't easy to stop, but you need to convince him if you want him to be with you into old age." He had patted her shoulder, but it hadn't eased the pain she felt.

She had known it all before he'd said it. She thought back to their life together, so many years and most of them good. All of them proud ones to be the woman standing at his side, the woman he had chosen. Over and over he told her how much she meant to him. He was a man who knew a woman needed words, and he gave them to her generously.

She thought back to the day that he had told her he wanted to marry her. She had gone out on the circuit, her first year to try barrel racing at more than local fair events. She'd known Nick at a kind of distance. That year though he had kissed her, and it wasn't like any boy ever kissed a girl. It was a man's kiss, and she had responded as a woman.

When she went home on a break, she never expected Nick to follow her. When she'd opened the door, she was in shock to see him standing there. She was seventeen and although she'd had a crush on him, big rodeo star that he was, after that kiss, he hadn't said much to let her know that he was thinking of her as more than another girl at the events.

They had sat on the porch as her parents weren't home, and her little brother and sister had been shooed away. For awhile it was in silence, then he said, "I've been thinking about something."

"What?" She still wasn't sure what he wanted with her, but she liked how he was beside her, the feel of his muscular arm against her, the scent of his skin, as they moved the porch swing back and forth slowly.

"I can't stay here long. I guess you know I am due in Dallas at the end of the week."

"No, I didn't know that. I hadn't entered there; so won't be going."

"I want you to go."

"I really can't."

He had sucked in a breath then. "I know this is sudden, but I don't have time for all the courting you have every right to expect. I want you to go with me… as my wife. Will you marry me?"

It had been a shock, knocking the breath from her. Before she could give a response, her father and mother had returned home and given him a look that would have sent him running if he'd been a weak man. He wasn't, and he looked back without animosity because he saw how they'd be feeling at him taking their little girl away. He was a man, and she was not much more than a girl.

"What's he doing here?" her father asked as he brushed past into the house.

"Sorry for his rudeness," her mother said. "We had some bad news in town is all."

"What?" Jean asked.

"They turned down the loan for the new equipment at the warehouse. It's okay. Not a huge deal but would have allowed us to expand. That won't be happening, and he's disappointed."

Jean introduced her to Nick and then her father when he came back outside.

"Sir," Nick had said, instantly setting her father's nerves on edge as it wasn't how he was used to being addressed. "I just asked Jean to marry me. She hasn't answered; but if she says yes, I want you to know I'll take good care of her."

"I thought you were a saddle bum," her father said, opening the beer in his hand. "How would you take care of her?"

"I promise that I will."

"Well it's out of the question," her mother had said. "Jean's just seventeen, just barely out of high school. No time for getting married this young."

"I think that's for Jean to decide."

"In our state, we'd have to sign for her. She's underage."

Nick had turned back to Jean. "What is your answer?" She saw it clearly that day that if she said no, she'd never see him again. If she said yes, her parents would be furious. She'd have to go with him without marriage at least until she turned eighteen. That would put her beyond the pale so far as they'd be concerned. She didn't have long to make her decision. It was how it would always be with Nick, but she hadn't known that yet.

He left that night without knowing, but she packed her bag and went to him. A few months later they were married in a little Arizona town by a justice of the peace on the second floor of a courthouse with only two cowboys as witnesses. It took two years for her parents to be reconciled to the marriage. When she had come to his motel that night, he had said, "You know it won't always be easy, babe?"

She had nodded, but she hadn't cared. He was her first love, would soon be her first lover, and the feelings she had had for him went beyond anything she had ever experienced. The pain that would follow did also. Seeing her man broken up, losing the babies she had wanted, giving up on any dream of a real home, none of it sounded like what a woman should want, but a woman takes what comes with some men and that was what came with him. She regretted none of it.

As she sat by his bed, knowing how many times she had done it, she prayed that God would help him see he had to give up this life, that he would accept it without bitterness. That God would help them find a way to live without the rodeo.

Nick's face was pale against the growing stubble of his beard. He always did have to shave again in the late afternoon to avoid the five-o'clock shadow. She brushed her hand against its sandpaper roughness finding it reassuring. Some things didn't change at least.

Now and then in his sleep, for it was sleep, he moaned. She hated knowing he was in pain, and she couldn't help. She hated the tubes connected to his body. She loved him more than life.

It was nearly four in the morning, and she had dozed in the chair. She'd left her hand resting on the bed beside his, wanting him to sense her physical presence wherever he was and to reassure herself he was still breathing. The pressure of his fingers on hers woke her. Looking up she saw those beloved blue eyes watching her.

"How do you feel?" she asked.

"Like I was run over by… a truck." His voice wasn't much more than a whisper. "I could use some water."

"Ice cubes, they said." She put one in his mouth.

"You look tired," he said.

"Some."

"I really did it this time, didn't I? I wasn't expecting I'd be waking up."

"You almost didn't." She felt the tears start again.

"Don't cry, babe. I'm sorry."

"A few tears won't hurt me... or you."

"How long do I have to be here?"

"Can't you ever wake up and ask anything else?" she asked with a smile.

"How bad is it?"

"You will recover and live. That's the important part."

"And ride again?"

"Do you have to ask?"

He turned away. "No. You were right. I should have quit before it got to this. I'm sorry, babe."

"Just heal now, okay?"

"Yeah... I think I'll sleep awhile."

She watched as he drifted off. She hated this. He would hate it. How would they manage? She had to have faith something would work, but what? Tears rolled down her cheeks as she thought about not just his physical pain but also the emotional agony for him of accepting he was finished with the thing he had lived with, loved, and known best. She could stand beside him, help in whatever way possible, but she couldn't do it for him.

When morning came and sunlight streamed in the window, it woke her. Looking quickly at him she saw he was already awake and watching her. "Should have woke me," she said grumpily.

"You needed the rest. Go on home. Take a shower. I'm going to be okay now."

"You promise?"

He managed a smile. "Yeah. It'll be okay. Quit worrying and give yourself some down time."

She knew he was right, and so she agreed. "But I'll be back later."

"I'm counting on it but not too early. I need to sleep too and not worry about you. Got that?"

She'd be more good to him when she wasn't so close to exhausted. She kissed him lightly on the forehead and left asking the nurse to call the trailer park if there was any problem. They would get word to her.

As she was coming out the front doors, she saw Billy driving up. "You are right on time," she said. "I need a lift."

"Hop in. How is he? I guess okay or you'd not be smiling and heading back to the trailer."

128

"He'll be okay. I thought yesterday that it was the end, but it's not. Just a new beginning."

At the trailer court, he dropped her off with the admonition to let him know if she needed anything at all. She was relieved he had been there and that he then understood she needed to be alone. Words weren't going to fix what was wrong in her life. She had to start coming up with a plan.

Inside the trailer, she threw off her clothes and took a shower. She stayed there until the water turned cold. Dragging on a robe, she lay down on her bed, immediately drifting into a deep sleep.

A few hours later, she woke and walked restlessly around the little trailer. It was almost eleven. She wanted to go back to the hospital but that would be a mistake. Nick wouldn't like it if she showed up too soon. He needed to sleep, to get a healing rest.

Everything she touched reminded her of him and what had happened. She could not let herself dwell on the accident, on how close she had come to losing him. A light knock at the trailer door was a welcome respite from her dark musings. It was even better when she saw it was Sara.

"I didn't want to bother you," Sara said as she came into the dining area.

"You're not. I kept thinking, and thinking right now is bad. I am just glad to see you. I keep... you know reliving the moment it all happened. Then I worry what comes next for us."

They sat in the small dinette and then Jean measured and turned on the coffeemaker, staring blankly at it. She needed something to do. Anything to not think.

"I called the hospital," Sara said, "before I came and they said he's doing better."

"He's a quick healer. I'll give him that."

"How about you?"

"I'll heal too but it's been touch and go." She forced a smile. "Talk to me about anything but the accident. "How about telling me something about you. Something I don't know."

"Well, you don't know that I paint. Not like walls," she said with a smile, "but landscapes, sometimes an abstract, but I am working on learning to paint people in their daily lives or at a job."

"Like rodeo people?"

"I haven't tried that. Rodeo is too new and moves too fast for me." Sara smiled. "But more on the street or waiting for a bus or children playing by a river's edge."

"I'd like that kind of painting. I never tried to do any kind of creative stuff myself. I'd like it if I could have, I think... other than when it didn't come out, of course."

"That is the hitch with it. Then it makes me angry at myself. I haven't gotten to a point where what I see out there, and what I visualize it should be, that they come out the same. It's frustrating at times."

"Would you like to be a professional painter or is it a hobby?"

"That's the question, of course. It's not easy to make a living at it. I've wrestled with the whole issue."

"Boy, tell me about that. The difficulty of making a living. I guess anybody who follows their passion has that problem to deal with."

"Did you follow a passion?" Sara asked wondering if that would come under the category of something not to discuss.

"I only had one. Nick. And yes, I followed that wherever it went. I still am."

"You didn't need something else, something for yourself?" Sara had been wondering about that. What if a woman truly desired a man, loved him, had made him the center of her life, how would that work out for her, for building her own life?

Jean was silent a moment; and Sara was about to bring up something else, when she answered, "I think I should have had something for myself. It probably would have been better for us both. He knew I was his center and it was a lot to lay on him. I think it was a life mistake of mine. If I was to do it all again, I'd still be with him, but I'd be for me too... if that makes sense."

"It's not too late for you to do that, find that thing for you."

"I know. Nick and I both have to change now."

"Does he accept that?"

"With that man, who can know for sure? He said it. I hope he accepts it. If he doesn't, I don't see how he can survive something like this again. People have to know when to let go when things aren't working. I should have said something earlier, but I didn't and that's my sin."

"Jean, you gave him freedom to follow his dream. How could that be bad?"

"Suppose I hadn't. Maybe he'd be with me right now."

"He is with you. He just has to heal, but he hasn't gone anywhere. The thing is we can't control someone else. You didn't try with him. Now what he needs is a new passion," Sara she finished thinking about how hard that must be even when the words were so easy to say. "Sounds like you both do."

"You're a pretty smart cookie for being so young," Jean said with a bigger smile.

"I have been getting a quick education." Sara laughed.

"Men will do that for you."

"It pushes all the buttons I never had pushed before. Billy has pretty well had it with me though."

"He'll be back especially if he said he wouldn't."

"How do you know that?"

"I saw how he looked at you. He's hooked. It'd take a lot to push him away now no matter what he thinks."

"It doesn't seem it has much long-term potential though. He travels. I'm here. He doesn't want anything serious. I am not sure I am ready for that either."

"Are we ever ready for the thing that comes along to change it all for us?"

"Wow, you really nailed that, what I have been thinking. It has changed me."

"Looks like in a positive way."

Hey, I forgot, I brought some food I thought you might like." She went back out to her car and came back with a sack which when she opened it, held croissants, muffins, sweet rolls, bagels, even some cream cheese. "I didn't know what you'd like, so I got a variety."

Jean smiled and took a croissant. "Mmmmm thank you. I had forgotten I was hungry."

Sara took a muffin for herself. "You have to keep strong," she said as she bit into it. "I may not know a lot about men, but I can tell that he's going to need your strength now—even more when he gets out of the hospital and only has you to order around."

Jean chuckled. "He'll do that all right. You seem to know more about men than you admit."

"This part might be guesswork."

"Have you had a lot of boyfriends?" Jean asked, "if that's not too nosy."

"Nothing serious but I have my father to look at. I've dated a few boys but nobody for more than awhile. I never knew a man the way... the way it is with Billy."

"You are a lovely woman but I suppose you get told that a lot."

"Sometimes."

"Sometimes!" Jean snorted. "Don't give me that modesty junk. It's got to be more than that. You are beautiful and you know it."

"I am going to be straight with you. My parents taught me beauty doesn't matter for life. I don't think I ever heard them even tell me I look pretty. It was more when I did good at something, when I said something they thought was intelligent, or helped out somewhere. It's always about what you do and especially what you do for others."

"Well, that's weird—but kind of sweet, I guess."

Sara smiled. "They said if people concentrate too much on what they look like, they will forget other things that matter more. Plus they don't like the idea of someone being conceited."

"Hmph. It's fun to be pretty, and I don't see why it's bad to tell someone they are."

"I don't disagree. Just telling you what they said, and it maybe rubbed off on me. I like physical beauty in people like say you. I admire it when I see it, want to paint it even. It's hard to evaluate your own looks though, don't you think?"

"This is getting deep for me," Jean said with another laugh. "Tell me about the boyfriends instead. I can handle that better." So Sara related a couple of funny stories involving boys she'd dated where it hadn't worked out so well. Jean laughed and that was what counted.

They moved into the tiny living area space with fresh cups of coffee and Jean's mood grew somber. "What I can't figure out is what we do next. What can Nick do? He'd die as surely in a store clerking as he would out in the arena. He doesn't know anything but riding. I don't think I'd mind clerking so much though."

"It's not bad," Sara said. "You help people find what they need, give some a chance to talk about their problems and yeah that is part of the territory at least in a small store. I have liked doing it although not sure how I'd feel if it was forever."

"My worry is more Nick. He's lived all these years on the fast lane. What does he do to equal that?"

"He's not an old man. He could go back to school, get some training."

"Most anything I can think of like that, he'd hate. He's been used to freedom, the adrenaline rush of the ride, what can supply any of that for him? Plus Nick loves traveling."

"Do you like the traveling part?"

"Actually it's not bad. We see a lot of our same friends at different events. I make this into our home wherever we are; so it's not like it's really leaving home to do it."

"How about living closer to your parents? Would you like that?"

"They are wrapped up in grandkids and their lives. They don't care if I'm around. I disappointed them and in some ways they never forgave me even though it's no longer discussed."

"Disappointed in what way?"

"Marrying Nick. They saw that as marrying beneath myself even when he was at the top. Now, well it'd be even more of I told you so. I sure don't need that."

"Parents do get their minds set on things."

"Yours don't think much of you seeing a cowboy?"

"They don't actually know what Billy does, and even then they weren't thrilled about him." Sara said with a sheepish smile. "It wasn't like it seemed it would matter. He said from the start he'd leave when the events were over. They really never had to know."

"Unless it doesn't end there."

"I can't even think that way. He said it would, and I have to accept that."

"Do you want more?"

"I want what is possible to have."

"Sounds practical and unrealistic," Jean retorted.

Sara was the one to laugh then. "If I tell myself it enough, maybe I'll believe it."

"You won't. Take it from an expert," Jean said with a laugh. "You can try to kid yourself but it never works. Better to be honest at least with yourself from the get go."

"Then," Sara said thinking before she spoke, "I want it. I want whatever of it that I can have, and I hope for more than a week."

"That's more like it. I guess I didn't help you any last night when I said you should get him to leave rodeo?"

"It's been in the back of his mind all along about me. It just put fuel under the fire."

"I'm sorry I interfered. I was feeling a rush of emotions that isn't really like me. He came by this morning, but he didn't have much to say other than checking to see how I was."

"Well I already knew the whole spiel before it started. It really can't work. Two different worlds—yada yada yada."

"Sometimes differences are good."

Sara stared into her coffee. "Whatever the case, it's not really my choice where it comes to him. He pretty much made it clear that was that last night."

"Are you going to the rodeo today?"

Sara laughed. "Despite how it might seem so far, I am not a masochist. It would just make it harder. If he had wanted me there, he'd have said so. I won't push him on this. Look, let's come up with something more positive to talk about."

Jean grinned. "Any suggestions?"

"My mind is blank. How about we do some cooking?"

"Like what?"

"How about cooking some spaghetti. Do you like that?"

"Very much but I don't have the ingredients here."

"I'll fix it at my house and bring it by."

"That sounds lovely."

"One other thing. If you need money, you let me know, okay? I can help out and I really do want to."

Jean smiled more broadly. "Thanks but I'm okay for now. And Sara, whatever happens with you and Billy, I hope you and I can be friends."

"I'd like that a lot."

When Sara left, she didn't drive straight back to her home. She detoured toward the rodeo grounds but didn't park. She could see the crowds, hear the cheers and then laughter, but she wouldn't go in. She had to let this end.

She put on her radio and damned if the first song it played wasn't *The Way We Were*. She should have turned it off, but she didn't. She hadn't had long enough to have that to which the song spoke. She hadn't had that history with Billy that would be something to cherish when she got old. It would be more missing what could have been than thinking of what had. She resisted crying, but it wasn't easy. It would be easier when the rodeo was over—she hoped.

Her home was cool and pleasant, both her parents gone as she went into the kitchen and began the marinara sauce she had promised Jean. It was good to cook, to have something to think about that didn't involve a man riding a bucking animal or telling her he'd call her sometime when he didn't mean it. Cooking was a release for the frustration she felt and she fixed enough to take some to Jean and leave enough for her parents' dinner.

With that simmering on the stove, she decided to call a friend, the only real friend she had made since moving to Pendleton. Cathy was quick to say she'd be right over and had nothing she was doing. When she arrived, the two girls sipped Cokes and chatted.

"What have you been doing?" she asked Sara.

"Nothing much. What about you?"

"Nothing much my foot. Troy said he's seen you twice with a cowboy."

"Word gets around fast."

"He got the feeling it might be serious. He said the guy was tall, some might say good looking, but he didn't think he was that good looking himself. Either way, that doesn't qualify as nothing much, does it?"

"No, it would be something if it was going somewhere, but it's not." She wasn't sure how to tell Cathy what she felt about it. How could she tell her that it might've changed the direction of her life anyway? That sounded naïve of her to think one encounter could do that. Better to say nothing until she was more firmly established in her own mind with what it had meant to have those days with him.

"What's he like? Where'd you meet him? I think Troy sounded jealous."

Sara laughed. "That seems highly unlikely. Troy only wanted to please his folks and mine. No way was he interested in me."

"Well what about this guy? Is he gorgeous? Troy would never admit it if he was. Is he one of the riders in the Roundup, traveling salesman? Come on tell me more."

The talk wasn't as distracting as Sara had been hoping. She didn't want to talk about Billy. "Have you been to the rodeo?" she asked Cathy hoping the conversation would go another direction.

"Not yet, but I figured I'd go Saturday for the finals. Come on, tell me about this guy. You saw him twice. Troy was jealous and that look on your face tells me it is not nothing."

"You know you meet a lot of people in life. Sometimes it sticks and sometimes you both just goes on. We went out a time or two but didn't have anything really in common." She was making herself sound so logical and totally in control when she knew she felt anything but. "Yes, he was one of the cowboys. Don't say anything about it though to… well anybody. My folks didn't know."

"Too bad it didn't work out," Cathy said with a small sigh. "It sounded neat, meeting a guy like that although I guess it would be going nowhere as they don't stick around long. He'd be back next year though."

"That would lead to quite a relationship," she said sardonically. "Every year for a week."

"I envy you. It's so boring here. What is there to do? I just want to get out of this town, and the sooner the better. I registered for some classes, but I don't know why." Cathy was pretty, soft features, light blond hair that was helped along some with lighteners.

Sara opened a package of potato chips to go with the Cokes. "So where would you go?" Sara asked.

Cathy shook her head. "I don't know. Maybe L.A. That's a big city with a lot going on. I sure don't want to be stuck here the rest of my life."

"What about Russ?"

"Loser loser loser. He only wants to run his parents' wheat ranch. If I got serious about him, I'd be stuck here the rest of my life."

"I thought you loved Russ."

Cathy shrugged. "What's love? Do you know?"

"It was enough to want to be with him five years.'

"Almost six but we are going to break up. I won't probably go to L.A. but maybe Seattle or Portland. I could get a job in an office. It's why I took shorthand and all that shit; and then… well who knows."

"You really dislike it here that much?"

"You wouldn't know because you only moved here a year ago, not even that. Wait 'til you have been here a couple of years; then you'll know it's no place to live. Nothing ever happens."

"I guess it depends on what you consider something worth happening. I like the country around here. It's pretty; the mountains aren't far off. The skies are fantastic."

"Phooey. Who cares about that stuff? I want night life, shows, entertainment. You wouldn't really get what I'm talking about beings you came from a big city. I should move to Vegas."

"Don't you think we bring with us what makes a place exciting or not." She laughed then. "That sounds so Pollyanna doesn't it?"

"Yes, it does. Seriously, you must be kidding. I want to try out a different world. Maybe I'd come back, but at least I'd know what was out there."

"Well I can't advise you on this, not that you'd listen to me anyway."

"Sara, it'd never have worked with Russ and me. People have to want the same things in life or it is a constant battle. I've seen plenty of that with my folks. It's why they divorced and not just them but you know Sandy, don't you?"

"Not well, she's single though, right?"

"She was married to Rick, and they got a divorce last year. He works at the feed store. I don't think he wanted the divorce, but she got bored their life."

"But she still lives here."

"Only until she gets a job elsewhere. She wants to move to Texas."

"Lord why? Well, you are right about one thing. I haven't been here long enough to really know what it's like year after year."

"So," Cathy said, "tell me more about your cowboy."

"He's not mine."

"Yours or not, he sounds like the most exciting thing that happened to any of us this summer. He's the one who got in the fight at the pavilion, right?"

"It wasn't much of a fight but yes, that happened."

"Was it over you?" she asked, her eyes alight with interest.

"No and how about changing the subject. I don't want to talk about him."

"You did like him then?"

"Of course, or I'd not have gone out with him but sometimes two people are just too different like you just said was the case with you and Russ, right?"

"I suppose. Want to go see a movie?"

"Not tonight. I have to deliver some food to a friend and then I think I'll stay home and read."

"Borrr-ing!"

Sara laughed.

Chapter Nine

Tired, his day over, Billy stood and smoked for awhile with the other men as they talked over the events, Nick's injury. He finally said, "We need to take up a kitty to help them as this is going to be rough economically."

"I ain't won so much myself this year," Jason said, chewing on a chaw of tobacco and spitting, "but you're right." He dug out a five and put it in the hat Billy had taken off his head to start collecting the offerings. Billy added two twenties as others put in what they had.

Denny came up then asking what was going on. "I could hold the money," he offered, "and get more. I am his best friend."

Some of the men looked at him skeptically, but Billy had no reason to keep it himself and dumped the bills, into Denny's hat.

"Before the rodeo ends, you give whatever you collect to Jean," he said.

Denny nodded somberly. "You really think... that is... is he going to? Well shit, you know."

"He's a tough old bird," Jack said. "He'll make it, and they will need some help until the insurance money kicks in."

"You think he belonged to the IPRA?" Hank asked walking up and throwing in two tens.

"He competed at Tulsa the first year they had the nationals. He had to be."

"That insurance will help some but not enough and not with living expenses." One of the other guys threw in a twenty and a one.

Billy finished off his cigarette, as he slowly walked back to his truck for the drive to the motel. It looked to him as though they had gotten just two hundred dollars. It would help with daily living for Jean but wouldn't touch the real cost of this catastrophe. He'd be able to offer more once he knew how he was going to come out of this Round-up financially.

It hadn't been an easy day although both of his rides had gone well leaving him well on top of the bareback and still in the running with the bulls. He caught himself several times scanning the stands wondering if she had come. No way would he know with the crowds. Better he didn't know probably, but he wondered anyway.

The bull ride had been the disappointing one. The longer he rode them, the more he knew he'd never be better than mediiocre at it. He hung on, but it wasn't pretty. Why the heck did he do it? Saddle bronc would be better and next rodeo he'd use better judgment. The bulls were one of those challenges he should let go. The sooner he quit trying to master the skill, the better.

Absentmindedly, he massaged his right wrist. It was stiff and had been twisted again in getting off the bull. It seemed to be okay, not swollen, but it wasn't what it had been or should be. That wouldn't help with any of his rides.

As he pulled the truck into the motel parking lot, he was glad to see Tice's truck wasn't there. Tice had tried to make peace that morning, and they were talking to each other. Billy knew it wouldn't be the same between them. When Tice had asked about Sara, Billy had shrugged him off.

This conflict really wasn't about Sara but about the changing relationship between the two men. For Tice it was about a changing lifestyle that he couldn't help but fight to hold onto but in the end he'd lose it. Billy would do what he could to help Tice when he needed it, but he wouldn't let him dictate anything to him regarding his own choices. He'd heard enough of the subtle digs to know Tice was only wanting to put him down as a way of lifting himself up. No more.

In the room, he lay down on the bed without showering, dusty clothes and all. He felt like a nap would make everything seem clearer. He had barely drifted off when Tice slammed through the door. He took a shower and came back dressed in clean clothing to stand over Billy.

"Look, I said I was sorry. You still holding a grudge?"

"Forget it. It's done. No grudge."

"It sounds like there is. Want me to apologize to her?"

"Forget it."

"Look, kid, I don't want trouble between us."

"There isn't any."

"You coming down to the bar tonight?"

"Not tonight. I'm tired and plan to go to bed early."

After Tice left, the room was quiet, but he couldn't find sleep again. He lay on the bed thinking he should shower but not moving to do it. He tried not to think. Usually he could manage but not this time. She was on his mind, and she shouldn't be. Everything was swirling together; and if he blocked Sara, Nick and death would enter the confusion filled arena.

Finally he gave up and took a shower, standing under the stream of hot water until it began to cool. Dressed in a clean shirt and jeans, he sat on the edge of his bed, looking down at the rug. Things had gotten out of his control. When had that happened? He lit a cigarette thinking he used to believe he ran his own life, made his own choices, but he was beginning to doubt that. Did a man ever know? Never mind, that train of thought was going nowhere.

He thought about her again. Those beautiful green eyes, the way her hair glowed in the sunlight, the feeling of her skin under his fingers. He wanted to make love to her. He should have except... would once be enough? He thought about how she had looked sitting in this room, watching as he had come out of the shower. If Tice hadn't shown up at that moment, they would have made love. Nothing was going to stop it. But then it had. He was just lucky Tice had not come in the middle of it.

It wasn't really what Jean had said. That was just added certainty to what he had already known. Oh he wanted to make love to her, knew she wanted it too. The thing was would it have been fair to make love to a woman like her if he didn't love her, when he'd be gone from her town in a few days? And then he thought of something else, something that scared him. What if he did love her? What if he wanted her to be waiting for him every day, every night?

Stupid thought. They had nothing in common and no way to work out a real relationship. She belonged with her family. He belonged on the road. She would want things he couldn't give her—not for years, maybe never. He thought about Nick lying crumpled in the dust and knew that could happen to him; and where would that leave Sara, even if she wanted a life with him? He couldn't do that to her. Best to let it go right now.

Thinking about Nick, about the accident, he then turned his thoughts to fate. Geesus Christ, he was on a destructive stream of thought. Fate, what was that? What made a man make it past death so many times and then boom, he would be killed and on a fluke? He sucked in the smoke, held it a moment before he blew it out.

Was this about fate? He didn't believe in a god who directed the world' but if not that, what was it about? Anything? Nothing? Why the hell was he thinking this way? He was the man who tried to live in the moment. How was that working?

In a way fate had put Sara in his path, and from the moment he had seen her, he wasn't going to let go. Stubbing out the cigarette, he lay back on his bed but couldn't seem to rest, finally giving it up to go get something to eat. Instead of getting into his truck, he walked uptown to the little café where he could get a dinner that wouldn't make him sick. He hadn't eaten all day and ordered a steak with all the trimmings, finishing it all.

By the time he got through eating, the street lights were lit. He walked along the sidewalk with no special goal in mind. At a certain point, he knew he was heading toward her house and that made no sense, but he didn't stop. Something was making him keep walking. He didn't plan to see her but just be near, he guessed. He sure wouldn't be knocking on her door. It was late anyway... Too late.

By the time he got to her house, there were no lights on, and he was glad. If there had been someone obviously home, would he have been tempted to knock despite what he told himself? For a man who normally considered himself to be focused, he felt scattered. What had pulled him back to be close to her? He lit another cigarette as he stood under the street light, leaning against the pole, smoking, and thinking again that it made no sense for him to have come.

He turned and began walking down the street but stopped at the sound of running feet. As he swung around, she stopped a few feet from him, catching her robe up around her waist. Her feet were bare. "You weren't coming up," she said, not making it a question.

"No lights on. I figured you were all gone."

"My parents are."

"Where are they?"

"Happy Canyons and some drinks with friends afterward. Why did you come?"

He smiled. "Heaven help me, I don't know. I started walking and... How did you know I was here?"

"I was looking at the window, watching the moon rise. At first I thought I was imagining it, about the time I realized it was definitely you and you were real, you had turned to go." She pursed her lips together. "You weren't coming up. You were leaving."

"I'd have been back." He dropped the cigarette to the ground and crushed it out with his boot.

"You would have?"

He opened his arms, and without saying a word, she came into them. He bent, taking his hand and lightly lifting her chin. His lips came down on hers, the kiss deepening, their tongues playing with each other. They stood kissing until a car's headlights picked them out, and they walked back to her house.

On the porch was a bench swing and she led him to it. They sat, holding each other, kissing, and it was like before for how he felt her melting into him. After a bit, she asked, "You really walked up here?"

His smile was chagrinned. "I really did but to be honest, I didn't have a goal in mind when I started out. Or maybe I did but didn't know it."

"Obviously I'm glad," she teased. "I missed you."

"It's not making any sense, but I missed you too. It doesn't seem possible I could miss somebody who I didn't even know last week."

She stroked his jaw. "How were your rides today?"

"I'm at the top of the standings on bareback and bull well less said about that the better. I stayed on is about all I can say about it. It wasn't pretty."

"I've never seen anybody ride a bull."

"I wondered if you'd be there today."

"You had to want me to be. It was your choice. I wasn't going to chase after you. I wanted to though."

He bent and kissed her. "I thought it would be best for you and for me if we didn't see each other again. Then I went and did this. For a man who likes to think he has a plan, knows what he's doing, I'm not making much sense even to myself these days." He shrugged.

She snuggled closer to him. She was aware then that when she had thrown on the robe, all she had under it was a thin nightgown. She felt very open to him, and although he hadn't begun to caress her, it would be so easy.

"This isn't the place for that," he said with a grin as though he had read her thoughts.

"There won't be much time for it though," she said knowing they both understood what they were talking about even if they didn't spell it out.

"We could work out something. I was supposed to head to Portland, but I might delay it."

"You mean stay around here for awhile?"

"I can't do it for long because the only chance I have for the finals will be that I win at enough rodeos. I can skip one though as it's been a good year."

"Or…" She was thinking. "What if I went with you for awhile?"

"You'd do that?"

"Let me think about it or even meet you at some city or another. Where do you go after Portland?"

"Oklahoma was the plan."

"I need to think about it, about how I'd manage it," she said as she took his hand and kissed the fingers one by one. "I think we can work it out… if we both want it enough."

"You believe that?"

"I don't honestly know," she said with a laugh, "but I am game to try. I don't want it to end here."

He sucked in a breath. "You are not part of my plan, baby."

"I know."

"But I don't want it to end now either."

"It might not work."

"It might not."

"I don't know much about the rodeo life and don't know how I'd fit into it if... well you know if I did travel with you for awhile."

"Your parents would blow their tops."

"That could be true. For a little while anyway."

"Sara... do you love me?"

She smiled. "Do you love me?"

"It seems a little crazy to even think it. I never said it to anyone before, never thought it but I can't explain this any other way. I am thinking I do. I sure didn't want to and yet from the start, I couldn't let go."

"I feel the same way. I love you, Billy. Can we really know it's the lasting kind? It's all been so fast. But I care for you a lot, and I don't want it to end for us, not here and not without seeing where it can go."

"It doesn't seem like it'll be anywhere good." His smile was rueful.

"If we knew that, we'd let it go. but we don't."

"I just worry like Jean said that it'll end up hurting you."

"She told me she regretted saying that. But you know, at the party that night, at their trailer, she said, I'd be more likely to hurt you."

"That could happen."

"Are you afraid to try?"

He smiled. "Definitely."

"A big strong cowboy type like you?"

"I know fear about a lot of things. Hurting someone else is definitely on the list."

"It's not your responsibility for that. I have to decide this for myself, but we don't have to decide it all right now, do we?"

"No, we don't."

"I think you better get to bed. You look really tired. I'll get dressed and drive you back to your motel."

"Not a chance. I walked here and can walk back." He stood and pulled her to her feet kissing her again long and hard, his hands firm on her back, running down to her buttocks pulling her against him where he could feel her soft curves against his hardness.

Yin and yang some would call that. They fit together good. He knew how it'd be if they went further, but no way was he sneaking up to her bedroom to do it or dragging her back to the motel where again Tice might interrupt. No, there'd come a time for it, but it wasn't going to be this night. When it happened, if it happened, it would be where there was enough time and the right place to do it right.

He kissed her lightly on the forehead and then headed down the steps. "Tomorrow," he said as he looked back, but he heard the door closing and she was already gone.

He hadn't realized until he started down the road how tired he was. He was thinking he should have let her give him a ride when a car pulled up alongside and slowed down. "Want a lift, cowboy?" she asked.

"I thought I told you to stay home."

"You did?"

"How's this going to work if you don't do what I say?"

"How's it going to work if you think you can order me around?" She laughed as he got into the car and sank back in the seat with a sigh of relief.

"All right," he said, "you were right... this time."

"Ah just this time?"

"I'm not admitting too much—just yet. Wonder if your folks will hear about this one too." He smiled tiredly.

"Will it matter if they do?"

"I'd like to keep a decent relationship with them. I am thinking I need to tell them what I do as a way to make sure it gets a better start than them just finding out."

"Hmmmm, you think so?"

"It didn't matter when we were talking about ending it with the rodeo. Now, yes, they need to know. I'd rather face it now than later."

"They won't be happy," she said teasingly.

"They haven't thought much of me anyway. How much worse can it get?"

"Likely they're hoping I'll dump you... or you'll dump me. I told my mother I'd be moving out though. She wasn't happy about that either, but she didn't complain much other than to hope it wasn't going to be to move in with you. I won't do that. I need some time living on my own, I think, and you aren't ready for me to tag along to all the rodeos, are you?"

"I wasn't thinking I was even ready for this much," he said with a tired smile.

"I told a friend about you."

"Someone who will tell your folks before you get a chance?"

She shook her head. "Cathy won't do that. You'll likely meet her sometime, sooner than later. She will be rooting for us to work out—especially if she ever sees you." She laughed. She turned into his motel parking lot and stopped the car. "If you weren't so tired, and if we weren't likely to have Tice show up, I'd be tempted to come in."

"There will be a better time," he agreed as he reached over to kiss her but lightly so their fiery passion didn't overcome his commonsense.

"See you tomorrow," she said happily.

He agreed and then locked her car doors as he got out. He watched as she drove off, turning a corner and disappearing. He found it hard to believe how much had changed in a few hours, but that'd pretty much been the way the last few days had gone. How would it end? He had no idea and was too tired to take his thinking further. Tomorrow. Maybe it'd be clearer tomorrow.

Chapter Ten

Friday

Billy didn't wake until sunlight was streaming in through a crack in the curtain. Tice was stirring as Billy got up and showered. They had nothing to say to each other as both dressed in silence. It was an uneasy truce that made Billy anxious to get out of the room. The two of them might have to talk someday but not now. Maybe they never would and the change had just been done without words.

Outside the wind was blowing, the dust thick in the air. Only eight-thirty and already hot. He wanted to see Sara but didn't know how he'd work that out. They had said a lot but worked out very little. Maybe today she'd have second thoughts. Maybe today he should have them.

He found a phone booth and dug into his pocket for Sara's phone number. The phone rang but no one answered. He hung it up. Maybe just as well. Inside the café, he ordered breakfast and then saw Denny walk in. This was not looking like his day.

The kid came over. "Hey, how ya doing?"

"Where's Susan?" Billy asked as Denny sat down without waiting for an invitation. Billy signaled the waitress for coffee.

Before he could get his first sip, Denny had started in. "You done good yesterday." Billy nodded. "Really good in bareback. Of course, bull riding is another story."

"Yeah, it's not been my event."

"Looks like you might win bareback though."

"Don't count your money until the last hand has been played," Billy said with a shrug as placed his order for breakfast. Denny studied the menu and then ordered the same thing. "Where's Susan?" Billy repeated.

"She wasn't up yet. You must be feeling pretty hot about now. Luck is what I see it as."

"Really? That's how you see it?"

"Sure. Get a good horse, and it's all set."

"Well there is always the possibility you could screw up even a good horse."

"Not me."

"No, not you," he said with a wry smile. "Somebody."

"I suppose. I guess you know I don't like you much," Denny said finally.

"You're kidding? And you hid it so well."

"Don't you want to know why?"

"Why would it matter to me?"

The kid ignored him but waited until the waitress had brought their meals. "It's Nick. He just thinks you're the best there is. All he could talk about is how you're going to take all around and be at the top the next five years at least."

"Nice of him to say that," Billy said as he began to eat.

"I seen you ride and don't think you're so hot. Especially not with the bulls."

"I already agreed with you about that. Did you have a point?"

The kid sucked in a breath. Clearly he wanted an argument, and Billy was in zero mood to give him one. He had enough distractions with Sarah. All he wanted this morning was to get his mind in sync for the events ahead of him.

"You been to see Nick?" he asked as he took another sip of coffee, his eyes hard on Denny.

"I don't like hospitals."

"And someone does?" He sipped his coffee before he added, "What about the money the boys put together, you give that to Jean yet?

"I will."

"You're in no hurry, it appears. I thought he was a friend of yours."

"He is… or was anyway."

"Bauer, is all you care about using somebody?"

"What makes you say that?"

"If you like Nick, if he has been a friend to you, then get down there and give him some support. That's what we do for each other."

"I might... but it won't be because you said to do it."

When he left the café, Billy had a bad taste in his mouth. He was also irked that the kid had managed to get him to pay for his breakfast. Forgot his wallet. Yeah right. Oh well, he wouldn't be seeing him that much longer as he had a feeling Denny wouldn't be long on the circuit unless he changed a lot of his attitudes.

He stopped by the trailer court to see if Jean needed a ride to the hospital. Driving up, he knew where Sara had gone as her car was parked in front. When he knocked, Jean opened the door with a big grin. Sara was sitting on the sofa drinking coffee. Jean poured him a cup and smiled even more broadly as she looked from him to Sara.

"How's Nick?" he asked lighting a cigarette.

"Sleeping better. They said he had a good night," Jean said.

"I tried to call you this morning," Billy said looking at Sara.

She smiled. "And I came by your motel before I came here. You weren't there. Another girl?" She was teasing.

"I was at the café for breakfast. I wish you'd been along to save me from that twit, Denny."

"Be sure you hide how you feel about him," Jean said with a laugh.

"He's got too much ego to notice… unfortunately."

"He's young."

"That might be part of it." He didn't want to argue with Jean or put down someone she liked.

"Actually," Jean said with a smile, "I am realistic about him. He's a hanger-on, a user. He hasn't been to see Nick or me. He and Susan are all about themselves."

"He might yet show up at the hospital," Billy said. "Maybe it is all about him being a kid and he'll grow up."

"I guess time will tell… So what does it tell about you two both showing up here? Coincidence?"

"Definitely," Sara said.

"At least this part is," Billy answered. They both grinned.

"I think you worked out your differences, is what I think," Jean said.

"For the moment," Sara said.

"Is Nick up to visitors today?" Bill asked to change the subject.

"He's got a cast and was walking some yesterday with help. Yes, I think he'd like to see you. He's wearing a cute little hospital gown and still hooked up to an IV, but they think they might disconnect him later today."

The hospital corridors were cool, the antiseptic smell strong, pungent in Billy's nose. His boots sounded louder to him than usual as they echoed in the hall. He tapped on Nick's door and heard the familiar voice saying, "Come on in."

"You look better than the last time I saw you," Billy said sitting on the chair next to his bed.

"I don't remember much about that. I… know I hung up... and then it's a blank."

"Not like you need to remember. The thing is you made it. It was a bad pile-up but you are going to get through it." Nick's face was pale, the pallor being enhanced by the stubble of his beard, the darkness of his hair as it curled damply around his forehead.

"I guess so."

"Think positive."

Nick managed a little laugh that ended in a grimace. "I've made it through a lot, but not this."

"What do you mean?"

"Rodeo and me had a parting of the ways with that ride... I just wish I knew what I was going to do now. Whatever it is, it's obvious it won't be... rodeo. I could've killed somebody besides myself getting hung up that way—like a green kid." He turned his face away as he clenched his jaw.

"It's happened to others."

"Yeah right. And they aren't still rodeoing, are they?"

Billy couldn't deny that. It was a bad kind of accident, and he was right about the risks to others. Stopping a horse in that situation was dangerous for everyone. It could have ended worse even though at the moment he had dived for the horse's head, he hadn't thought of the risk.

"There are a lot of things to do in this country," He said to try and buck them both up.

"Funny. I can't think of any offhand."

"Give me some time, and I'll come up with some ideas."

"Let's not talk about it. How is it going? I mean the standings?"

"I think John Kittering has first money sewed up with saddle bronc. You remember him. He's from Billings."

"Yeah, I do. A nice young guy."

"Well it's not a done deal as Tice has got good numbers too. Billy Mitchell has it for bull riding unless something goes wrong. I am way back there on that one although so far I've made all the rides."

"You're too tall for it."

"I keep telling myself that but then keep entering. I am not sure why."

"Sure, you know why. You like the rush."

"That or I'm a masochist. I wouldn't put money on either possibility right now," he said thinking of some other self-destructive actions he'd taken without thinking through where it might land him. He wouldn't be mentioning that unless he had to. "Anyway I didn't see who was at the top of bull dogging or calf roping but so far I have the top numbers in bareback. Gene Evans is hot on my neck though."

"How about Denny?"

"I thought he might've come by to tell you himself."

"Not yet." He hesitated a moment. "I know, he's cocky and not as good as he talks or thinks." Billy didn't want to add what he thought; so he kept his mouth shut on it. "He's not as good as you... or as I was. He isn't realistic..."

"Time will tell, I guess."

"Speaking of time... How's it going with your gal?"

So he couldn't avoid that one after all. He was tempted but didn't pretend he didn't understand. "Up and down at best. We likely have too many differences for it to go anywhere. When I leave, I'll be leaving alone."

"So it's over?"

"No."

Nick consider that a moment with a tired smile. "You haven't had long to get to know each other."

"We're opposites on pretty much everything that counts."

"Sometimes what counts most ends up surprising us."

Billy looked at Nick's crooked smile. "Okay, I do know that," he said finally. "I'm not trying to tell the future where it comes to her. So far that's been a lost cause anyway."

"Good."

"She surprised me when she talked about maybe coming on the circuit with me sometimes—us not being married. I don't know if that'd work. She's been raised different with parents. Well, you know."

"You're young to get married. She's even younger."

"Damn straight. I thought I'd get to that after I quit rodeoing. By that time I figured I'd have enough for a little ranch. You know the dream. Start small and grow it up with the work and years."

"You know what plans are like."

"Lately."

"Life is what happens while we're making... those plans. Seems like I heard that somewhere and have lived it a lot."

"Tell me about it. She and I've only known each other a couple of days. We can't make a life decision; and yet if I leave, how do we figure out what we could have had? The truth is she's the kind of woman I always thought would be there, but it was in the someday category."

"Lousy timing," Nick agreed with another faint smile.

"Wrong time and maybe right woman," Billy added.

"You sound so confident." Nick managed a laugh that became a groan. "You know, it's not all up to you."

"You're not going to preach to me, I hope."

Nick shook his head. "No, I got no answers for you. Not even for me. Nothing ever worked out quite like I wanted. Damn I sure want a cigarette."

"They not let you smoke in here?"

"Not with my injuries, I guess. Hard way to quit."

Despite his best intentions, Billy went back to what he was wrestling with the most. "The thing is rodeo is hard on marriages with the exception of you and Jean. I've seen a lot of divorces just in the short time I've been in it."

"Marriage, huh?" He gave a little laugh.

"Well not like the word has been used."

Nick shifted in the bed, giving a low groan. Billy said, "Want me to call the nurse?"

"No, it's okay. Just... You know how it is."

"I should go and let you get some rest."

"I will but just want to say one thing. You know it's not always been gravy with me and Jean. We've had our rough patches."

"But you and she have something special. The thing is Jean wanted rodeo too, didn't she? Sara, she doesn't know much about it."

"I don't know if Jean always wanted it. She wanted me. It was a package deal. I didn't think I could do anything else. Guess I'll find out now."

"Sara has been pretty sheltered. She'd get a crash course in life if she sticks with me—already has in some areas she never figured."

"She looks to me like she's tougher than you think."

Billy looked at him skeptically but saw that Nick was spent. He patted his shoulder and said he'd see him later.

Sara was sitting with Jean in the lobby, watching as Billy walked up. "How can you drink that stuff?" he asked looking at her cup of coffee from the vending machine.

"It's what is there," she said practically.

"How was he?" Jean asked.

"He sounds stronger. Like he'll be okay. He was going to sleep when I left."

"I'll slip in quietly. Thanks for taking time with him. I know you're busy."

"He's a friend."

"Others claimed that too, but they haven't shown up. You are the real deal, and I appreciate it. Nick too, I know."

"Anything I can do for you?" he asked, but Sara could see his mind was already elsewhere.

Jean put her hand on his arm. "Nothing. You take it easy today, okay?"

"Always," Billy said with a grin. He turned to Sara. "Are you coming with me or staying here?"

She gave Jean a hug and followed him out to get into his truck. Since there was little time before the first event, they had lunch at the rodeo grounds. As they ate their hotdogs and sipped a shared Coke, she saw how far from her his mind was. She didn't see it though as upsetting this time. She had come to realize it came with the territory as he prepared himself for the challenge ahead. Taking a last sip of the Coke, she said, "I'll be up there." She pointed toward the bleachers that were filling up.

He smiled and bent to kiss her. When their lips met, it was as magical as it had been the first time. Their gazes met, and she touched his arm lightly, then his neck. "You do good, okay?" She knew it was trite but she could think of nothing else to say.

"Sure. Hey, baby, let's have pizza tonight." He pulled out a cigarette and lit it, blowing the smoke away from her.

If she had learned one thing in this week, it was that sometimes, she had to pretend to let go of her fear or at least not show it in front of him. He had his own way of dealing with the tension of the ride. "Sounds yummy," she said and made herself smile. She kissed him again, and knew his mind was a long way from her. She went to the bleachers, climbing up the steps to where she would have a good view of the chutes and the arena.

Not long after she got seated, she was surprised to have Susan Bauer show up. "Hi," she said, "mind if I sit down?"

"Of course, not. How are you, Susan?"

"Great. Denny hasn't been as lucky as Billy but today's going to be his day. I just know it."

"Well, good luck."

"Thanks but he won't really need that. I mean it's all about his ability, right?"

"You know honestly I am not that much up on what rodeo is about, but my guess is it's a mix of luck and ability. Things do go wrong sometimes in life or anywhere." She knew she was repeating what Billy had told her. Her new life philosophy. She smiled to herself-- uncertain if she liked that idea or not. This business of finding her own life when she was tying herself to a prairie wind, well she wasn't so sure it was going to be easy to hold onto herself. She'd sure give it a shot.

Susan was going on, but Sara had stopped listening because she had caught a glimpse of Billy behind the chutes. He was kneeling, putting on spurs, then rose and adjusted his chaps. She felt her heart skip a beat. He was fluid, like that wind, and she felt a huge pride that she was the woman he wanted to be with-- well at least for now.

Why was it that whenever she saw him, she felt that surge within her chest that moved to fill her whole body? Would it ever change? Would there come a time that he'd be somewhere, she'd look over, and not feel warmth filling her being? She felt him everywhere. Love didn't seem like a big enough word for that or was it the only word that could possibly explain what this was? If there was no such thing as love at first sight, what was this?

She forced her attention back toward the arena and saw the preliminaries beginning. The parade was fun and then came opening events. Color, sound, movement, like one painting after another. From the program, she knew he would be riding early, the first real event that got it all started. She heard the radio announcer as he talked of the background of bareback riding, explaining how the scores were tallied.

The first rider out of the chutes was bucked off before the buzzer. She applauded loudly along with the crowd understanding more how much they put into what they were doing. Denny Bauer was next up. To Susan's screams of excitement, he made his ride to the buzzer and drew a respectable score. While it wasn't world record, as one might have thought from Susan's reaction, it was nothing for which to apologize. 'At least he made it to the buzzer,' Sara thought cattily but kept the words to herself.

She watched the riders with interest, trying to decide what made a good score. "Next rider out on Surprise is Billy Stempleton from Bend, Oregon. Billy has scored consistently high here at Pendleton and is the rider to beat. This cowboy has been rodeoing professionally for five years."

Coming out of the chute, Billy spurred high on the horse's shoulders. Rhythmically he spurred Surprise on each buck. She knew by now that the spurs weren't sharp. Keeping his legs high like that had to make the ride more difficult and with only balance and the rope to hold onto. As the animal twisted and hit the ground hard, Billy was right with him. He made it look easy as he never lost connection with the animal.

The whistle blew and she felt a surge of relief, but it was only momentary as she realized that even though Billy's legs were now down, hugging his horse, he still had to get off that bucking animal who was no less eager to throw him than he had been during the countdown.

The pickup man came alongside, trying to give Billy a chance to grab his waist, but Surprise lived up to his name and twisted away. Then she saw Billy let go, throw his leg over the animal, landing with a side roll. In a matter of seconds he was up, dusting himself off, and walking toward the chutes. The applause was deafening. The top score of 79 came as no surprise and led to more cheers.

As he had walked across the field, he had looked up toward her. She smiled, unsure if he saw her. She felt some of the excitement and fear mixture that she guessed might be part of the rides for the men. Vicariously, it had been an adrenaline rush. She was pretty sure his gaze was on her and for that moment he was sharing the results with her. She tried to label her emotions and found they were jumbled together with pride. Was that foremost or was it relief?

"My," Susan said, "he did well. Lucky again, wasn't he?"

"More so than your husband." She heard it announced that Billy had scored highest leaving him only one more day to secure being top cowboy for that event.

"I just hope Denny gets a good horse like that one tomorrow."

"And if he does, that he isn't bucked off," Sara retorted. She settled back then to watch the other events. She felt a little calmer about the whole thing until she remembered the bulls were last, and she had no idea what that would be like-- other than everyone agreed dangerous.

The events seemed less stressful when she didn't know anyone riding in them. She watched the milking contest with amusement as two men would go running out after a cow, have to secure and milk it, racing back with the milk first. Between that and the clowns, the rodeo was giving an emotional respite before the last event.

Looking toward the chutes, she saw for the first time the kind of bulls the cowboys would be riding. The Brahmas seemed larger and meaner than any she had seen in fields. What kind of animals were these? She felt a rising tide of fear that Billy would be mounted on such an animal. She heard one crash against the fences and it gave her some idea of how strong they were, how angry they were at what they were being forced to do. They weren't just big and vicious looking, but they had long, wicked looking horns. The men getting them into the chutes were jumping away and then back down to get the animals set for the cowboys to mount them.

She began to realize, as she heard bits of conversations, that most of the people around her were once again connected to the rodeo, relatives here for the events, friends, spouses, but they talked of what was going on and in terms more technically than she would likely have heard out in the larger stadium.

Luck of the Draw

"Hi," a pretty dark-haired woman sat down beside her.

"Hi," she responded wondering if she had seen her at Jean's and if so, should she know her name.

The woman chuckled. "No, you don't know me. I am Jacey, married to Hank Peterson. He's the clown out there." She pointed to a tall man with shorts, a kind of phony skirt and scarf attached at the waist, suspenders and a clown face.

"As you can probably tell, I'm a newbie here," Sara said. "I keep trying to understand but it's a little beyond me."

"Everybody starts sometime. Hi Susan."

The two women exchanged a couple of words as Sara continued to watch the events behind the chutes more than what was going on in front of them. Billy was smiling often as he talked to different men, then knelt to change his spurs. She had no idea why he needed to do that but other riders were doing the same thing, so evidently it was part of the event.

Jacey turned back to Sara distracting her mind if not her eyes. "Someone told me you're with Billy."

"Well as much as you can be with someone you only just met."

Jacey chuckled. "It happens two ways here. One is you grow up with him. That's my kind and Susan's here. The other is you meet, and it's a whirlwind. I can point to four or five women around you where that's how it was. Those guys don't have much time and don't waste what they do." She giggled again.

"I am beginning to understand that... and I guess a woman doesn't either if she wants to be with such a man."

"They are a unique breed."

"Which works out best? I mean the ones who grew up together or those who meet and get together virtually overnight?" Sara asked with a smile.

"The one that lasts," Jacey joked. "I think... in all seriousness, it's the one who can accept not only the man but the rodeo."

Sara noted that Jacey's gaze also never left the arena as she was watching her husband do antics for the crowd. She saw one other thing now that she watched more closely. Hank kept one eye always toward the chutes, watching for what would happen next. He moved fast and was quite the athlete with all the make-believe humor of fear and terror. It was hard to believe this was the same man who had been drunk in the cafe her first night with Billy. He was now all business.

The noise from behind the chutes was growing more a factor as the bulls were pushed into the various chutes, kicking and butting their horned heads against the sides. How on earth did men ever get on such animals?

Rain Trueax

"Bull riding is made more dangerous by the fact that these bulls will go after anything on foot," the announcer began his spiel, changing from one of humor to one of facts about what the audience would soon be seeing. "A horse cannot be used for pickup as they are no safer near the bulls than the riders. Bulls are fast and agile. The only thing standing between that cowboy and the bull, once he hits the ground, are the clowns."

Hank Peterson ran around the arena pretending to hide, but Sara saw what he was really doing was placing barrels strategically. From where she was, she could see his expression. Behind the painted on clown mask of a smile, his lips were set.

"Hey Hank," the announcer said, playing along, "you get back out there. Where you going? You say home? You can't go home! Quit! What do you mean you quit!" The dust was heavy in the air along with the noise. Sara felt a fear growing in her belly. Billy was going to ride one of those animals... and then have to get off it, an animal that would want to kill him if it could. This was madness.

Billy was not the first rider out of the chutes, and Sara divided her attention between watching him and the first rider out on his bull. The gate swing open and then out they came with dust and fury. Billy had climbed the fence alongside the chutes to watch, and she realized it was for more than watching but ready to help if needed. When she saw him moving from that position to one of the chutes, she knew he would be riding soon and felt a greater surge of fear fill her chest-- as greatly as the love had earlier.

The announcer's attention then turned to the next ride. "Up next will be Billy Stempleton, an Oregon cowboy, on a bull called Corkscrew. Hey boys, help him get down on that bull. He looks like a mean one. Folks, you might ask why that name? It's not like he's for opening wine bottles, folks, no, it's because he goes in tight circles. You'd be amazed how tight, well you won't be in a minute, but bulls like these have a spine that lets them twist in tight circles. Every bull has its own temperament to make the ride more of a challenge to the rider as if it isn't already. Corkscrew, well he has a reputation for not being ridden. Let's see if today that changes."

Hank had now moved closer to the chutes where he'd be ready for whatever happened. Sara turned her gaze back to Billy's chute where she could see men on the rails above the bull and Billy in their center, lowering himself down.

"He has to get the rope just right," Jacey whispered. "Sometimes that takes some time."

"And then?" Sara swallowed hard.

156

"He'll signal when he feels he's ready. See Hank is closer now, out of the way; so he doesn't interfere with the ride but close for when he'll be needed."

Sara hated those words, be needed because of what they meant. But he would be needed. It was a big horned bull, and he wasn't happy at being there.

Then the chute swung wide, and Billy was out on the bull. Although Sara wasn't experienced in any of it, she saw he was in trouble right away. The bull had begun a spin right outside the gate, barely beyond it, then switched direction. Billy was holding on but by now it was obvious just barely. He had managed to straighten himself again when the bull kicked out behind, changing momentum and then another of those spins. How could anybody stay on an animal doing that and all of it right in front of the heavy wooden chutes? Would they be a help or a barrier he'd be slammed into if he was thrown? Could Billy jump off to them for safety? Would he even try or could he again try to right himself and stick out those eight seconds?

A second later, the answer came as she watched him flung from the bull as though he was a doll. There was no soft dirt landing as he was thrown against the hard wooden railings. It was a hard fall as he crashed into them, sliding to the dust. The bull had turned then and was heading back to finish the job it had started. He would gore him and nobody could get there in time to stop it.

"Hey hey Bully boy," Hank yelled dashing in to slap the bull on the butt. Sara felt Jacey's hand reach for hers as they watched now as the clown began to taunt the bull enough to give Billy time to get his senses together or the men who were now behind the fence be enabled to safely drag him over it.

With Hank's baggy skirt flapping, the bull was indecisive, looking from fallen cowboy to the irritating man and then made up his mind and turned toward the clown. Hank ran for one of his barrels as the bull began butting it with his horns trying to dislodge the irritant. He rolled the barrel for a moment but then turned back to the cowboys who were now on the ground, dragging Billy toward the fence. He seemed stunned from hitting the fence so hard. How badly had he been hurt?

She saw several more cowboys vault the fence, reaching for him, getting his arms as they got him to the other side before the bull returned to slam into the fence again. Another of the clowns had come forward and was now taking turns with Hank in teasing the bull. Sara knew only one thing, she had to get to Billy. How badly had he been hurt? Jacey gave her a little pat but only said, "Good luck," as Sara scrambled down the bleachers.

Behind the chutes, she saw Billy on the ground. Tice was also there and two men she didn't know. She heard Tice ask, "How bad is it?"

When she heard Billy's voice, even before she understood what he was saying, she felt a surge of relief. He was conscious, then she saw the blood on his forehead. Tice said, "I think you hit your head on the fence when he tossed you. Might need some stitches."

She didn't try to run to him but to instead stay out of the way as others assessed his injuries. She saw now he was trying to get up and being held back. "Give it a few seconds at least, boy," Tice was saying with a chuckle.

"I'm fine," she heard Billy protest.

"Not fine. This needs a doctor looking at it. You coulda busted a rib the way you were slammed into those boards." Billy swore. "How's this feel?" Pulling open his shirt, Tice was touching his chest on his left side.

"Like you shouldn't do that." He pushed himself up onto his elbows and caught his breath at the pain.

"Give it some time," another cowboy said. "Pass out and you might send that rib right through your lungs."

"Okay okay," he managed. "Is Corkscrew out? The guys okay?"

"Oh you know Hank, he played him awhile... if you can call that playing, but he's out now. Next ride's going on."

"Corkscrew would've nailed me if not for him."

"He's saved pretty damned near all of us over the years."

Several men she didn't know were standing by Billy readying to help him to his feet. She moved closer then and saw when he recognized her. He forced a smile as he met her worried gaze. "Now you know what I meant by not pretty," he said attempting a joke but not seeing her smile in return.

"Are you okay?" she asked knowing it was a dumb question. Of course, he wasn't. The other men looked toward her as though not sure who she was or what right she had to be there.

"Shook up mostly," he answered. "Just give me a minute. I'll be fine."

It was obvious that it was a lot more than that, and he wasn't fine as she saw him grimace with pain. What was the role of a rodeo man's woman in such a situation? Did she say, of course, you're not, you idiot. What did you do to yourself this time? Or was it tenderer, and oh darling, are you hurt? Nothing sounded right, and she was feeling a little shock herself. This wasn't the sort of thing for which any event in her life had prepared her.

Two medical attendants came up with a stretcher. "You need help getting onto this?" the older of the two asked.

"You got to be kidding me," Billy growled. "I don't need that. I just need to catch my breath and I'll be fine."

The attendant ignored that and knelt to feel of his side, examine his head, ask if he saw two of anything.

"Yeah, two of you," Billy said.

"Smart ass cowboy," the younger said with a grin.

"You need to have a doctor assess those ribs," the older objected.

"I do not."

Sara knew she probably would make a lot of the men there angry at her interference and one cowboy in particular, but she couldn't keep quiet any longer. "You do need to have your head examined... among other things. You're bleeding, and you can't evaluate a broken rib yourself, Billy."

He grimaced, the look on his face saying he would hate this worse than being thrown. "Okay but no ambulances. I can walk." He forced himself unsteadily to his feet and then taking a deep breath that made him wince again, he said, "See, I'm fine."

"Then shall I drive you to the hospital?"

She saw he didn't like it but he nodded. "I don't need it but all right." As his voice grew stronger, his mood seemed more determined.

She bit her lip but wasn't going to argue with him further about how badly he'd been hurt. The doctor in ER could do the convincing. At least he was standing even if a little uncertainly. The lines around his mouth were tight, the muscle in his jaw twitching as she had seen it do under stress. It would be best to help him do what he had set his mind to do and not waste time arguing.

Tice came up. "You going to be okay?" he asked with genuine concern in his voice. "That was a nasty spill. I ain't never seen that bull rode and looks like I might never."

"Not by me today anyway," Billy agreed forcing another smile.

Sara put out her arm then to give him some support if he wanted it. He did as he put his own arm over her shoulder.

"You sure you don't need us?" the younger EMT asked.

"I do not," Billy said through gritted teeth showing his impatience at being coddled.

"You keep a grip on him," he said to Sara, repeating his warning to Billy. "If he falls and his rib is broken, it could go right through his lungs."

"You can talk to me," Billy snapped. She saw on his face that it was bad enough to be thrown from the animal, worse that he got hurt, but even worse that people were making a big deal over it. This was clearly a man not comfortable with being seen as weak.

The medics shrugged. Obviously they were used to seeing cowboys walk off with serious injuries if there was any way at all. She just hoped Billy wasn't being foolish and letting that pride prevent his better judgment from coming into play.

It was a long walk, or seemed that way, to Billy's truck but they made it. Then came the next obstacle. "I need your keys," Sara said without much certainty as she had never driven a gearshift like Billy's.

"You ever drive one of these?" he asked giving her a doubting look.

"How hard can it be?" she asked. "You just rode a bull. I think I can do this."

"I didn't ride it very long," he differed.

"I can do this, my dear."

"You have to do one thing first."

"And that is?"

"Help me get these damned chaps off." That process led to so much fumbling on her part that it almost made her give up on the truck driving. Worse was when she realized he'd also need help getting off his spurs. What did she know about spurs? She learned.

"Okay," she said finally. "Where are your keys?"

His look was skeptical but he pointed to his duffle bag where a side pocket held the keys. It wasn't like she wanted to drive the huge thing, but she knew he shouldn't not with yet undiagnosed injuries and even possible shock. He had hit his head and there might yet be a delayed reaction to that. Hopefully he didn't have a concussion and his ribs weren't a compound fracture, but either way he should not drive yet and she could do it.

She gave him help into the passenger seat and then walked around trying to catch her breath. She could do it. How much could there be to it; and surprisingly once she got it in gear, there wasn't a lot and she drove them relatively smoothly to the hospital. In the waiting room, she picked up the papers for him to fill out. His head was working well enough for him to give the required facts, and then they waited to be called.

A short while later, the nurse ushered them back to a small cubicle, took Billy's blood pressure, his temperature, measured his pulse, and gave a cursory look at his head. "What else is injured?" she asked with a tired voice that sounded like she'd seen too many of these.

"My side," he answered, his breath coming a little shortly now which worried Sara and the nurse.

"Doctor will be right back. Help him off with his shirt." And then the nurse was gone. Sara hadn't had much experience with undressing adults, but she found it was not that hard to do the shirt, glad it had already been unbuttoned by Tice as she eased it off his shoulders and thought there'd be more pleasurable reasons for doing this. The smile on his dusty, blood streaked face told her he was thinking the same thing.

Finally a young doctor came in and gave him a speculative look as he glanced down the chart. "So what is exactly the nature of your injury. How did it happen?"

Billy gave him the cursory details as the man was examining his pupils, feeling of his jaw, and then probing his side from where the pain was coming. "I suppose you already know that you likely broke a rib with this kind of swelling, where you hit the board," the doctor said.

"I had guessed it was possible."

"I can't tell if it's compound, whether it'll pull apart under stress. Let's get you some X-rays."

"And what will they tell?"

"If the break is clear through, then you probably will need to check into the hospital and we'll do more tests."

"No, thanks."

"I am giving you my recommendation."

"Can't you just tape it?"

"Rib fractures are not taped these days," the doctor said with some impatience. "If I taped your chest tight enough to actually do some good, it would make you at risk for pneumonia or pleurisy. The only suggestion I have for a rib fracture is what I just said; and if not that, then bed rest, pain killers, and the suggestion that you not take any more falls for a couple of weeks."

"You aren't giving me a lot of help here."

"The rib will heal itself if it doesn't pull apart. You just have to give it a chance."

The doctor then examined the cut on his head, cleaned it with something that burned and applied a bandage. "There is some swelling here, but you seem to have normal reflexes. I don't think you have a concussion; but again, you won't have tests, and I can't provide the guarantee."

"Life doesn't come with guarantees anyway, does it, Doc?"

"Not yours for sure. You do understand. Oh never mind, I know you do and do it anyway."

Billy was in no mood to hear a lecture about that. None of this day was going as he had hoped. This was the last straw.

"Keep track of any symptoms of concussion," now the doctor was directing his comments to Sara. "If he is dizzy, faint, or too sleepy with increased pain tomorrow, get him back in here, okay?"

"I'll try," she said aware that she wasn't going to have much to say in that from the stubborn jut of Billy's jaw.

"You allergic to any painkillers?" he asked Billy.

"No."

"I have a sample here that I can let you have but no prescription for more because if it's that bad tomorrow, I want you coming back in to see me and get a prescription, got it?"

"I won't need that."

"We'll see about that." The doctor gave the pill container to Sara. "These will knock him out; so be sure he's somewhere he can sleep before he takes them. Sleep right now is a good thing."

"What should he eat?" she asked

"No problem. Once he takes those pills he won't want anything before morning and then just keep it light unless he's worse and then you know what to do—get him back here one way or another." His tone brooked no nonsense.

He turned back to Billy. "Don't be a macho hero about this if the pain is worse. If it is, it'll mean you need to get in and have those x-rays you say you don't want. Got it?"

"Got it," Billy grunted as Sara helped him get his shirt back on. She didn't bother trying to button it.

"How are you?" she asked when they got outside as she saw his grimace of pain.

"I'll be glad to be to the motel where I can lie down, is about all I can say."

"The pain is bad?"

"Not good, baby. I usually don't like taking painkillers but... tonight, it's likely to be the only way I'll sleep." He staggered a little and she could tell by the dazed look in his eyes that he was spent as well as still suffering some shock from the hard slam he had taken. When she helped him into the passenger side of the truck, he laid his head back against the seat to rest.

As she drove toward home, she relived it all. One moment everything was okay. The sky was blue overhead, a few thunderheads off against the mountains. The world was going on as it always did. Then it all changed in an instant and this time it was for Billy and her that the change had come. Life wasn't very predictable is all she could think with what was left of her mind to think.

The one thing she knew was she was not taking him back to his motel. He needed to be with someone who could make sure he didn't have a serious head injury. She would take him to her home. Looking over at the dust and blood, there'd be no hiding from her parents what he did or how he had been hurt. They would just have to accept it. She hoped. Otherwise she'd have to go back to the motel with him and brace herself for Tice's appearance later. One way or another, she was staying with him.

Chapter Eleven

At her house, Sara saw that one of the cars was gone. That was good at least. She vaguely remembered something about them going out but had no idea where or for how long. It didn't matter. She could get Billy inside without their help.

"We're here," she said touching his shoulder. His eyes opened and were for a moment blank.

"Where's here?"

"My house."

"No thanks."

"I will not leave you alone, and I don't want to stay at your motel room with Tice in and out. Here is where it needs to be."

He gave her a long disbelieving look. "Your parents are here."

"Well not at the moment. One of the cars is gone. I don't remember what they said but something was planned for tonight."

"And when they come home, they see me there like this?" he snorted. "I don't think so."

She did have to admit he looked pretty disreputable with his shirt open, blood and dust on his clothes, a bandage on his forehead. He also was sexy as hell, and they'd probably dislike that even more than the dirt. It was the only option though, and they would just have to accept it.

"Geesus, baby, I can't stay here," he said when he recognized she meant it.

"You might have a concussion. Someone needs to be with you. When you take the pain killers you'll be out of it; so it has to be me, and it should be here. You think my parents would like me staying overnight in your motel room better?"

"So they learn I'm a rodeo rider this way? They'll never forgive me or you."

"You don't know them. They talk a lot, but they'll come through in the end."

"It took years for Jean's folks to accept Nick, and they still aren't close."

"My parents are not hers. Besides if it takes that long, so be it. We are going in, and you are going to let me win this one because you know I'm right."

She saw him start to say something more and then set his jaw. He did know she was right. So he unenthusiastically nodded and let her help him out of the truck.

In the living room, she tried to ease him onto the sofa. "Not on your life or mine. I am not going to get blood and dirt on your mother's sofa."

He was obviously not giving in on this, so she left him for long enough to get a blanket to lay over it and a pillow to make him more comfortable. "Now?" she asked. He let himself down with a sigh of relief while she went into the kitchen for a glass of water to take the painkillers. When she got back, he was staring at the ceiling.

"Is the pain bad?" she asked handing him the pills and then the water.

"Not good. I've had broken bones before... but no ribs. They make it hurt to breathe deeply."

"Are you dizzy?"

"Maybe a little. I better warn you that when I take these, I'll be out for the count. You sure your folks will want to find me sleeping on your sofa."

She thought maybe a little teasing was in order. "Better than my bed."

He managed a short laugh as she'd hoped. "I'd rather be in your bed though."

"And I'd rather you were. I don't want to put that off too long, okay?"

"We won't... but long enough to get over this. I don't want to disappoint you for your... first time." He swallowed the pills with a couple of sips from the glass. Then he laid back with a sigh of relief.

She sat beside him, stroking his hair back from his forehead.

"Sorry to disappoint you today," he said. "I wasn't very impressive as an introduction to bull riding."

"If it was my last to see, I'd be happier," she said. "That was frightening. Why on earth does anybody do it?"

He shrugged and then winced. "It's hard to answer something like that—even when I am thinking clearly."

"I better get your boots off before you can't help me," she said and went to the foot of the sofa to get a hold of one of them and with a tug and his help, they soon were both sitting in the hall where he insisted they be put. He was right, they were pretty dusty but then so was the rest of him and for now there wasn't much they could do about that. He was in no shape for a shower.

She brought in a damp washcloth and washed the dirt from his face and chest. She thought he had gone to sleep but then he opened his eyes and looked at her, reaching out his hand. "I want you to know... I appreciate you... being there for me like you were today."

"Where else would I have wanted to be?"

"I jokingly said you'd never be a woman a man could lean on. I was proven wrong."

She smiled and reached down with her other hand to brush his hair again with her fingers. "You were, weren't you?"

"No pizza tonight." She could see he was fading fast.

"We will save that. There'll be other nights."

He smiled then even though his eyes were half closed. "A lot of them." In a few minutes she could tell he had fallen asleep. The big house seemed suddenly so quiet. She liked sitting beside him, watching him when he didn't know, wasn't alert or aware. The lines around his mouth had relaxed and she hoped that meant the pain was lessening with the pills.

She walked back into the kitchen and made coffee. She'd have to stay awake through the night, and it would take caffeine to assure that as she was already tired from the stressful day. Scratch that, the stressful week. So many nights she hadn't slept well, had lain awake thinking about what she was going to do. What was possible. What was impossible.

The irony was, where she had no idea where any of this was going, it all revolved around a man she hadn't known last week. How crazy was that! If life was supposed to make sense, to be logically ordered, hers has lost all sense of it.

Waiting for the coffee to perk, she moved restlessly around the room from the stove to the refrigerator, circling around the table that sat in the middle of the room. She couldn't stand to sit as nervous energy filled her with no place to put it. She listened for sounds from the living room. None came. She wondered if that meant he didn't snore. She guessed she'd find out about that someday. And despite him being hurt she felt a sort of quiet satisfaction in having him with her now.

At least he'd be safe for awhile. She knew he'd go back to rodeo, but he'd have to heal. That would give them time to get to know each other right here in Pendleton while he recuperated without the pressure of having to move on so soon.

When there was a knock at the door, she went to it quickly to prevent it waking him even though she doubted anything would wake him after he had taken the pills. She was surprised to see Cathy standing there.

"Hi," she said, ushering her back into the kitchen.

"What's up?" Cathy asked and Sara realized she didn't know anything about what had happened at the rodeo. It's not like it'd be a big enough story for the newspaper even if there'd been time. She tried to think how to explain any of it.

"Well, you remember that cowboy?"

"How could I forget? The one at the dance."

"He's in the living room."

"You're joking."

"Not likely."

"And your folks will say?"

"That's a bit undefined at the moment." Sara explained cursorily what had happened and saw Cathy's interest growing. "Can I see him?" she asked. "If he's sleeping, it's not like he'll know."

"Cathy, he's not a zoo animal. You'll meet him someday if... well if everything continues between us; but I won't let you go in there and watch him when he's sleeping."

"That's kind of selfish," she said but then Sara saw she was teasing. "Okay, okay, I'll go. You promise I get to meet him; and if he has any cute friends, them too. A hot rodeo cowboy, yeah I could go for that in a big way."

Coffee cup in hand, Sara walked back into the living room and settled into the big chair to watch him sleep. How far she had come to find herself a woman who would enjoy just watching her man sleep. What was that about? Would it always be like this? Was this what Jean had felt and still felt? How about her mother for her father? She didn't think it was like that now, but had it ever been?

Five days. This had all begun five days earlier. That fact kept coming back to her. That wasn't long enough to make a big difference in a person's life. But then she knew it had for Nick and Jean. It had for Billy in eight seconds when it could have ended his life. Definitely. Life was tentative. It was on loan. Everything a person knew could be changed in a split second.

Seeing his body hurt had crystallized what she had already known about what she felt. Was this love at first sight? Could you meet a person somewhere, like she had Billy in the store; and know, without knowing why or how, just who he was to you? She had thought of herself as a logically based person and what was happening to her made no sense using that gauge and yet… and yet.

She had never had a life purpose set out for her that apparently Billy had or as had Nick. She had been drifting along, taking some classes, doing some jobs, but nothing had dared her, forced her to operate on higher levels.

Even her painting hadn't been a challenge because she wasn't putting it out into the world, trying to sell it, letting others judge it. It had all seemed so easy and then it wasn't.

She recognized until now she had been taking the path of least resistance. Those days were finished. Caught between the energy of Billy and that of her parents, where was her own energy in it all?

Wanting a man didn't mean living with him for the rest of a woman's life. So many people ended up thinking they had it all figured out and then bingo, it changed again, and overnight they didn't want what they had. Love certainly wasn't all someone needed. Couples needed to want the same things from life. Even Cathy had seen that.

Perhaps when a woman was like her, not sure what she wanted, and she came across an irresistible force, perhaps she got carried along by that wind and would only realize years down the road that she hadn't wanted it at all. Maybe it explained divorces. It might be because the person hadn't known what they wanted in time, or even who they were. Doubts flooded her mind along with the love she felt for him.

Billy had said he never believed she could be the kind of woman he could rely upon. She couldn't deny that until this week she hadn't known she was either. Through these few days, she had learned something different about herself. She could also be a risk taker. Wow, from where had that come?

Why would it take Billy to bring this knowledge to her? She guessed it was the energy between them but something more. He was the one she had been looking for in some mysterious way even when she had not known and certainly never guessed who he would be when she found him. It wasn't like a search for a life mate. It was a search for that energy.

There were recognizable traits that she saw as admirable. Those she would have always been drawn to in any person. They were things like a strong sense of purpose, a way of treating people. She liked his long range dream. He seemed to know where he was going and how he'd get there. Well maybe he'd be wrong. Maybe he couldn't get there this way, but he was on a path that was possible to define and had the potential to do it for him. She knew nothing like that for herself.

She could not pretend none of this was physical. She could feel him even as he slept under the influence of those painkillers. He was a handsome man but it was more than that. Even asleep, he looked powerful with that long, lean, rangy body and the ropy muscles. His strong jaw was covered now with some bristle. With his eyes closed, she didn't see the vitality that shone from them. His eyes told her so much of his moods from narrowed with irritation to soft with desire.

She sipped her lukewarm coffee having nearly forgotten it in her intense stream of thought. So she could figure out, more or less, why he was the one, but what did she offer in return? Did he see her realistically for who she was or would he soon be disappointed? Clearly he was physically attracted but was that all? He had every reason to worry that she could not fit into his life or that she might try to distract him from his purpose. She worried about that too. It was a very strange thing to watch people pit their physical selves, their skills against death. What kind of people did that? That put an elemental quality into Billy's life that she had never experienced.

Then there were her parents. Okay she had reassured him that she thought they would accept this, but she wasn't so sure herself. She did not want to lose them in her life. Jean's parents hadn't ever accepted the relationship, and the end result had been a loss for them all. How would she feel about losing relationship with the people who had been part of her life from birth? It was a lot to give up especially when it was for a man who might not survive what he did. One day out there, it might be the last. Maybe he'd change his own mind about whether he wanted her. She could give up her parents and lose him too.

There was one thing she knew for sure, and it had been reinforced this week. Love wasn't all that was needed to make a relationship work. Did she and Billy have the rest of it? Despite seeing him like this, feeling her love growing so that it seemed it would overfill her, she knew there had to be more. She wasn't sure if she had the strength to go the distance given what that might mean.

She dozed off and woke with a start when she heard the kitchen door slam. She hurriedly went in to see both of her parents looking at her. "We saw his truck out front," her father said not needing or wanting to use Billy's name. That was enough upset for one day, but she knew they'd soon be getting more.

"He's in the living room," she said to start and unsure what would make sense to them.

"You and he were in the living room?" her mother repeated putting down her purse.

"We agree you are an adult, Sara," her father said starting sternly, "but for God's sake, entertaining young men here when we aren't home doesn't look good to the neighbors."

"And with no lights on," her mother echoed.

"I wasn't entertaining him. He's sleeping. Look, we haven't had much chance to talk the last few days, but Billy was hurt today and that's why he's here."

"Hurt?" they both echoed.

"He probably broke a rib and has a head injury."

"His truck didn't look like it'd been in a wreck," her father said,

"It wasn't an auto accident. He was hurt riding one of the bulls at the rodeo. Actually Corkscrew did it." She wasn't trying to be funny, but in a way she almost felt like laughing, a nervous way.

"So he *is* a cowboy?"

"Yes, he is."

"A rodeo cowboy. And you didn't tell us," Ann added unnecessarily.

"The day he came here to dinner, I actually didn't know. He told me later that night. Then when I knew, it didn't seem it mattered as I had no idea I'd see him again. Tonight, he didn't want to come here because he knew we hadn't told you and he wanted to be the one. He had already told me he wanted to do that, but then this happened. I insisted he come here since he could have a concussion, and he shouldn't be alone. I couldn't go to his motel again, could I?"

"That part at least made sense," her father agreed but didn't seem mollified.

"So what would you like us to do now?" Sara asked as the wisest question she could imagine.

"Us? It's you and him?" her mother asked with disbelief in her voice.

"Yes, it is."

"You barely know him," her father objected.

"I know the important things and will learn more."

"Important, like he's good in bed?" her mother snapped.

Sara glared at her. "I don't think that's a question you have a right to ask."

"We are your parents."

"Parents of an adult. Look, I don't see going on with this. Do you want me to move him tonight and go back to the motel with him?"

"No," her mother retorted, pursing her lips. "Are you in love with him?"

"Yes, I am."

"And he says he loves you?" her father asked. She could tell he was trying to make his voice sound calm, and she appreciated the effort, as he didn't wait for her answer before adding, "Do you have plans?"

"We have talked some before he got hurt. I am not sure now. I really don't want to discuss this more as nothing is firm."

They moved to the table and sat down, the three of them, as they had so many times through the years. It gave Sara a sense of nostalgia that nearly made her teary. Would this be the last time for such a gathering? Her mother freshened her coffee and then poured cups for them. This was a big change for them all—a lot to digest.

"Guess he doesn't think much of us," her father finally said.

"Why would you say that? He doesn't know you."

He managed a crooked grin. "He knows what I think about cowboys."

"Well he did take into account you didn't know any back then."

"An out. I like a man who thinks of outs." He smiled again with a sigh. This was actually going more calmly than she had anticipated.

Sara tried to think what would make this easier for them. 'You know, actually I have learned there are a lot of good things about cowboys and especially him. He doesn't see what he does as wild and woolly but an athletic event, a skill he has which he makes money by doing. He doesn't plan to do it forever."

"Most likely that's not an option," her mother put in. "I heard one of them got hurt pretty badly there the first day."

"People get hurt in football too, right? It's a sport if a man treats it that way. He has good values. Doesn't drink much. Doesn't go to the bars to carouse. He works hard and has goals. He could have won all around on bareback until he got hurt." Although smoking was a vice of sorts, she didn't mention it and didn't think it would count against him anyway since her father smoked a pipe.

"Seems to me that's the story of that life—almost wins," her mother snipped and then grinned apologetically. "Sorry."

"So he's come close to winning all around?" her dad added. "Was that a career accomplishment?"

"It's a means to an end. It's about making enough to buy a ranch. He said down along the John Day. It'd take awhile to get there, but he's saving toward it."

"It's a lot to take in," her mother said with a sigh. "A week ago none of this and now a man in our living room who might be our son-in-law someday."

"He and I have not discussed marriage, not that you were suggesting that. And not sure if that will make you feel better one way or the other."

"What have you discussed?"

"One day at a time actually." In a lot of ways she was surprised they were doing as well as they were. Practically speaking they had already surpassed what she had expected as they discussed this without raging emotion. Maybe she hadn't known them as well as she had thought.

"As a parent, this is a lot to take in," her dad said but he was managing a smile at least even if it did appear a little sick.

"He is a gifted athlete, really he is. It's beautiful to watch him ride when... well when it doesn't go badly like with the bull." She told them a bit then about what had happened when he got hurt.

Her father walked over to the coffee pot and refilled his cup. "I have to tell you that I think you are fooling yourself about this. He's not your kind. He's seen things, done things that you never probably will. I think someday it'll show up if not sooner than later."

"I can't predict the future where it comes to where this is going," Sara said not wanting to argue nor go too deeply into where she did feel it was going.

"Can I say the rest of what I am thinking?" he asked pleasing her again that he wasn't barging right through and instead was treating her like an adult.

"Of course, and I'll think about it. I promise that."

"No matter what he says about it being a sport, I think it's something more than that. It's not a team like football where people learn certain moves and they follow them. It's a violent sport with each man against the animal. He's been drifting then from rodeo to rodeo every year, always on the move, no home at all. I am guessing he doesn't have a permanent base. What he wins one day, he can lose the next. He has to put money for the travel and the fees and then loses it all when something happens like this. Supposing he does get hurt badly sometime and then cannot do it full time? He's used to being his own boss, doing what he wants when he wants, having freedom. Will he turn to drink then, be bitter, resent that he has to work 9 to 5, and will he then take that out on you?"

"Your points are valid and I have heard them all, some from Billy himself. Why don't we talk more about this another time, after you have known him a bit better?"

"You really are not rushing to marry?"

"No, I am not." She didn't feel a need to mention what they had been discussing doing because her parents were unlikely to look favorably on that either. It would be back to what looks good to their community; but she'd cross that bridge when she got to it.

Her father took a deep sigh, waiting a moment before answering. "We don't have much choice, do we? We raised you to think for yourself. Now we find you doing it, but it's a bit much to take in without us really knowing all that's at stake. The point in the end is we don't want to lose you. You are our only child. You see this man as someone special to you. I am not sure how we will see him, but maybe you can give us time to find out?"

"To hear you say that means a lot to me. I don't expect you to tell me something you can't know yet. I think the time will come and you'll like him and someday be glad of having known him as I am." She realized she was putting it in the past tense, but she had to stay realistic. This wasn't apt to be for the long term between them even if it would color the rest of her life for what it had been.

"If you get into this and it doesn't work out, well we will be here for you... and if it does work but he has to leave the rodeo sooner than he expects, he could always work in the store someday."

She laughed then, her first spontaneous laugh in hours. "I think that might be his biggest fear."

"Well sometimes we draw that biggest fear to ourselves. At any rate, we will be here for you, honey. You know that."

She had gotten more than she had hoped, and she hugged them both in gratitude.

"In a practical sense now," her mother said as she took their cups and put them over onto the counter, "we need to get him off our sofa and into a real bed. The downstairs guestroom will do."

They made up the bed and then walked back into the living room to the sleeping cowboy. Sara touched Billy's shoulders lightly.

His eyes blinked open and he tried to remember where he was. When he remembered, he knew he should not be there. "Sorry," he mumbled, as the pain in his side and head reminded him what had happened.

"We have to get you into bed. We made one ready for you on the main floor. Can you walk there?" It was not Sara's voice, and then he realized it was her mother's. Not good.

"I shouldn't be here." He knew though there was no way he could leave under his own power.

"Of course, you should," Ann Connors cajoled, "we wouldn't hear of you being by yourself tonight. Come on and let us help you." Her tone was considerably warmer than he would have expected. Either that or this was a fever induced delusion.

When he sat up, he discovered that wasn't too bad. Dizzy—check. In pain—check. Exhausted—check. Pretty much that covered it. He could stand though. He did it, and the world suddenly went black as pain knifed through his chest and he half fell. Sara, who had been standing close by, caught him. They might both have fallen under his weight if George Connors hadn't caught hold of Billy from the other side.

"This is ridiculous," Billy said feeling a little steadier on his feet. "Sorry about the trouble."

They helped him to get down the hall to the guestroom and then laid him back onto the bed which he sunk into with a grateful groan. He held his hand to his side to try and lessen the pressure on the cracked rib. He wasn't sure it helped but lying flat was good.

He looked up and saw Sara's worried face. He wanted to reassure her but wasn't sure how when the pain was so strong. She left the room and came back with the pills and a glass of water which she helped him take.

"It's okay," he said, "don't look so glum. This really is nothing."

She bent and kissed his forehead despite the fact that her parents were watching. Obviously the cat was out of that bag. He wanted to apologize to them for something but could barely remember what. His energy was rapidly waning as the pills were having their desired effect of causing his physical world to move away leaving him in a land confused between reality and dreams.

Mrs. Connors came back with a basin of soapy water and a washcloth. "I think you'll rest better if we get you out of that shirt and wash off some of that dust and blood." They eased the shirt off and then Sara began washing his chest and arms.

"Your bruise is really something," she said. "It pretty much covers half your side. I think I better not touch that as it looks sore enough as it is."

"Thanks he grunted, relieved to be feeling cleaner if still in pain. He felt himself drifting off and didn't know anything more.

Chapter Twelve

Saturday

The next thing Billy knew was sunlight streaming in a window. He was alive. That was the good thing. He was in Sara's home. That was not a good thing. He had been vaguely aware during the night that someone had looked in on him, but he had not had the energy to react to it.

He watched the shadow of the leaves on the wall as the wind moved them. He had no drive for doing anything, but he would find it. He was aware of pain, but nothing with which he couldn't live. There was no dizziness, at least as long as he wasn't moving.

Slowly he eased himself onto his elbows to test how that went. From there he sat. 'Not bad,' he thought. 'I can do it.' After last night he had been unsure if he'd be able to pull it together by today. He had to and was relieved he could.

He saw his clothing, washed from the looks of it, hanging over a nearby chair. He was in no hurry to get up. The bed was soft, the sheets smooth. He lay back watching the birds in a big old oak tree outside the window. With their chattering, he felt more and more a part of the normal world that he had left the day before for a short time. It looked like it was going to be a nice day. He could see blue sky through the leaves. Maybe this one wouldn't be so hot. He wondered what time it was.

At a light tap on the door, Sara came in. "Hi, beautiful," he said, reaching out an arm for her to come to him. She was wearing the same robe he had seen two days before, her hair looked tousled from sleep as though she hadn't bothered to brush it before checking on him. Dark circles under her eyes told him she had been at least one of the ones he had sensed during the night.

"How are you feeling?" she asked. He saw she had a glass of water and more of the painkillers in her hand.

"Water is good but no pills," he said firmly.

"It won't hurt to take them again today. You won't get addicted this fast."

He smiled. "I also don't need them and they knock me out; so no more."

"How is the pain?"

"Tolerable."

"Tolerable? What does that mean?"

"It means it's going to be okay. I am a quick healer."

She made a face but handed him the glass then set the pill container on the dresser before she sat beside him. "You look better," she said.

"Anything would be better than yesterday," he said with a smile. "I am hungry." He pulled her to him being careful to keep her on his right side. The movement cost him some pain but was worth it when he felt her soft body in his arms and claimed her lips with his own.

"Sorry," he said as he released her, "I keep forgetting where we are. Your folks still around? Are they ready to string me up?"

"Not quite yet. A shotgun was mentioned though," she teased.

He sighed. "I don't blame them. I guess they know the whole story now."

"Not much way to hide it. And it's actually looking okay."

"You are kidding?"

"They are trying to be understanding," she corrected herself.

"It's a lot to take in for them. Geesus, it's a lot to take in for me. Excuse my language."

"I don't mind some salty language, and yes, it is for all of us."

He kissed her again. His kiss growing a little stronger and showing more ownership. "I could get used to waking up with you there," he said when she lifted her head.

"I sure hope so," she teased.

"So they know... everything?"

"Did I say that?" She laughed. "They know what they need to know for where we are today."

"I'm surprised they didn't throw me on the street last night."

"I think the thought crossed their minds, but I'd have had to go with you and they knew that too."

"Well, I would have understood."

"I'm just glad you seem so much better today. It's a relief. How bad does it hurt? Oh wait, I asked that, and you didn't tell me."

"It hurts like I'd expect it to hurt, but I think it'll be fine now that I am past the first day."

"I hope so. That doctor really wanted you to have X-rays."

"And what would they have settled? It's going to be okay or it's not and it looks like it is."

"Do you want breakfast?"

"You mean instead of you?"

"Yes, instead of me. My parents are understanding but not quite that understanding."

He grinned. "Then whatever you have for breakfast would be great. I am hungry. All I had yesterday was that hotdog. Will I see your parents if I go out there?"

"You were considering sneaking out the backdoor?"

"It could yet be done if you get any smarter with me."

"They are in the kitchen and yes, you will see them if you come out with me—after you get dressed that is."

"By the way, who took off all but my shorts? You, I am hoping?" he teased knowing it would not have been her with her folks right there.

"I would have liked to do it but thought it might be pressing my luck."

"Wise girl. You know this is hard for me to get because they should want to kill me."

"What have you done to deserve that?"

"I want their little girl."

"Well they did say something about you being a drifter, irresponsible and a play around."

"Ah so they do have good judgment."

"They say they trust mine… and it is mine in this case that has to matter most. They raised me to make those choices. And, I have not told them all the things we've been discussing as it won't come up right away, will it?"

"No, probably not."

"What would you like for breakfast now that we have taken care of all of that?"

"Bacon, eggs, toast, coffee… or as close as you can come to all of that."

"I think we can handle that and maybe even some pancakes at Casa Connors… Do you need help getting dressed?"

His smile was pure male. "I really could use some."

She laughed. "I'll send Dad."

"On second thought I can manage."

"In that case, I'll settle for bringing you breakfast when it's ready. Sit back, sir."

"Nothing doing. I am getting up and want to face your folks anyway sooner than later."

"Well, I'll see what is in the house. Come out when you are ready… unless you need help after all. Bending might be kind of tough. Oh and the bathroom is the door to the right of yours when you go out in the hall."

"Thanks. I'll take it slow and I'll be there when I can." He kissed her again and then let her go.

As he dressed, he felt more and more sure his body was not going to let him down. There was pain, but no more than he'd had before. He was used to functioning with varying levels of discomfort, sometimes worse than this. His arm was sound, his mind alert, his hand, his legs strong, and they were what counted.

Dressed but barefoot, he padded out to the kitchen which was a large sunny room with old, glass-fronted cupboards. At the table sat George Connors with Sara, now wearing jeans, and her mother at the counter and stove. He smelled bacon cooking.

"Would you like coffee?" Ann Connors asked with a friendly tone to her offer. "Sugar and cream are on the table."

"Thank you, ma'am," he said as he eased himself down into one of the chairs.

"We're mixing up pancakes. Do you like them?" Sara asked.

"Nature's perfect food," he said as he accepted the coffee from her.

"And please," her mom said, "no ma'am, remember. We're Ann and George."

"Sorry about putting you folks out last night," he said unsure of how you start talking to people whose daughter you want to steal.

"It was okay once Sara explained the situation. It was the sensible thing to do. No dizziness this morning?"

"No, ma—Ann."

George looked at him without a smile. "So you ride in the rodeo?"

"Yes sir, for five years professional and then years before that when I could."

"You start straight out of high school?"

Another sore point probably but one that had to be faced. "I was drafted at eighteen. I went to 'nam right after training. I was there a year, got out of the military as soon as I could and then began riding."

"You saw combat in Vietnam?"

"Yes sir. Some."

"You probably assume I didn't support that war."

"I thought that might be the case."

"But I sure as hell support the boys who fought in it. You did your duty and I admire that." He stretched out his hand to take Billy's. "Tough time, wasn't it?"

"Yes sir."

"Remember to call me George." And then he finally smiled. "I guess we'll be getting to know each other a little better soon, won't we?"

"That is my hope… George."

"Sara," George said, "you concentrate on those flapjacks, or they'll be burning. I won't hurt this young man."

"It's okay, baby," Billy said then wondering if that nickname would break the fragile truce between her parents and him. It appeared to be holding. "I don't mind your dad asking me some questions considering how we have been talking."

She grimaced but turned back to the stove.

"So, if you do say take on responsibility for Sara, say take her away from us, how will you support her?"

"Daddy, it's not like I can't earn money also."

Billy smiled but decided her father deserved an answer. "I have money saved from these years."

"Not likely much given rodeo," George said with some disbelief in his voice.

"Normally I'd not tell a man something like this but I have a little over $50,000 in CDs and another $20,000, or about what it was last month, in the stock market."

George was clearly taken aback. "From rodeo?" he asked a little aghast.

"I haven't made as much as I will if everything goes as it is heading. You start out slow and it builds."

"Unless something happens like with the bull."

"It is like any sport. It can go wrong sometimes, and that was one of those times. I should have quit entering bull riding. I'm not good at it. I did it for... well I admit, the rush and trying to prove I could. I kept thinking I'd get the feel for it but I haven't obviously."

"You don't blame it on that particular bull?"

"He didn't help," he said with a grin, "but my bull rides have been in the category of barely there. Saddle bronc and bareback would have, should have been enough."

"Enough for what?"

"Well the real money is in nationals. Then there's advertising if a rider gets to the top. Little here and there. It all adds up."

"You could lose it all."

"I couldn't because I don't do it that way. If something changes, I'll let it go. What I told you is not my operating capital. I travel cheap or did anyway. I mostly just have food, gas, a cheap motel and the entry fees that I could lose. Each year I have set aside so much cash for that. It's my test. If I ever lost that all, I'd give it up."

"That's a surprisingly responsible attitude for a young man and not what I'd have expected from... Well, I admit I am surprised and not just in how much you have put aside at your age."

"I had a goal even before Sara. I knew this wasn't the life I wanted or could have forever. I also knew I couldn't get what I do want without working at something that brought in a lot of money."

"A ranch, she said."

"Yes. That's at least five years, likely more away. I will buy it before I can stay there full time. It's going to take years to make enough operating capital to make it work. I think I can ride up until my mid-30s if need be, and then the body starts losing it for the kind of events I enter. I won't stay with it until I am broken and can't do anything else."

"We might be able to help with the ranch, you know change how long it takes you to get together the funds for it," George said thoughtfully.

Billy took in a deep breath. "I want to get along with you folks and understand your offer, appreciate it, but I will do this myself."

"Without me as a factor?" Sara asked as she had been taking it all in.

"Well, of course, if we are together, I would take you into account," Billy said, "but if it works out for us; and if you decide to travel with me someday, there are not a lot of ways you could earn money. I don't think we could count on that although if you get good at the painting, that might add up to something." He tried to judge if this kind of conversation was upsetting her parents, but so far they seemed to be looking at it from a practical, not a controlling manner.

"And if you are injured again?" George asked. "What about then?"

"When it's serious, there is Rodeo Cowboy Association Insurance."

"What if you were badly injured and had to quit?"

"I'll face that when it comes. I hope by that time, I have the money for the spread I want. I won't make promises I can't keep, and in this case, I really don't know for sure what I'd do. I won't kick a dead horse though and stay too long. I like Nick a lot but I am not him."

"Do you actually know anything about ranching besides bucking horses?" George asked which at that point, Ann interrupted with telling them the first hotcakes were ready and enough business was enough.

When Billy got his plate, he put syrup on the hotcakes but before he took a bite, he said, "I wasn't ready for this to be honest. Until I met Sara, I figured this was all five or ten years down the road before I'd get serious about a woman." He smiled ruefully. "Even after I met her, I was thinking still a long way off, but I am learning things don't always come when we plan."

"It's good to take some time, be sure you are compatible, have the same values and all."

"She and I are talking about that... or starting to anyway."

"Not much time to do that."

"We will have. It's been a fast readjustment for us both."

"One more question," George said and his voice became uneasy. "Are you a Christian, Billy? We are church going folks."

Billy managed a smile. This family didn't beat around the bush. In a sense he liked that even if they wouldn't appreciate his answer. "I am not a church-goer. I do believe in God but not the way you maybe do. I don't see a need to be in a church." He considered a moment and added, "I don't pray or anything like that if that's what you were asking."

Ann said, "You two need to start eating before it gets cold. I think that's enough from our end, and Sara and Billy can work out the rest."

"But--" George started to say.

"No buts, dear. These two have to decide what matters in their lives. We did that and now it's their turn."

Billy was a little amazed; but if he had been expecting to have a meddling mother-in-law, he was getting his expectations rearranged. As they ate, the meal became more pleasant, less pressure and more genial. The strain was gone for the moment, and Sara's parents seemed mostly content with the direction it was heading—at least for now.

"I imagine this was a setback not being able to finish the events here," George said as he refilled everyone's cups.

"I'll finish," Billy said. "Originally I had planned to go to Portland for the expo but that will probably depend on several things. One of which will be how the rib heals."

"What do you mean finish here?" Sara asked clear upset in her voice.

"I won't ride the bull today. Obviously I can't win there, would be at more risk if I tried, but I still have a good shot at it with bareback. I won't let that go without at least trying."

"Are you crazy?"

"Not last time I checked. I can do that without being thrown, without taking another fall. You don't expect me to just give up, do you?"

"It's not giving up when you have been hurt." Her tone was a mixture of anger and hurt. "Did you listen to what the doctor said?"

"I heard it."

"Just in case you were too dazed, he said you probably broke a rib which could easily pull apart and puncture your lung."

"That was if it's a compound. He didn't know that was the case and neither do you."

"Billy," she snapped, "that's why you didn't want an x-ray isn't it? You didn't want to know so you could do this if you were capable of standing at all."

"I didn't think it was necessary to know."

"Oh I get that now." She sounded furious. "To you taking it easy means just not riding a bull. I cannot believe this. I absolutely cannot believe it."

His eyes narrowed. "I didn't hurt my right arm or shoulder. I can do this. That's how it'll be," he said his voice lowered.

"You're being foolish. Dad, tell him!"

"Oh no way, not on a bet," George said. He looked at Ann, and they seemed to be of a mind as they both rose from the table. "We cannot settle this issue between you two and don't know enough about it to give an opinion even if we had one. It's a lose-lose for us to even discuss it. We'll be in the living room if you need us." And they walked out of the kitchen. These parents were definitely not the kind Billy had been expecting.

When they were alone, Sara walked to the stove staring down at it. After a moment, she said, "I never dreamed this is how it'd be."

"You don't know enough about it, what I can do. This is a thing I have to decide. I believe I can do it without hurting myself."

"Believe? Oh that's reassuring, and I have no say in it at all. That's what you're saying."

"About something like this, no. Can't you just trust me? Is this how it's going to be is a good question. It's all your way or no way?"

"You'll be killed."

"I won't have any more chance of it now than any other ride." That wasn't such a smart thing to say but it was too late to take it back, and it was true. "I think if the break was compound, it would have already moved. It didn't which means it's like a simple fracture—if even that. I make it to the whistle, the pick-up man will get me off, and then I can take a break for awhile."

"If you make it to the whistle," she said her own voice now lower and more depressed sounding.

"Sara, this is what I do. I will not give it up for your fears." He thought about moving over to her, trying to take her in his arms, but this was a point they would have to get through or it'd never work anyway. He wouldn't stay home because of her panic. If she couldn't take it, then better now than later. "It is who I am."

"Who you are could kill you."

"You're reacting out of fear not knowledge."

"And you're using such logic?"

"I am basing it on experience which you don't have."

"Logic has to be based on facts. Facts are you were hurt yesterday, badly hurt."

"It looked more scary than it was."

"I was there."

"It was a new world to you."

"This is insane. You have a broken rib that they said could well go through your lungs."

"Maybe just cracked. I think by the level of pain, which is a lot less, that it was mostly the bruise. Nobody dies from a bruise."

"I have tried to understand your world, how you think, but it cannot be like a totally foreign one. There have to be some things that we all can agree make sense. Taking a fall like you did needs time to heal from."

"You don't understand."

"Oh so now I'm stupid."

"I would say more ignorant." Not that he realized that was going to sound better. He was beginning to grow angry himself. This was a time he needed her support not her challenging him and trying to force him to go her way with it or ... Or what?

"If you do get thrown, what do you think will happen?"

He shrugged feeling the responding ache in his side. "I will roll and still make it okay. Then I'll go get an x-ray." He tried for a smile but couldn't make it work.

"I can't believe any of this." She turned from him and folded her arms over her chest. "I understood what you did was risky, but I also thought you would use good judgment on when to add to that risk."

"And I am."

"I guess I never did know you."

"Sara, if you can't accept who I am then that's right. Can we can talk about this again after the ride?"

"There won't be any after the ride for us." Her tone was remote, unemotional. She'd gone from trying to convince him to giving up. Was that giving up on everything?

"You don't mean that."

"I do mean it. I can't live with a man who goes out of his way to get himself killed."

He lost patience with her then. "I am going to go now. I will come back afterward and see if you have changed your mind. I can't argue with you more about it now."

"You're still in pain. I can see it in your eyes and how you are moving. You're not in shape for this. You will be killed. You won't be back because you'll be dead."

He sucked in a breath. He did understand some of how she felt, but he simply could not let her decide this. He could win. It would increase his odds of taking all around. If he took some time off, didn't go onto the next rodeo to spend it with her, he weakened his chances for the big one. He needed this ride. He didn't even have to make a champion ride out of it. He just had to stay on.

"I can win here and you want me to throw it away."

"It's about money? This is all about money?"

"Sure, some of it. It's also about finishing what I start. It's about the satisfaction of being the best at something. It's about the men I work with respecting me for what I accomplish."

"And that matters more than what I think?"

"You, baby, are new to this. You don't know this world yet. You have had a tough week. I get that. The stress of it happening to Nick. Hearing how that all impacted Jean. Then you and me how it grew so fast, finally my getting hurt. I understand it hasn't been easy for you, but understand something else. This is who I am. I couldn't respect myself if I let you decide something like this for me, if I let you change me. Do you really want that responsibility?"

She had tears in her eyes. "I want you to live and us to have a chance, and you aren't going to give us that if you do this. You'll be killed, and I'll never have another chance for something like this."

"It won't be that way. I love you, baby, but I can't give up me for you. I wouldn't like myself if it was any other way, and I don't think you would either."

"What if I can't stand this?"

"What do you mean?" he asked quietly.

"I can't take your life as you are saying it has to be. I love you, but I can't live with this."

"You making this a choice between you and rodeo?"

"And if I am? Okay I don't mean permanently but just now for when you're hurt. Later it'd be different."

"It won't be different. There'd be something else. I know you're scared, but that isn't all this is."

"It is."

"This is an excuse. You will be scared every time. I do understand how it must be. A strange world for you." He had used up his patience and knew he couldn't keep doing this. She was wearing him down. Not changing his mind but taking his energy. He had to put it to an end, or he'd ride and be thrown. "I am going to finish what I started."

"Then that's it."

"If you make it so, then I guess you're right. I won't be the first or last cowboy to ride with cracked ribs. Men have ridden with about anything broken you can name. That's what rodeo is."

"I'm sorry for you all then. I want nothing to do with that kind of life."

He felt sick inside at the loss, but he couldn't change it. She had to do what was right for her. He couldn't force her to see things his way even if he had wanted to. "If that's how you want it."

"It isn't how I want it. It's how you want it. I want you."

"You don't want the me who exists, the whole package. You want what you could create, mold. I am who I am and it's take it or leave it." He was trying not to be angry but it was past that with anger mixed with frustration and disappointment that this wasn't going to work. He had come to really believe it could. He had ignored his own doubts, and this was to be the end result.

She turned away staring out the window. "All right," he said, "I don't hold it against you and won't try to change your mind. I will say I am sorry. I thank you for what you did for me yesterday and today. Thank your parents." He thought about reaching over to kiss her, but it was too late for that.

He walked back to the guestroom and hoped she'd come after him, but she didn't as he wrestled on his boots. His forehead was shiny with sweat by the time he got it done. Standing he knew he'd be all right though. He would make this, survive the ride and this loss. After all, it'd only been a couple of days.

Driving toward his motel, he tried to tell himself it had been for the best. Sooner or later it had to come to this. She was just too different. The life he led wasn't for her. This pain would heal just like his rib. Just going to take time.

Shifting gears hurt his side, but it was okay. He wouldn't take a pill for the pain as if he did that, he'd not have his reflexes at their peak. Pain wouldn't stop him but slowness would. His head was clear. He hadn't told Sara, because he wasn't sure if the doctor would agree; but he had an idea to increase his chances to get through this by getting his torso taped. All he had to do was talk the doc into it. First he went to the motel.

In the room Tice had on the television. He looked up. "You okay?"

"I've seen better days."

"Where you been?"

"Spent the night at Sara's."

"Wow, injured and all? That babe is really gone on you."

"Pick your mind up out of the gutter, McGraw. Her folks are good people and took me in last night."

"You could have come here. I'd have looked after you." Tice looked aggrieved.

"To be honest, I wasn't thinking clearly, and Sara did the thinking for us both."

"Figures. How you feeling? I gotta say, you don't look too good."

"Thanks. A shower will help that. What time is it?"

"Little after nine."

He went into the bathroom and took a long shower which helped to restore him even more. When he came out, Tice was still there and sitting in the chair, the television off. "You see a doctor?"

"Yep."

"And?"

"He thinks I need a mother."

Tice cursed. "I was trying to be helpful."

"I am fine, cracked rib maybe. No concussion."

"You leaving Pendleton now?"

Billy shook his head. "Probably tomorrow morning. I ride bareback today."

"Is that smart?"

"Hard to say, but I'm doing it. Not the bulls though. I already lost that anyway. No point in trying to finish it and having them finish me."

"Well at least that sounds smart."

"Thanks." Billy smiled.

"Your ribs might pull apart if they were broken... when you ride, I mean. I seen that happen."

"And I've seen more rides when it was just fine."

"The breaks, I guess."

"They do come along that way. Look I need to go. See you at the chutes."

"Wait a minute," Tice said coming out of the chair and taking Billy's arm.

"For what?"

"Where we going next?"

"I haven't decided that. You better make your own plans."

"It's her, isn't it?"

"It's not her. I haven't decided what I do next is all." He was going to have to do some healing one way or another. Maybe he'd have that x-ray after the rodeo was over and that would help him decide what came next. He could head back to Bend for a week or so, not to see Martin though.

He began thinking about the High Cascade lakes. He could go up there, sleep in the back of the truck, look up at the stars, do some fly fishing. He hadn't fished since he was in his teens. It wouldn't be warm up there in late September but he had a good sleeping bag. There was peace to be found in those tall pines and deep blue lakes. It had always helped him, and he might look for it there again.

There were a lot of things with which he needed to make peace. His childhood, his brother, that year in Vietnam. He tended to put things aside, not try to work them through but maybe the time had come where he should change that. Going straight ahead, not stopping to think where he'd been, what had gone wrong, it was not probably the smartest move for the future.

Yes, he'd give himself time to think about his life; but come October, he would be in Portland at the Expo. He liked that rodeo, indoors, well run show, good purses. He'd look up his sister and see what she was doing. He didn't know that he'd get along any better with Nora than he did with Martin. He barely knew her now and maybe that was for the best, but he'd find out.

When Tice left, he lay back on the bed trying to get some rest. The problem was all he could think about was Sara, seeing her picture in his mind. Like at the river, when he was at Jean and Nick's with her, her on this bed, the feel of her breast under his fingers. Then there was watching her walk toward him after he'd been hurt.

The ride had gone all wrong, right from the start. Coming out of the chute, he knew he'd lost his balance and couldn't seem to get it back. Abruptly Corkscrew had lived up to his name by turning a tight circle before he abruptly switched the opposite direction. Billy hadn't even be sure how the bull's back could articulate that way but didn't have time to wonder more than hold on and try to stay with the turns. The third twist and he was tossed knowing it was too close to the fence. There was no time to break his fall or protect himself as he was slammed hard, nearly losing his senses even while he knew he couldn't let that happen. The bull was still there.

In the distance, he had heard the screams of the crowd, felt the pain, the grit in his teeth and the overwhelming urge that he had to get up and get over that fence except he had been stunned by the fall and his body was not obeying his commands. Blackness came but only for a few seconds. With returning awareness had come two things—one pain, the other that the bull had turned back for him. It all had to have happened in a few seconds but it seemed to have stretched into an eternity.

And then Hank had been there, yelling at the bull, insulting him, hitting him on the rump as he darted in, further taunting the bull with a cloth he was waving. He had yelled again, running in circles, mimicking Corkscrew. The bull had been indecisive only for a second, another slap on his rear decided him as he had turned to go after the moving figure ignoring the still cowboy. It was enough time for Billy to try to get up and over the fence and find others were there, grabbing his arms, helping him climb.

Moments later he was back on the ground, lying beaten in the dust, and then he'd seen her coming toward him. He had wanted to be her hero and not end up the one needing help, but had learned then the strength she had. It made the loss now even harder. But there wasn't a thing he could do about it. She had to do what was best for her. He kept telling himself that, but it didn't get any easier to accept. How could a woman cause him this much grief in a week, not even a week? He guessed there were no rules for that sort of thing. She had come along at the wrong time, but he had known he'd hold on if he could. As it ended up, he couldn't to her anymore than Corkscrew.

It wouldn't be a good time to take a break from the rodeos as he had been building something there; but suddenly he wasn't sure if he had the fire for it. He could hire on at a ranch for the winter instead of driving to the Southwest. The desert sounded good too, a lot of big rodeos down there. It was hard to get firm about the future, but thinking about it helped him not think about her.

He had let a woman get under his guard. He had known that was stupid; but, for reasons he couldn't fathom, he'd done it anyway. He had used his defenses against her, but they hadn't worked. Was he being a fool now to let it all go when all he had to do was let her decide this one thing? Except it wouldn't be one thing, and he knew it. She had not been able to accept the rodeo life. This was a big thing if she wanted to be with him. He wouldn't be signing on at a ranch. He knew what he had to do, and he'd do it.

He glanced at the clock realizing he had to get going. When he rose, he felt pretty fair, stiff but not overall bad. His stiffness could be worked out. If he wanted to talk to the doctor about strapping, he'd have to get with it.

Outside, the sky had clouded over and thunderclouds were building up. Maybe a storm by afternoon. Stepping off the curb, he lit a cigarette as he walked to his truck but before he got there, he heard his name called. It was the kid from the motel office. He waited for him to come up to him. "I thought I was paid up," he said.

"I saw you ride yesterday and yes, you're paid up. That bareback ride was really something. I just wanted to tell you how much I admired what you did."

"Thanks." Billy was anxious now to get over to ER as if he didn't have time, he'd have to ride anyway.

"I'm glad you weren't hurt seriously with the bull. Just wanted to say that."

Billy remembered when he had first seen the young clerk and how superior he had felt. He was the one riding the adventure while the youth was stuck at a dead-end job. He wondered now who was the smart one. Oh he was free all right but he also hurt and might be hurt worse before this day was over. The woman he wanted didn't fit into his life. He tried to remember the kid's name but couldn't. never was good with names. "Thanks... uh..." Billy took a long draw on the cigarette.

"Scott. Scott Wingate. Guess you won't be riding today."

"Don't know why you'd think that," Billy said with a touch of sarcasm.

"Well good luck then or break a leg or whatever it is you guys say to each other."

"It's definitely not break a leg," Billy said with a grin. "See you around."

Chapter Thirteen

At ER, Billy had to wait to see the doctor who had treated him. Trying to explain the whole thing to anybody else would be ineffective at best. He hoped he had time to wait as he looked at the clock evaluating how long it would take.

He was ushered into a cubicle and within moments the doctor was coming in. "Back for the pills, huh?" he asked with a grin.

"I don't need that. I want something else from you. Something you said you'd not do."

"Taping your chest? I told you why that's a bad idea."

"It won't do damage if it doesn't stay there long, will it?"

"No, but what good would it do?"

"It'd get me through a bareback ride."

The doctor leaned back against the counter and gave him one of those you are a fool looks. "I don't want to be party to that decision. Tape is no guarantee of anything if you have a compound fracture. It might even be two ribs broken. You refused the x-ray to find out."

"Because I knew that wouldn't determine my riding. I figured it was a waste of time and money. I am riding today. I will do it no matter what you decide right now, but I think my odds are better if you tape me up."

"I won't take that responsibility."

"How about the responsibility of my riding without you doing what you can to help me live through it?"

The doctor muttered under his breath as he considered the request more seriously. "It's foolish. I hope you know that." He sucked in a breath. "If I do that, you come back here for x-rays, have the tape removed if you survive it all, and promise not to sue me." He laughed.

"Sounds fair enough and definitely no lawsuits." He grinned.

"Take off your shirt. I'll be right back," the doctor said.

The doctor came back with tape, rubbing alcohol and a nurse. He again examined Billy's chest, probing the bruised area, feeling of his ribs and giving a humph once in awhile. "Nice bruise," he said finally.

"Want to photograph it?" Billy asked with a grimace. "That really hurt, I hope you know."

"Nothing compared to what's coming," the doctor said kindly. After cleansing the area, he and the nurse ran gauze around his chest first and then wound it with tape enough times to make Billy feel like a mummy. Still he could move what needed to be moved for the ride, and it would be worth it if it held a rib together.

He stood a little shakily as he shrugged back on his shirt. "Thank you, I think."

"I hope you can say that later today," the doctor said skeptically.

At Nick's hospital room, Billy thought about not stopping but then decided he owed it to his friend. He knocked lightly as to not wake him if he was sleeping, admittedly hoping he would be. The last thing he needed now was more emotional storms. He heard a stronger voice than he had expected saying to come on in.

"How you feeling?" Billy asked, noting the enlarged pupils and line still running from an IV to Nick's arm.

"There have been better days," Nick responded forcing a smile. He was sitting up in bed though which seemed a good sign.

Billy gingerly lowered himself into one of the chairs beside Nick's bed. At the other end of the room was an old man snoring.

"Jean told me you got busted up some yourself," Nick said.

"The breaks of the game—pardon the pun." He smiled.

"So I'm not the only one who lost out."

Billy wished for another cigarette. "Could be although that's not decided yet. I won't be taking all around, but I can still win overall in bareback."

Nick studied him. "You... edged into that chair kind of cautious. What got broke?"

"Maybe ribs. Doc wasn't sure."

"And you know how many men are under ground from a rib through their lungs."

"I didn't come here for a lecture. I got other places I can get that and they're prettier."

Nick managed a grin. His face was still unshaven and very pale. "All right. Lecture over."

"How long you going to be here?" Billy asked.

Nick's face paled even more. "I can't afford to be here even now. So soon as I can get out."

"The boys have anted up a kitty to help you and Jean out. I'm not sure how much is in it, but she should have it by now. It won't be a lot but maybe it'll help."

"We don't need charity."

"Nobody said it's charity. It's one person helping another as you'd do if it was the other way and you damned well know it." Nick pursed his lips together, not able to argue but unwilling to agree. "You figuring in the IPRA insurance?" Billy asked.

"I forgot about that."

"Well be damned glad they started providing it. It might not cover everything..."

Nick interrupted, "They're talking physical therapy."

"All right, so it likely won't but it'll help. You gotta quit feeling sorry for yourself on this and start thinking what you can do."

Nick glared at him and then managed a smile. "All right... all right. Hell, I get a day to feel sorry for me though, don't I?"

"Not much more than that. It's time to cowboy-up."

Nick sucked in a breath. "The thing is I keep coming back to that. If I don't ride, can't ride and I admit, that's done, what can I do? I don't know anything but it and now it's gone."

"You will figure out something. Geesus, you can still ride, just not a bucking horse. You got a lot going for you, not the least of which is Jean. You are a lucky man to have a woman who has always been there for you. You be there for her now. Get on your feet and then start worrying over the next step." He rose then. "I gotta go, but you take care, and I'll be back to make sure you do."

Nick reached out his free hand. "Thanks—for all of it. I needed the slap to wake me up."

Billy drove straight to the chutes. Several of the guys kidded him about showing up and thinking they were rid of him, but he knew most of them would have done the same thing. It was the cowboy creed– they finished unless they were laid out flat.

"How you doing?" Hank asked coming up and slapping his shoulder enough to cause Billy to wince tape or no tape.

"I'm alive thanks to you. It's not the first time either."

"What are you doing here? Not back for the bulls, I hope."

"Nah. I give that up for awhile at least. I have a good shot at bareback though and I am going to take it."

"Wait'll Jack sees you. He had money on Gene Evans."

"Serves him right for betting against me."

Billy did some simple stretches, testing out his muscles, seeing what his limitations might be from the bruise and ribs. He put on his chaps and spurs, taking a little longer but getting it done. The activity was building in the stadiums and behind the chutes.

Then Denny was standing in front of him. "What are you doing here?"

"What were you counting your money too?" Billy retorted.

"I saw how you got slammed yesterday, heard you broke a rib. You can't be here to ride?"

"Seriously, I can't? Wow then wonder why I am here."

"I don't know."

"I got a tip for you. Never trust rumors. You know how they are for truth." He walked off with Denny trailing behind.

"Hurt much?" Denny asked in the friendliest tone of voice he had yet used with Billy."

"What do you think?"

"You really riding?" Denny repeated.

"Nah, I am actually here for the dance. Do you know when it starts?"

Denny spit off to the side. Evidently he had picked up chewing tobacco as another bad habit but Billy said nothing.

"I'm surprised is all," Denny said finally.

"You didn't go see Nick yet."

"I will... after today."

"Did you get the money to Jean?"

Denny shook his head. "I been meaning to do that too. I've been busy is all."

Billy managed to swallow his anger. "They need that money."

"I know. I'll take care of it. Tonight. Where you going next?"

"I haven't decided."

"Me either."

Billy got it then. Denny saw Nick as done for and he was looking for someone new to glom onto. It wasn't going to be him. He kept his answers short and was glad when the kid walked on.

Billy lit a cigarette listening to the opening events with one foot on the first rail. The world was a strange place is all he could think. People used each other or sometimes helped. It wasn't always easy to tell which was which. Maybe he had also used some on his way up like Tice. Using and being used seemed to go with life. He didn't have to like it.

Without wanting to, Sara came to his mind wondering if she really had meant what she said. He could go back there after the events were over. Or maybe he shouldn't. Maybe he ought to just let her go, that it'd be best for them both.

He worked through his mind what he knew about the horse he'd be riding. Lucky Days. Not much information on him but that wasn't necessarily bad. Maybe it'd be his lucky day. He wished he felt more optimistic about it. He had to make this ride. He drew deeply on the cigarette as he remembered the feeling he had had when he drove to Pendleton that this place might be bad for him or at least life changing. He didn't think he was doing something that dangerous with the ride. He could do it in such a way as to lower the risks.

Idly watching the activity around him, part of it yet or not, Billy leaned back against the fence to conserve his strength. His hat was slanted down over his eyes, one boot on the fence behind him. He tried to pretend there was no pain, but there was and he had to get past it.

Then he saw her. A feeling of momentary disbelief came over him as he thought he had conjured her from wanting her so badly. He straightened so quickly that it sent a surge of pain through his side. She stopped a few feet from him. He dropped his cigarette, grinding it into the dust; and then she was in his arms, face against his chest. She was right where he needed her to be, when he needed her to be there.

After a few moments, she stepped back and said, "You are a stubborn man."

"I'm stubborn?" he retorted.

"You're really going to do it, aren't you?"

"You know I am."

She looked up into his eyes. "And it is that way or no way for us?"

Now he was wondering why she had come. Was it one last chance to change his mind? "I am riding in a few minutes."

"All right."

"All right?"

"Yes, I want what you and I can have together for however long it will be. I want to be with you. If you still want me after this."

"You know I want you."

"Do I?"

"You should." He smiled and pulled her back into his arms. Kissing her, feeling, even there with all the cowboys watching and a lot of them were, her tongue delve into his mouth, teasing and lighting up his body with the warmth of that kiss as she melted into him.

When they broke apart, Jack, who had been standing nearby, joked, "My gawd. I guess this must be your woman." He laughed along with several others who had watched the kiss.

Billy heard in the background the announcer beginning to discuss the bareback event. His mind wasn't on it but on her. He knew he had to switch his attention to what was coming next, but he didn't want to let her go. He only wanted this woman in his arms-- his need to focus on the ride ahead, everything else was pushed to the background.

"Mom and Dad came down with me and are watching their first rodeo." She smiled and reached up to touch his cheek. "So you better do good."

"Ah no pressure," he teased.

"Not much anyway." Running her hands down his back, she became aware of the tape. She looked up questioning.

"A deal between me and doc. He did it for me if I agreed to come back afterward to get it removed and take an x-ray to see what's really going on."

"Wow, he agreed to that. He was so against it."

"He didn't like it, but he saw there was no arguing me out of riding either way. It's my extra insurance. See I'm not totally reckless."

"It better be enough," she said kissing him again. "I suppose I have to leave."

"You can wait back here if you want."

She pursed her lips together. He saw she was trying to be strong. "Okay," she managed. She was the kind of woman who if she had to shed tears, they'd be after he'd gone. He needed not to see them; and so he left her then, tightening his chaps, climbing the fence of Lucky Day's chute. Tice had come up to help him get adjusted. It wasn't quite his turn to settle down on the horse and so he waited without anything to say.

"You sure this is a good idea?" Tice asked again.

"Does it have to be?"

"Reckon not."

Billy watched the gelding as it shifted its body around the box. The horse was edgy but not showing the flightiness that sometimes made them impossible to give a good ride. This one seemed to be waiting out what it knew it had to do. Good, they were two of a kind.

He needed a good ride but not too good. All he had to do was last out the whistle. 'Just give me those eight seconds,' he suggested as he moved out over the horse's back. Lucky Day stood still, dancing his feet a little but not trying to buck. The gelding showed no enthusiasm for what was coming, but he also wasn't going to fight it, not yet anyway. Billy lowered himself onto his back, adjusting the strap to his satisfaction and then moving forward until he was sitting on his hand. It all felt as balanced as it was going to get.

Another rider was bucking out onto the grass in the middle before he was tossed from his horse. That meant he'd be up next. He heard the announcer saying his name.

"Billy Stempleton from Bend, Oregon is at the top of the rankings here today. He was hurt though yesterday in bulls. Not surprising that he'd be back today because that's how these cowboys are. They never say die."

Billy was wishing he'd quit talking, and especially not use that word die even when he didn't mean it that way. Now he just wanted to get this over. "Easy boy," he said not wanting the horse too calm or too skittish. Some days he wanted all the show he could get but not today. Today he just wanted the horse to buck and for him to finish the ride in one piece.

Deciding he was as ready as he'd ever be, he nodded to Tice, who yelled, "Let'er buck." When the gate swung open, Lucky Day was out and doing his thing. Billy spurred high on his shoulder with the dulled spurs, making the ride count, no longer feeling any pain as the adrenaline kicked in.

Lucky Day surged across the ground, landing hard on his front feet and kicking out with the back. Bucking he circled back. He was putting on a show and giving Billy a ride he could manage. From the first buck, Billy caught his rhythm. He and the horse were one, even with different purposes, even with one trying to dislodge the other. When they hit the grassy center, there was an instant change of motion, but Billy was ready for it and didn't miss a beat.

Bucking, twisting, turning, and coming down hard again on his front legs, Lucky Day was giving it his all. Billy was past doing anything but reacting with his own instincts that matched the horse's. He felt it as he always did how it was like flying with the wind, testing his strength and ability against this powerful animal. It was all about the moment.

He heard the whistle then, saw the pick up man coming toward him and he put his own legs down around the horse's belly. When he swung off, grabbing the rider's waist before letting himself drop to the ground, he felt it had gone as well as it could and then the pain was back. Not worse though. He was tempted to throw his hat in the air as a sign of victory, but few in the audience would have understood.

This was the kind of ride he had needed. The score would be good enough. It had looked like a good ride, but it wasn't too hard. The horse, now freed of the irritating strap around his middle had quit bucking and gone galloping for the exit

Luck of the Draw

The crowd was cheering. As Billy made the exit himself, he heard his score—74. That would do it. The stands were cheering even louder as the announcer said that would put Billy at the top with no way for the remaining riders to catch up. He would win bareback at the Pendleton Roundup for 1974. It was why he did it but for something more—for knowing it was something he could do and do well. This time, for the first time in his life, he was sharing that victory with someone.

Out of the arena, he looked for her and then saw her at the edge of the cowboys who had come to congratulate him. He strode straight for her as she came running toward him. He'd have to go to the ER but even that was okay. It was more than okay when he took her into his arms.

Chapter Fourteen

Sunday

"One week ago, I drove into your town," he said, "with no idea what I'd find."

"It had to be more than a week," she disagreed but she knew it wasn't.

"You sure your parents are okay with this?" he asked as he drove the truck toward the mountains, tent and camping gear in the back.

"I don't know how they feel or what they'd prefer except one thing. They repeated that I am an adult. It is my life and I have to live it."

"We could wait." It was all moving pretty fast.

"If your ribs don't feel up to it…"

"They're fine. The doctor verified that with the x-ray. Just a hairline fracture and no reason to limit my activity. Taping and then getting it off hurt worse than it does now." He grinned as he glanced over at her.

"Well if your ribs are okay, then I want this time together. We won't have much after it as you said there was a rodeo in Portland, right?"

"Yes, and I will enter it. I need the points since bull riding is off the menu for at least awhile."

"Awhile?"

"Sara, I don't know that I will again. I am not good enough at it, but if I decided to do that, you'd go along with it, wouldn't you?"

"I suppose." She made a face.

"I will support you in what you do which is your painting." His tone was patient but with humor in it. He did get it. "It's why I insisted on you bringing your oils along with us for these few days. We both are young. We have to make our lives all they can be. Right? Use our skills."

She pursed her lips but nodded. "It seems like being an artist is less dangerous."

He laughed. "Depends on who you paint maybe?"

"Jean looked good, I thought, more relaxed," she said as she brought up the visit they had had with Jean and Nick before they had driven out of the city.

"Less worried by the day, I'd guess," he said. He was still steamed over what had happened to the money the other riders had put together to help them. Denny would take care of it. Yeah right. Denny took care of it all right.

"What are you thinking of?" she asked. "Your face turned dark as a thundercloud.

"The money everybody put together for Nick and Jean."

"But you handed her $400. Wasn't that enough? So what was the problem?"

"It wasn't what the guys put together. Damn that Bauer, the bastard. He disappeared right after the events. Nobody saw him. He pulled out, and the money was gone with him."

Her mouth dropped open. "I can't believe it. What a worm."

"If he has the nerve to show up at another big rodeo, I can hear him now claiming he just forgot or even try to say he gave it to them and they lied. He's done with rodeo. Actually I hope he does show up again. He'll get the beating of his life if he does."

"You will tell the others who donated."

"The beating will come from me. Damn that would give me pleasure. And yeah, I'll tell others later if I hear he's ever shown up anywhere so he can't pull anything like it again. I hope to God I don't see him again."

"Where'd the money you gave them come from then?" She looked at him and then back at the road. "Oh."

"I won this time." He grinned over at her. "In a lot of ways. I could afford it, and Nick would have done the same for me."

She put her arm through his and laid her head on his shoulder. "I do love you, cowboy."

Billy chose a wilderness campsite and set about putting up the tent while she got out the stove and cold box for a makeshift table. She felt nervous about what was going to happen that night, and yet totally determined that her new way of stepping out toward life, would begin with him up here. To do that, no words needed to be said over them. For a few years maybe they wouldn't live as a married couple might be expected, but they would grow together and apart.

There had been a time she wasn't sure how it would be for them, but now she knew. Someday they'd have a real life together like normal people, a family. In the meantime she had things to do, and some of it should not be in either her parents' home nor Billy's. It was time to make something of herself so she could be a fit mate for this strong man.

When the site was set, the folding chairs out, the sleeping bags and air mattress inside the tent, they sat with a glass of merlot looking toward the small creek that bubbled past their site.

"What are you thinking?" she asked as she saw a resolute look on his face.

He shook his head. "Just about this week. When I came to Pendleton, I was sure I knew what I'd be doing. I did feel the place would change my life but was afraid it was a jinx."

"You did get hurt."

"But not badly. It wasn't a jinx. It was a new beginning when I found you."

"I never dreamed what a week could do to my life either. It wasn't even just finding you, but it was seeing how you were so directed, knew what you wanted. I wanted some of that for myself, not just that you had it but that I could also."

He laughed then lit a cigarette watching the burning tip for a moment before he took a deep drag on it. "I am not sure I was all that directed. Maybe in some ways. I did a lot of it without thinking. I think you knew I didn't want to talk about my dad much and 'nam not at all. There were things I didn't want to tell you about, especially not before the rodeo when I needed to concentrate on it, but now..."

"I'd like to hear whatever you want me to know."

"I am not sure what that is. You know after I got out of the army, I put a lot of what happened aside, didn't let myself think about that year. When I came to Pendleton, I had that and then my dad's goals, all of it mixed up with mine. I likely sounded more sure of myself than I was."

"You could have fooled me."

"A person fools themselves too."

"I've done a lot of that with letting myself drift, taking the easy road—up until I met you." She smiled at him then. "Do you want to talk to me about the war now, now that there is no rodeo in front of you for awhile."

"I'm thinking about it." He ran his fingers through his hair.

"I think if we are going to be together, because I believe we are mates, well you need to tell me whatever you think I should know." She put her hand over his.

He told her then pieces of it. The memories raced back in a way he had pushed aside for years. There were the firefights. He never really could explain to someone who hadn't been there what it felt like to hold a gun to be facing a jungle environment that was strange where that day was likely to see the end of someone's life. It could be his own. Whoever was out there, it would be a stranger, but someone who wanted likely the same things in life he did.

She curled into his arms as he went on to tell her about the positive side to the experience-- the comradeship as there was with the rodeo. *You stuck together. You were there for your friends, the men alongside you.*

"Do you have flashbacks to it?" she asked.

He shook his head. "It comes to me when I think about it but mostly I don't think about it. I don't know if I did the right thing to go or not. But you know I did what I felt I had to do."

"I believe that."

He didn't add to it the details that she understood he would carry with him all of his life. She was glad she wouldn't know all he had gone through, what he had seen. Whatever it was, had been, he had not taken joy from it. He had done what he did with everything— what he had to do.

"I will be here for you," she said when he stopped talking. "I want to hear the things you need to talk to someone about. I want to tell you my secrets. I will be softness to your hardness, yin to your yang. Moon to your sun."

He smiled. "You know I tried to understand that all once but never did."

"You are someone who doesn't need to understand it. You live it. I want to live it too."

He bent to kiss her and the kisses deepened as he pulled her into his lap. They sat on the folding chair for awhile, the kisses growing longer, ones she felt through her whole body, her hands moving over his body, opening his shirt. "Does it hurt when I do that?" she asked as she ran her hands over his chest.

"It would hurt if you didn't," he murmured. When she moaned, wanting more, he carried her to the tent, pushed open the flap with his knee and laid her on the sleeping bag before he zipped the tent door closed.

Their love making was slow and relaxed, one step leading to another. By the time he entered her, broke through where no man had gone before, she was so ready that it barely hurt. What followed made any possible discomfort completely forgotten.

As they lay together afterward, their limbs entwined, she kissed his chest. "I am glad I waited."

"Well you didn't wait as long as you're supposed to," he teased with a light kiss of her fingers.

"I know... bad girl. So bad, I want to do it all again." And they did.

Later after they had eaten their evening meal that she had managed only to slightly overcook, they sat down by the little brook. They lay back to watch the stars come out. "I want you to come with me to meet my sister in Portland but first my brother," he said. "He'll be in shock."

"That you have a woman?"

He chuckled. "No, that it's a woman like you."

"You still have some ground to work with him, don't you?"

"We might never be able to do it, but I will try again. You have given me some ideas which might help on my end." He was silent awhile. "My family wasn't what I thought or knew it should be. I hope if we have one someday, we can make it different."

"We will."

"I came here for ending something and instead find I am beginning something."

"Are you sorry about that?"

He grinned. "Do I look sorry? I am a lucky son of a bitch, and I know it."

"Me too and it's not like I have everything worked out either. I have to deal with my parents, move out of their home, figure out what I am doing in this life."

"We can help each other with that."

Her smile broadened, the twinkle in her eye almost the equal of the stars overhead. "Yes, we can help each other a lot of ways."

Epilogue

2004

Billy rode into the ranch yard, his mind on the cattle the Travis boys and he had just moved down from the higher pasture to the one nearer the barns and corrals. He unsaddled his horse, gave him a pat on the rear as he sent him trotting off into the corral nearest the house. He was pleased with the tally and the good calf crop. They had lost far fewer calves this year to the first timers. He'd have to remember to tell Nick to be sure and pick up the vaccines when he was in town.

As he dusted off his clothes outside the house, he walked in without removing boots even though he knew how much Sara preferred he do that. When he saw her on the phone, he smiled and headed straight for her. From her end of the conversation, he knew she was talking to the gallery and the news was irritating her. He put his arms around her and kissed the top of her head, smiling as he knew she wanted him to leave her alone at the moment.

When she hung up, he asked, "What's up with Sherry?"

She growled and turned into his arms. "The usual. A disagreement on the date for the next show, and she wants me to do a joint one with Jason Southwick. His work and mine don't go together at all. So what's that all about?"

"Don't ask a dumb cowboy," he teased.

"Yeah right," she said with a grin. The passing years hadn't done much to dim the red of her hair. Her figure was as slim as before she'd had two boys and a girl. "You smell like cattle and horses," she assessed as he lightly kissed her lips.

"And you smell like roses, soap, and is that turpentine? What the hell were you using turpentine for?"

He opened her lips with his tongue as he felt her respond to him, her body melt into his, her kiss aggressively meet his own.

"Cowboy, I have things left to do. I just got the house straightened up," Sara protested slapping his chest but her eyes saying something very different.

"So I see. And you too." He grinned as he kissed her again.

"There is not time for that," she objected but not very much.

"Jake won't be here for an hour."

"But I have things to do before that like finish the dinner."

"More important than this?" His kiss went deep into her soul and once again distracted her from whatever she had been thinking.

Thirty years together, twenty-five married, and nothing had changed for how his kisses seared her and pulled her away from whatever she had been intending to do. She didn't object and she did follow him upstairs.

He stripped his clothing as he walked into the bedroom. "Want me to shower first?" he asked

She was already stripping off her own clothing and by the time he was naked, she was back in his arms leaving no doubt as to what she wanted. There was no need for foreplay or anything but falling onto the bed and into each other. Her climax was only barely ahead of his.

"God," she whispered as she came back to herself. "I thought you were tired after a day out with the cattle."

"I was up until I saw you." He grinned and headed for the shower, her not far behind.

Half an hour later, she was back in the kitchen when their son's truck drove up. Jake and his latest girlfriend were in it, both visiting during college break. Billy pulled his son into his arms, the two men equally tall and strong.

"Place looks good," Jake said as he introduced them to Rachel who was very lovely and shy.

"We had a good season so far. You going to be back for branding?"

"Do you need me?"

Billy considered a moment. "We can always use an extra hand. You're best at roping, but Nick and Jean will be here. I can get Wes if he's not already committed elsewhere. The other ranches. We can get by without you if you don't have time."

"A lot depends on finals, but I will make it if the dates work."

The ranch bordered the north fork of the John Day River. Just as Billy had spoken of years before, it had good grassland for making winter hay, timbered hills above the house where the cattle could graze through the summers. It was a good place for cattle and for raising the family they had started right after they formalized their marriage. Three children followed quickly and now all were off to school in different colleges and states. The money Billy had made during his rodeoing years had been wisely invested in more than the ranch, which enabled them to get educations for their children.

He thought about Tice then, the life that had been cut short by a drunken drive that ended in his truck rolling. Maybe Tice had wanted it that way as he had no dream beyond the rodeo, and it was at the end for him.

While at first Billy had had to stay on the circuit, to bring more money to the ranch, Nick had come to the land to act as its foreman, a position that he still held. It had worked well for them all. Even better when Sara's parents had retired and moved closer to the ranch to be more of a factor in the life of their grandchildren.

As Billy heard his son and his girlfriend laughing and talking with Sara, he remembered the day he had walked into her father's store and luck had determined it all. He could have so easily missed it with a different choice that day. It was all the luck of the draw.

THE END

See the video trailers for Rain's Books at

http://www.youtube.com/watch?v=3_Yzcr3ocFY&feature=plcp

Other Books by Rain Trueax

A Montana Christmas
Arizona Sunset
Bannister's Way
Desert Inferno
Evening Star
From Here to There
Hidden Pearl
Moon Dust
Second Chance
Sky Daughter

Rain Trueax

ABOUT THE AUTHOR

Rain Trueax is the author of contemporary and
historical novels based in the American West which has
been her home country since birth. Living on a ranch in
the Oregon coast range with her husband, writing stories
of the west has come very naturally. Some of the stories
have continuing characters, but all stand alone in their plot
and development.

Beginning with "Arizona Sunset", and three months
later with "Tucson Moon", Rain is bringing out her first
historical romances. The Oregon based books will be
available in 2014.

www.ingramcontent.com/pod-product-compliance
Lightning Source LLC
Chambersburg PA
CBHW021035130626
46552CB00005B/1853